D0441573

30 Second Death

Also by Laura Bradford

The Tobi Tobias Mysteries

30 Second Death

Death in Advertising

Bradford, Laura.
30 second death : a
Tobi Tobias mystery /
©2017.
33305239945698
mi   09/19/17

30 Second Death

A Tobi Tobias Mystery

Laura Bradford

LYRICAL UNDERGROUND
Kensington Publishing Corp.
www.kensingtonbooks.com

To the extent that the image or images on the cover of this book depict a person or persons, such person or persons are merely models, and are not intended to portray any character or characters featured in the book.

LYRICAL UNDERGROUND BOOKS are published by

Kensington Publishing Corp.
119 West 40th Street
New York, NY 10018

Copyright © 2017 by Laura Bradford

All rights reserved. No part of this book may be reproduced in any form or by any means without the prior written consent of the Publisher, excepting brief quotes used in reviews.

All Kensington titles, imprints, and distributed lines are available at special quantity discounts for bulk purchases for sales promotion, premiums, fund-raising, educational, or institutional use.

Special book excerpts or customized printings can also be created to fit specific needs. For details, write or phone the office of the Kensington Sales Manager: Kensington Publishing Corp., 119 West 40th Street, New York, NY 10018. Attn. Sales Department. Phone: 1-800-221-2647.

Lyrical Underground and Lyrical Underground logo Reg. US Pat. & TM Off.

First Electronic Edition: July 2017
eISBN-13: 978-1-5161-0208-2
eISBN-10: 1-5161-0208-8

First Print Edition: July 2017
ISBN-13: 978-1-5161-0209-9
ISBN-10: 1-5161-0209-6

Printed in the United States of America

For Joe and Lynn, my very own Carter and Mary Fran.
You make my world brighter just by being in it.

Chapter One

Hell had officially frozen over. And, oddly enough, there was no swell of background music, no thunderous blast like I'd always imagined.

There was simply crunching.

Loud, deliberate crunching.

In fact, it was the cruncher and the crunchee that had turned the fiery flames of the dreaded underworld into the clichéd icicles referenced at the end of virtually every nasty breakup.

In English?

My best friend, Carter McDade, was standing less than five feet from my sofa eating a bowl of Cocoa Puffs.

That's right, Carter McDade—the same guy who lectured me daily on the gaps (okay, seismic gullies) in my eating habits. The same guy who could draw a textbook food pyramid in mere seconds. The same guy who'd willingly and happily choose broccoli in a head-to-head with a Caramello bar.

Which is why his puff-crunching pointed to one indisputable conclusion: Carter was stressed. Big-time.

A rarity in and of itself, Cocoa Puffs or no Cocoa Puffs.

My upstairs neighbor was the most positive human being I'd ever met. One of those happy-go-lucky, always-has-a-smile types. You know, the kind of person everyone needs in their life, but few are fortunate enough to have.

I was one of the fortunate.

I was also dumbfounded. Utterly and completely dumbfounded by what to say and how to say it. So I took the not-so-subtle approach.

"What's wrong, Carter?"

"Uh-in."

Now I'll admit, I have a leg up when it comes to deciphering puff-talk (it is, after all, my second language), but I was feeling pretty proud that I could decode it from even the most novice of crunchers.

"Nothing? Nothing?! Do you realize what you're eating right now?"

Carter looked at the bowl in his left hand and then the spoon moving toward his mouth with his right. "Uh-huh."

"They're *Cocoa Puffs,* Carter! Co. Coa. Puffs. As in *chocolate*—or as you call it, sugar central. You know, void of roughage. In fact, if I do recall correctly, you refer to them as the downfall of mankind. The reason for society's ills."

I guess I thought if I really hammered home the point, it might sink in. Then again, I was living proof that tactic failed. Just ask my mother.

Besides, it was hard to hammer home drawbacks when I didn't believe a word of what I was saying. Why? Because I, Tobi Tobias, am a chocoholic. And proud of it, I might add.

So I did what any good chocoholic would do. I sauntered into the kitchen, grabbed my Bugs Bunny melamine bowl and matching spoon, filled it to the brim with the last of the crunchy brown puffs (don't worry, I've got four more boxes in the cabinet over the stove), and headed back into the living room. I mean, let's face it, the expression "If you can't beat 'em, join 'em" was coined for a reason, right?

Not that my commiserating helped. In fact, when I returned, Carter showed no signs of having noticed my departure or subsequent return. His facial expression was still void of its trademark smile, and his eyes held a vacant look. Somehow, though, I managed to coax him onto the sofa.

"C'mon, Carter, spill it. It's Fiona again, isn't it?"

Call it a lucky (or, really my *only*) guess, but it was worth a shot. And judging by the look of complete mortification on his face as my words (and thus, his choice of food) registered in his subconscious, I'd hit the jackpot.

"Oh, good God, please tell me I'm not eating what I think I'm eating." Carter squeezed his eyes shut, then opened them slowly, cautiously. A tortured gasp escaped his mouth, along with a partially chewed puff.

"It's okay, Carter, really. It's been a long time coming. And it's not a good idea to keep depriving yourself of the finer things in life." I reached out and touched his shoulder, a teasing smile tugging my lips. "Thanks for letting me be a part of your spiritual awakening."

If looks could kill . . .

He rolled his eyes upward and then frantically wiped his tongue with the sleeve of his cable-knit sweater. "Ugh, how on earth can you eat that stuff?"

"Same way you just did, my friend. One yummy spoonful at a time." I winked and popped some puffs into my mouth. I knew I was being ornery, but I couldn't help myself. Let's face it, I'd endured more pontificating about my eating habits from this man than I could possibly recall. So this was, in a way, sweet justice. Payback. Come-uppance at its finest . . .

"My mind was compromised." Carter released a long, slow sigh and wiped his tongue one more time. "I swear, Sunshine, that woman will be the death of me yet. Mark my words."

I took the bowl from his shaking hand and set it on the end table to my right. It never ceased to amaze me how fast the sugar rush hit the chocolate virgins. Especially the stressed ones.

"What'd Princess Fiona do *this* time?"

"In the interest of time, it might be better if I tell you what she *didn't* do." Carter pushed off the couch and wandered over to the window. Drawing back the curtain, he peered outside. "Have you ever noticed the way Ms. Rapple kinda looks like Gertrude? Around the eyes and snout—I mean, nose?"

That did it. I laughed. And snorted. Loudly.

Damn.

"I'm serious, Tobi. The eyes droop in almost the exact same spot, and the nose, well, it's a perfect match. Right down to the persistent wetness."

Ewwww . . .

Thinking about my next-door neighbor, Ms. Rapple, was enough to make my stomach turn. The old biddy was something of a thorn in my side and had been since the day I moved into my apartment at 46 McPherson Road. In fact, I'm not sure I'd even turned the key in the front lock before she'd descended on me with her over-the-top questions, mean-spirited honesty, hideously bad breath, and her yippityyappity dog, Gertrude. Fortunately, having Carter in the apartment above me, and Mary Fran and Sam Wazoli living above Ms. Rapple, made the situation more bearable.

Still . . . was I wrong for hoping she'd win the lottery and move out into the countryside? Or, even better, to another continent entirely?

Carter, I knew, felt the same way about our elderly neighbor, though he tried his best to smooth over her abrasiveness with his normally sunny disposition. When that didn't work, he resorted to other things. Like ducking to the side of windows in true surveillance mode.

"You better come away from there, Carter. If she catches you looking, she'll be knocking on my door looking for some conversation." The thought made me cringe.

"The only conversation she's interested in these days is one that involves talk of your grandfather."

I shivered. "Don't remind me. She stops me every single day to ask when he's coming to visit. It gives me the heebies."

My Grandpa Stu was my rock, my grounding force. We'd been nearly inseparable since the day I was born—he teaching me how to navigate through life, me offering sticky kisses and half-eaten lollipops in return. The closeness we'd shared during my formative years hadn't changed as I grew into adulthood. If anything, it had strengthened as I went from *thinking* my Grandpa Stu was the smartest man in the world to *knowing* it.

But we no longer had uninterrupted days and a common front porch at our disposal. Instead, we had weekly phone conversations and a handful of visits each year—times I cherished as much as any from my youth.

Except maybe the last visit.

Don't get me wrong, having my Grandpa Stu in my apartment for a week had been wonderful. He'd helped me through a trying time that included a dead body and my professional reputation (don't ask). Unfortunately, that same visit had also marked the beginning of a budding affection between my once-smart grandfather and my perpetual thorn. He called her "Martha," his voice softening whenever he said it aloud.

Needless to say, I've had my share of nightmares since that visit. The worst, though, was the one in which my grandfather was sporting a hand-knit sweater identical to one worn by both Ms. Rapple *and* her dog.

I shook my head against the unsettling image and forced my thoughts back to the subject Carter was working valiantly to ignore.

"C'mon, Carter. What's the deal with Fiona?"

He let the curtain slip through his fingers, his body stiffening in response. "Okay, okay."

I scooted over on the sofa to make room as he dropped his wiry body down with a thud. "I told you we just started casting for Rapunzel, right?"

"Yup."

Carter stretched his feet out and propped them on my new-to-me coffee table. "I like this table by the way. Nice lines."

"Impressive topic shift, but it's not gonna fly." I bent my legs at the knee and pulled them under me, hugging a throw pillow to my chest. "So . . . Ra-pun-zel?"

He stuck his tongue out at me and rolled his eyes. "Okay. So, of course, the Frankster wants the lead to go to his amazingly talented niece."

Did I sense a defrosting in Carter's opinion of his one-and-only nemesis?

"Correct me if I'm wrong, but did you just call Fiona amazingly talented?" I asked for clarification purposes.

"The boss's words, not mine. I'd choose something more, oh, I don't know—*fitting*. Like world-class troublemaker, evil's lone spawn, or irritant extraordinaire."

So much for defrosting.

"I take it you'd rather she didn't get the part?"

"This is *Rapunzel*, Sunshine. Fiona's hair barely touches her collar. And she won't even consider hair extensions." He stopped, inhaled sharply, and then threw his head back against the couch. "She wants to wear a wig."

The reason for Carter's unexpected tumble off the broccoli wagon was suddenly crystal clear. If anything, I was stunned it had stopped at Cocoa Puffs. This little development could have landed him at the checkout counter of Death by Chocolate on North Euclid.

"A wig? Does she not realize what you *do*?"

"Oh, she realizes it. She just gets her jollies out of pushing my buttons. Has since the day her precious uncle—aka my boss, aka the Frankster—introduced us. Probably because my greeting lacked a bow and the obligatory peck on her hand."

It's true. Carter is, hands down, the nicest, sweetest, most genuine guy I'd ever met. But he doesn't kiss up to anyone. Ever. He speaks with his heart twenty-four/seven and doesn't give a hoot who you are or what you do for a living.

"Are you going to let her use a wig? I mean, isn't the whole hair thing why you're there in the first place?"

He pulled his legs off the table and sat ramrod straight. "Exactly! And I was salivating at the idea of doing this show. Not just because there's a chance it could be our last show ever at the theater, but because it's *Rapunzel*, Sunshine! Think about it—the extensions, mixing up just the right shade of golden blond, creating soft curls that are the envy of all . . . Oh my God, it was going to be so awesome."

It was hard not to notice the way his wistful tone morphed into anger as he continued, his voice growing deeper and more wooden with each subsequent word. "But now, I'm not sure I'll even make it past Monday morning, thanks to Princess Fiona."

I'd never seen Carter quite like this before. Sure, he was theatrical; it was part of his shtick. But there's a difference between being theatrical and being a drama queen, and Carter was suddenly blurring the line.

"C'mon, Carter. Just because she doesn't want you to do her hair doesn't mean you're going to lose your job. You know that." I tugged at a loose thread on my throw pillow and waited for him to come to his senses.

"You might've been right, Sunshine, if I hadn't let her bait me into a fight. *With* her uncle standing less than ten feet behind me."

Uh-oh.

"You didn't know he was there?" I asked, though why I'm not quite sure. The answer was obvious, wasn't it? Carter had, after all, resorted to *chocolate*.

"Nope. Not a clue. But Fiona did, I'm positive of that." Carter pushed off the sofa and wandered around my living room, stopping from time to time to look at a few framed photographs he'd seen a million times over the past two years.

"But you just *disagreed* with her on the hair stuff, right?"

Carter snickered. "Disagreed? Oh no. Let's just say I kinda unleashed the past six months of Fiona-inspired frustration. And once I started, I couldn't stop."

I gulped. "How bad did it get?"

"Depends on what you call bad." Carter stopped at my draft table and picked up a sheet of paper with colorful block letters across the top and rough sketches in a series of hand-drawn boxes along the bottom.

"Try me." I tossed the throw pillow onto Carter's empty spot and stood. I'd spent the better part of the day working on my campaign ideas for Pizza Adventure but wasn't necessarily ready to share them with anyone yet. Even Carter, my biggest fan of all.

"Well, let's see—I told her how sick I was of her temper tantrums during rehearsals, her constant screaming at the lighting guys, her Gestapo-like tactics when it comes to making sure no one even so much as *thinks* about eating something with peanuts anywhere in the building lest she break out in hives or whatever the hell happens to her, and, of course, her blatant hogging of the press anytime the theater actually gets *show* coverage these days."

My mouth dropped open.

"Wait." He held up his hand, crossing guard style. "Trust me, Sunshine. It gets better."

"There's *more*?" I asked.

Carter nodded. "I called her a spoiled brat with no chance in hell of ever making it as an actress."

Ouch.

Okay, so maybe the notion of a new job wasn't so drama-queenish after all.

What to say . . . what to say . . .

"Bad call, huh?" Carter cocked his head to the left and studied the paper that held hours of my brainstorming and subsequent doodling. "Say, this is cool. That's a kid dressed like Batman in that second box, isn't it?"

"Uh, yeah." I reached for the paper, but Carter pulled it away and read the words in the box aloud. "Nah-nah-nah-nah-nah-nah-nah, Nah-nah-nah-nah-nah-nah-nah, Pizza Cave!"

I looked around his shoulder and followed along as he came to the next box. "And now he's having his party in the cave with his buddies, right?" Carter asked, pointing.

I nodded. "So, what do you think?"

"I think it's awesome. They do parties for thirty-four-year-olds too?"

"Actually yeah. Though you might prefer their beach locale."

"Hey, I like pizza as much as the next guy, but I'm not driving to the coast to get some." Carter turned and leaned against my draft table, crossing his legs at the ankles.

"You don't have to drive to the coast." I nudged him to the side and pulled a photograph from the bulging envelope to the left of my shading pencils. I handed it to Carter, pointing at the large, warehouse-like space that would soon be known throughout the metropolitan St. Louis area as *Pizza Adventure—You pick the place, we'll bring the pizza*. A catchy little slogan if I must say so myself. "Dom and Gina Paletti have big plans for that space."

"*This* is the pizza place?" Carter crinkled his nose upward and nudged his chin in the direction of the picture. "Looks kind of industrial or something."

"It *did*. But look what they're doing with it." I reached for the envelope and extracted a mixture of hand-drawn sketches and actual rudimentary photographs I'd gotten with my point-and-shoot. "Here's the cave. And see? Those are the tables you eat at inside the cave."

Carter grabbed the picture from my hand and whistled under his breath. "This is amazing. Wow, wow, wow."

"Wait. It gets better." I handed him the next picture, one that depicted a Drive-in Movie room complete with tables inside car-like shells and a full-sized movie screen in front. "If you sit in this room, you can watch old cartoons like Bugs and Road Runner while you eat your pizza."

"Did you say *Road Runner*?"

I laughed and passed him the next photograph. "Now let's suppose you weren't a cartoon kind of guy. You could opt, instead, to eat on an island with thatched-roof tables, tropical birds, and bongo drums playing in the background."

He whistled again. "How many of these rooms are they going to have?"

"The plan is to have eight to start with. If it takes off as we think it will, they have room to add another four or five."

"Think they'll have a hairdresser room?" Carter handed me back the small stack of photographs and pushed away from the draft table. "I may be looking for employment sooner rather than later."

I hated seeing him so defeated, so unhappy. It was like the world had slipped off its axis and it was up to me to set things right. How to do that was anyone's guess, but I knew I had to try.

"Sorry, no hairdresser room, but there *will* be a castle."

Carter stared at me blankly.

"As in a room with princesses. And a wicked witch, of course," I prompted.

Still nothing.

"I was thinking maybe Dom and Gina might offer *Fiona* a job. Get it? Wicked Witch. Fiona Renoir ..."

My stab at distractive humor finally seeped through, earning me a slow nod in return. So much for the whole axis-righting thing.

"I wish it were that simple, but Fiona's not going anywhere. Not until she lands a real acting gig. And unless the little princess has a yet-to-be-discovered uncle living in Hollywood, or happens to stumble across a role that doesn't require a whole lot of depth or ability, I'm toast at the theater." Carter shuffled over to the four-by-four-foot square of linoleum that denoted my entry foyer and grabbed his navy blue parka from its perch on the door knob.

An acting gig ... A role that doesn't require a whole lot of depth ...

And then it hit me. Maybe *I* could get Fiona a job—the kind of job that would make Carter look like a hero and save his sanity at the same time. Sure, there'd be a few kinks to work out (like rescinding a semi-promise to someone), but if I could pull this off it might—

"I think it's time I face facts, Tobi," Carter said, his voice strained and tired as he slipped his arms into his coat and zipped it to his neck, his eyes meeting mine for the first time since he'd walked through my door an hour earlier. "Short of a miracle, I'm doomed at the theater."

Chapter Two

If I'd known I'd be running that morning, I'd have dressed more appropriately. Perhaps, oh, I don't know, in maybe something other than two-inch-heeled ankle boots and a long, fitted skirt?

But, truth be told, I hadn't really counted on the thirty-mile-per-hour wind gusts that had been conspicuously absent during last night's weather forecast on KNPW (*let's get it right, people!*), nor had I considered the almost kite-like shape my portfolio assumed when cocked slightly to one side.

Which brings us to why I was running (not walking) down North Euclid at eight-fifty on a Monday morning in my red mittens, black wool dress coat, and winter hat, chasing a large rectangular object like it was a thousand-dollar bill on steroids. Because, in a way, it was.

With my company on more stable ground now, thanks to Zander Closet Company and New Town, the proposal currently sailing down the streets of the Central West End was the closest I'd ever gotten to shifting the notion of car ownership from the overcrowded pipe-dream corner of my brain to the underused almost-a-possibility section.

I gave Jack Fletcher an obligatory wave as I approached his stand at the corner of Euclid and Maryland, eliciting a knowing eye roll and cockeyed grin in return as he wrestled with the stacks of paper and magazine displays that made up his (and his father's before him) livelihood.

"Jim Beasley sure missed another forecast, huh?"

I snorted my agreement as I rounded the stand in pursuit of nearly fourteen hours' worth of creative brainstorming and execution (with a little head-to-wall contact thrown in for good measure). Granted, I would have rather spent my Saturday and Sunday with a certain tall, attractive, sandy blond named Andy, but we won't go there. Suffice it to say, Carter wasn't the only one who'd been drowning his sorrows in chocolate over the weekend.

The wind died suddenly, sending my portfolio and its contents crashing onto the concrete sidewalk about three feet in front of me. I slowed to a trot, reached down, and... landed on my backside compliments of Sandy, Mr. Houghtin's overeager golden lab, who'd play fetch with just about anything. Even, apparently, a large brown, kite-like portfolio that bore absolutely no resemblance whatsoever to a Frisbee, a ball, or a stick.

"Sandy, no!" I heard the pitiful sound of my voice as the wind once again whipped upward and sent my dreams of a cute and sporty car skirting down the sidewalk with Sandy in hot pursuit, tongue wagging and collar jingling. Mr. Houghtin, of course, was missing in action.

My guess? Sandy's owner had been waylaid by Valerie Mollner, the sixtysomething neighborhood hottie who knew just how to bat her eyelashes and shake her derrière to make the single (and not-so-single) geriatric (and not so geriatric) set take notice.

But that was neither here nor there at the moment. What mattered was the fact that Sandy had caught her target and dropped it (dripping in drool) at my feet, her eyes staring into mine, waiting for me to launch my portfolio into the air once again.

"Sorry buddy, not gonna happen," I murmured as I grabbed hold of the thick brown paper envelope with both gloved hands and stumbled to my feet, daring the wind to mess with me and my portfolio again. I glanced back at Sandy, a pang of guilt coursing through my body at her sad eyes. "Hey, thanks, girl. I owe you one. Big-time."

By the time I made it into the office, it was almost nine-thirty. My face was windburned, my backside was sore from its canine-induced collision with the concrete sidewalk, and my gloved hands were numbly locked in a death grip around my frozen, drool-lacquered portfolio.

It was, as my Grandpa Stu was fond of saying, shaping up to be a banner day.

Any hope that my early-morning misadventures would remain private was squashed the moment JoAnna looked up from her desk, her eyes widening as she took in my disheveled appearance. I stood quietly (or as quietly as I could with my teeth chattering) and waited for the visual inspection to be complete, my mind making bets with itself as to what would be the first words out of her mouth.

"Good heavens, Tobi, couldn't you and Andy wait until *after* work?"

"JoAnna!"

The sixty-year-old woman who, for all intents and purposes, had hired *me* to be *her* boss, shot me her infamous hands-on-hips, don't-mess-with-me look. "You show up, with your stockings around your knees, your coat half-buttoned, a mere strand of blond hair hanging on to what I imagine started out as a French braid, and I'm supposed to think you came straight here this morning?"

Okay, so I hadn't noticed the stockings . . .

I reached down, hoisted my coat and skirt upward, and then pulled my stockings into their upright and locked position. My hair would have to wait.

"I'll have you know that my appearance has nothing to do with Mr. Andy Zander. Absolutely zilch. Nada. Zip. Goose egg."

"Uh-oh."

Ah geez. Call it a momentary loss of memory, but I'd forgotten I was speaking to JoAnna Kincaid, resident eagle eye, elephant ear, and meltdown magnet (she can sniff out a personal problem from a mile away—and drag it out of the sharpest, most stoic personality).

"Oh, no you don't. I look like this because Jim Beasley makes entirely too much money as a weather forecaster, and for some unknown reason, Sandy sees me in much the same way a bull sees the color red. And now I have to make sure her teeth didn't ruin my Pizza Adventure pitch before my presentation in . . ." I pulled my coat sleeve up and looked at my watch. "Fifty-five minutes."

JoAnna stared at me for what seemed like an eternity before she finally came out from behind her desk, pried the portfolio from my still-clenched hands, and gave me a power hug.

"You go fix your hair. I'll check the pitch sheets."

I allowed myself an extra hug-moment to regroup and then backed up. "Thanks, JoAnna. You're a lifesaver. As for the rest . . . I just can't talk about Andy right now. Maybe later. After the pitch. And *after* I see if I can save Carter's job."

"I read about the theater's money troubles in the paper a few weeks ago, but it doesn't make sense to me. Every show I've been to has had a packed house, and—"

"I'm talking specifically about Carter's job, not the theater as a whole."

"Oh?"

"It's been a bad weekend, JoAnna." I felt her squeeze on my shoulder as I turned and headed toward the tiny bathroom located just outside the conference room at the end of the hallway.

I smiled in spite of myself as I passed the four small shadow boxes mounted to the wall. The first box contained a tiny closet with a miniature skeleton hanging from the rod, a gold plate across the trim work below displaying my slogan for Zander Closet Company: *When we're done, even your skeletons will have a place.* It had been a gift from Andy that I would treasure for the rest of my life.

The second box was from JoAnna, who had liked Andy's line of thinking so much that she'd had one done to reflect my work with New Town. The inside of the box contained miniature houses and shops lining a beautiful town square, the gold plate at the bottom sporting their slogan: *Where vacation and life become one.*

The next two boxes were empty but warranted—one for Pizza Adventure, and one for Salonquility.

Salonquility.

I glanced at my watch again and noted the time. If I could find a way to get my outward appearance under control *and* de-drool my pizza pitch in the next ten minutes, I might be able to make a few phone calls in the hopes of saving Carter's hide.

Stepping into the bathroom, I flicked on the light switch and stared at my reflection in the oval mirror above the sink.

Yikes. So much for having time to make a few phone calls . . .

My green eyes looked tired and lifeless, and my blond, shoulder-length hair was no longer in the French braid I'd worked so hard on that morning.

I pulled my backpack onto the edge of the sink and rifled through it, searching for a comb, some lipstick, and, with any luck, a new face (preferably one that would enable me to see an R-rated movie without being carded).

"Here, let me help, sweetie."

I looked into the mirror, blinking rapidly against the tears that suddenly stung my eyes.

If JoAnna noticed, she didn't say. She simply took the comb from my hand and began gliding it through my hair, her quiet, gentle strokes enveloping me in a warm, armless hug.

"I lost him, JoAnna." The words spilled from my lips in a raspy voice, one so quiet I wasn't sure she'd heard.

"Andy?"

I looked into the sink and stared, unseeingly, at the circular top of the drain, my heart twisting in my chest. I knew she was waiting for an answer, but the lump working its way up my throat made it difficult to speak.

"Why do you think you lost him?" She began twisting the hair at the top of my head, her hands moving quickly and skillfully.

"Because I can't compete," I finally said.

"Compete? Compete with whom?"

"Brenna."

JoAnna's hands stopped for a moment as she met my eyes in the mirror. "Who on earth is Brenna?"

I swallowed against my tightening throat. "Andy's ex-girlfriend. They dated for four years."

JoAnna began twisting again. "If she was that important to him, he'd have married her."

"But that's just it, JoAnna. He *wanted* to marry her. But she wanted to chase her career and see where it would take her."

JoAnna finished my hair, reached into my bag for the mini hairspray bottle, and sprayed my braid ever so carefully. "And now?"

"And now she's back. Walked right up to our table at Lewis and Clark's Friday night—and, well, you should have seen his face." My voice cracked as I continued. "The hurt, the surprise ... it was all there in his eyes."

JoAnna grabbed hold of my shoulders and spun me around until I faced her. "The hurt makes sense, doesn't it? And if he wasn't expecting to see her, so does the surprise. But that doesn't mean you'll lose him. He adores you."

"But he *loved* her, and she's breathtakingly beautiful. I can't compete with that." I knew I sounded pathetic, but I couldn't stop myself. Despite all my instincts to guard my heart where Andy was concerned, I'd fallen head over heels.

JoAnna spun me back to my original starting place and guided my face upward with her right hand. "Do you not see who I see?"

"Huh?"

"Her." JoAnna pointed into the mirror with her left index finger. "Tobi Tobias."

I pulled my eyes from JoAnna's reflection and studied my own—the tiny spray of childish freckles across the top of my cheeks, the less than desirable chest measurements beneath my sweater, and the impossible-to-miss sadness in my eyes at the certainty that I was about to be dumped once again. My heart sank. "Oh, I see her."

"Well, if that's true, then you see a woman who is the most determined, hardworking go-getter I've ever met. If that's true, then you see a young woman who has the most loving heart of anyone I've ever encountered. And if that's true, *really* true, then you have to see that Tobi Tobias is breathtakingly beautiful all on her own. Inside *and* out. An unbeatable combination."

I swiped at the tears that spilled over my cheeks as JoAnna continued. "Andy Zander is a smart man, sweetie. He may have loved this—this Brenna girl—at one time. But he hadn't met Tobi Tobias yet. Things are different now."

I wanted to believe her, to believe in myself. But it was the "myself" "part that always got in the way when it came to matters of the heart.

Slowly, I picked up my comb, hairspray, and lipstick and deposited them back into my overflowing bag with as much determination as I could muster. "I need to focus on Pizza Adventure today. If I don't, I'll blow this meeting. And we both know that landing another client will help us breathe a little easier around here."

"And get you to quit borrowing my car?"

I flashed a shaky grin at JoAnna in the mirror and nodded. "Yeah, and get me to quit borrowing your car."

JoAnna turned me one last time and kissed my forehead. "You know I'm here for you. Always."

I squeezed her hand and managed to eke out a tear-free "always" in response. Baby steps . . .

"So what's this about Carter's job?" JoAnna asked as she followed me down the narrow hallway toward my office.

I recounted Carter's Saturday at the theater as he'd told it to me, cringing at the words he'd used on Fiona.

"*Our* Carter said that?"

I nodded.

"So he's officially out of work then, I take it?"

"Not as of yesterday, but who knows what today will bring."

I opened the door to my office and stopped, my eyes taking in my desk, picture-frame-covered shelves, and paper-strewn draft table in one quick sweep. A parade of pink sticky notes decorated my computer screen.

"Who called?" I asked as I strode over to my desk and reached for the top note.

"Mary Fran."

I tilted up each subsequent pink sticky note, Mary Fran's name sprawled across the top of each one. "Is she okay? Did something happen to Sam?" I could feel the panic starting in my chest as I looked up at JoAnna.

"She's fine. So is Sam. She's just stressed. Something about the animals being too loud at night."

I felt my shoulders relax, my breathing slow, and a snort-accompanied laugh escape my mouth. "And by animals we mean Rudder Malone, I imagine?"

JoAnna shrugged.

But it didn't matter. I already knew the answer. Rudder Malone was bad news. He was arrogant, obnoxious, and loud. He was also a bird—an African grey parrot, to be exact. And he was the star (or so he thought) of Mary Fran's pet shop, To Know Them Is To Love Them—the same pet shop where I'd worked on occasion while trying to keep my struggling agency afloat.

"So how are you planning on saving Carter's job?"

"Carter?"

JoAnna put her hands on her hips and shook her head. "Yes, Carter. *The young man who lives above you.*"

Leave it to the taskmaster to get me back on track. I shook my head against the image of a bandana-wearing Rudder Malone and reached for the Salonquility file on top of my desk.

"I'm going to take Carter's glowing recommendation and get Fiona a job on the Salonquility commercial."

JoAnna's hands dropped to her side. "Wait, what? Carter recommended her? I thought he said she had no talent."

I waved my hand in the hair as I consulted the handy information sheet JoAnna had compiled on all of my clients. The list included office and cell phone numbers for each client, as well as numbers for everyone else associated with that account—like the studio where we'd be shooting the salon's commercial on Friday. "Carter just *said* that to make the other actors feel less threatened by her unparalleled genius."

"O-kay. I think I see your plan, but what about that girl you already talked to about the role? Rachel, right?"

Which brings me to the one big stumbling block in my Help Carter Save Face campaign . . .

I slipped the receiver under my chin and closed my eyes. I *had* basically told Rachel she could have the job. But that was before this whole thing with Carter. And I owed him for so many things, with his unwavering support and loyalty top on the list.

I opened my eyes, sucked in a long, deep breath, and squared my shoulders.

Rachel Clark was the art director brought in for the last two commercials I'd created—one for Zander, the other for New Town. From the very first pre-shoot powwow we'd had together, I'd been impressed by her creativity and her innate eye for detail. In fact, I don't think we were halfway through that first shoot when I was convinced Rachel was the only AD I'd ever work with from that day forward.

Which is why I'd been floored when she admitted to me all she'd ever really wanted to be was an actress . . .

By the time I'd yanked my jaw off the ground, she was on the then-empty New Town set giving a mind-blowing, scriptless run-through of the commercial we'd wrapped thirty minutes earlier. And after seeing her work, I'd had to admit Rachel Clark was one multi-talented chick.

Unfortunately, fears and internal second-guessing had kept her from pursuing her dream. And that's when I'd come up with the ingenious idea to give her a role in my upcoming Salonquility commercial. The plan would (a) give Rachel something concrete to show an agent, (b) give Sara, the studio intern, a crack at Rachel's AD job for the day, and (c) help two people reach for a dream in the process.

A stellar plan until Carter opened his mouth and shoved both feet firmly inside.

"I have to help him, JoAnna, I just do. I owe him." I rubbed my left temple in an attempt to ward off the dull headache that was brewing beneath my skin. "Besides, there'll be other commercials, other chances for Rachel, right?"

JoAnna didn't reply. Didn't nod. Didn't reposition her hands on her hips. She simply mouthed a "good luck" at me and backed out of my office, pulling the door shut in her wake and leaving me alone with my conscience.

I nibbled my bottom lip inward and slowly punched the studio's seven-digit number into my phone.

Carter was in a bad place—a place that was affecting his spirit and his happiness. Giving Fiona some commercial work would make things right for him.

I knew that.

Believed it with my whole heart.

So why, then, did I feel like such a heel?

Chapter Three

No matter how prepared I was, or how confident I felt, pitching to a new client was always high stress. Always.

Like a first date in a lot of ways.

You know, where you close your eyes and imagine every wonderful moment you'll have together . . . minus, of course, the part where he looks at you a beat too long and you're suddenly convinced something's hanging from your nose or stuck between your teeth.

It's how I felt at that very moment as I opened my easel and turned to face Dom and Gina Paletti—the final hurdle between me and a set of my very own car keys.

I'd gone through the pitch over and over into the wee hours of the morning, forgoing sleep in favor of finding just the right words and the perfect inflection with which to deliver them. But despite it all, I was still struck with an overwhelming urge to run my tongue across my teeth and to sniff deeply. You know, just in case . . .

Instead, I pushed a renegade strand of hair behind my ear and flashed what I hoped was a confident, easy smile.

"Oh, Tobi, don't be nervous. We won't bite, will we, Dom?" Gina Paletti made a soft noise that sounded an awful lot like an *awwww* under her breath and then elbowed the plump man sitting beside her. "Isn't she sweet?"

"Jesus, Regina, watch that arm."

Gina rolled her eyes, then elbowed her husband again. "Ah, quit your bellyaching. You've got more than enough cushion to handle an elbow." To me, she said, "Your hair is darling in that braid, Tobi."

I grinned. From the moment I'd first met the Palettis, I'd liked them. They were honest, hardworking, family-oriented people. Sure, they bickered once in a while—okay, *a lot*, but it didn't take long to see it was all surface stuff. Dom and Gina Paletti were precious together. And very obviously in love.

"Thanks, Mrs. Paletti." I wiped my hand on my skirt and tried the confident, easy smile again.

Gina waved her hand in the air. Dom cringed in response.

"Good Lord, husband, would you chill? When I'm going to poke you, I'll poke you. Like this." She elbowed him again and then leaned over and kissed his cheek. "See?"

"Thanks for clearing that up," he grumbled.

"No problem." She kissed him again and then looked at me. "Now no more of this Mrs. Paletti stuff, Tobi. It's Gina. Not Mrs. Paletti. Not Regina. Just plain Gina. Okay?"

"Okay. Gina it is." I relaxed my rigid stance and cleared my throat in an effort to dislodge any nervous dust bunnies that had accumulated during my idiotic self-stressathon. "Shall we get started?"

"There's plenty of time for that. How's that young man of yours—"

This time Dom threw an elbow. "Yes, let's get started." He dropped his voice and said, "Regina, this poor girl has a company to run. She can't sit here and discuss hairstyles and dating."

Gina shot a glare (and a harder, more precise elbow) at Dom and then shrugged her shoulders at me. "Okay, let's hear what you've got. Mr. Ants-in-His-Pants over here gets bored if conversations don't entail Nascar and beer."

"What else is there, dear?"

I waited a moment to see if there'd be any more appendage throwing and then slid my storyboard and slogan onto the easel, their cover sheets still securely in place.

"Okay. As you'll remember during our first meeting, we discussed the uniqueness of your restaurant. It's this uniqueness, this *creativity* that we want to focus on in our campaign." I poured three glasses of water from the pitcher JoAnna had placed on the table in preparation for the meeting and handed a cup to Dom and to Gina. "This isn't your run-of-the-mill pizza joint with crumbs all over the floor and three round tables covered with red and white checkered tablecloths shoved into a poorly lit corner."

They looked at one another and nodded.

So far so good. I'd reminded them of their selling point. Now I just had to hook them.

"We want to get people excited about driving to South County for a pizza. Yes, the pizza is good—superb, even—but to the average person flipping through the paper or watching your commercial from their couch, a pizza is a pizza when you're talking about a ten-, fif-teen-, twenty-minute drive."

Dom shifted in his seat, thrust his elbows onto the table (thank God) in front of him, and rested his mouth against his two-handed fist. "So how do we convince them it's worth the drive?"

Oh, how I loved it when I cast the net and the client jumped right in.

"We *show* them you're different. Different in a way they can see, different in a way that'll pique their curiosity enough to make that drive. Once they're inside, you can convince their stomachs that it's worth coming back."

"I can do that," Dom said.

Gina shot a hand onto her husband's back and gently massaged his left shoulder. "Of course you can, Snookums. No one makes a better pizza than you do."

Snookums?

I stifled the urge to laugh (and snort), opting instead for a non-committal nod. The net was being lifted from the water . . .

"What's different about your restaurant for the guy on the couch, or the mom reading the paper, is your restaurant itself . . . the fact that you've gone the extra mile in creating a destination . . . something en-tirely fresh and fun." I pulled the cover sheet from my slogan board and stepped to the side. "Pizza Adventure—You pick the place, we'll bring the pizza."

Gina raised her hands upward, muttered something in Italian, and broke out into a smile as wide as the room.

Dom puffed out his cheeks and nodded his head with big, dra-matic movements. "I like it. Like it a lot," he said, his gruff voice suddenly tinged with a hint of softness.

"Like it? *Like* it? Would you prefer Pizza Adventure—we cut it in triangles?" Gina shrieked.

This time it was Dom who shot his hands in the air and muttered something in Italian, then, "I said I like it, didn't I, Tobi?"

Ah geez . . .

"Don't drag her into this. She just came up with a slogan that's going to make you a very rich man, Dom Paletti. I want you to show her some enthusiasm. Some en-thu-si-asm. Pretend she has four wheels and a number on her chest."

I shifted foot to foot, unsure of what to say and how to say it. So I opted for nothing.

"Four wheels and a number, huh?" Dom's face broke into a wide grin as he winked at me. "Wooooo! Wooooo! Great slogan! Great Slogan! Wooooo! Wooooo!"

That did it. In a flash, my professionalism was gone, pushed to the side by one of my infamous shoulder-heaving laughs (complete with a snort, of course)—a shoulder-heaving laugh that stopped all bickering between the couple and earned me a double-face stare.

"Good heavens, Dom, did you hear that?"

"Sure did, Regina. Sounded like one of those hogs on your dad's farm back in Italy."

Gina's clucking ceased. "Oh, Tobi, you need to break that habit if you want to keep your young man."

"I'm trying, Gina." I stopped, wiped my moistening hands against the sides of my jacket, and then slunk against the edge of the table. "Believe me, I'm trying."

"Good." Gina touched a hand to her chest and nodded. "Good. Good."

Dom rolled his eyes. "So what do we *do* with the slogan now?"

Relieved to be back in comfortable waters, I returned to my feet and dove back in. "*Now* we use the slogan as a springboard for our print campaign. We can run weekly ads highlighting a different destination room each time, or a single ad that shows all the destinations at once. But regardless, we want to run them often these first few months. We want them in the *Post-Dispatch*, the various *Journal* papers, and *St. Louis Magazine*. And I think a few well-placed billboards would be smart too."

Dom pushed back his chair and hiked his left foot across his right leg. "We just use straight photos of the room? Like the ones you took last week?"

"No. We create the scene we want with the help of a professional photographer."

"Sounds expensive." Dom's foot began to bounce.

"Actually, it's not. I use a photographer who needs the experience to build his portfolio. Yes, he'll charge, but trust me, he's reasonable."

"We don't need to be going cheap on this, Tobi. We're willing to pay for the best if it will help the business." Gina shot another elbow into her husband's side. "Isn't that right, dear?"

I sat down on the arm of a chair. "My photographer *is* the best."

"Sold," Dom said.

"Great. I'll set him up for location shots next week. In the meantime, we need to find some people for the photographs—kids, teens, young couples, families, and retirees."

"Leave that to me. We'll ask people from our church." Gina pointed at the easel. "What's that larger rectangle behind the slogan? Is that for us?"

I stood up, pulled off the slogan board, and removed the cover sheet from the storyboard. Gina gasped.

"Oooohhhh, look at the little boys eating pizza in the Batcave . . . and the teenagers at the car tables . . . and the adults in the beach room . . . and, oh my! Did you draw those?"

"Yes, I did."

Gina elbowed Dom in the ribs again. "Have you ever seen that kind of talent in such a petite package?"

Surprisingly, Dom ignored the elbow and simply shook his head, a pleased expression on his face as he peered at the poster-topped easel. "No, I haven't. Tobi, those are incredible."

Judging by the look on Gina's face at her husband's choice of words, my numbered chest and its four wheels had just crossed the finish line.

The rest of the afternoon was a blur between the impromptu celebration JoAnna and I had over lunch (complete with an assortment of car brochures she'd picked up over the weekend) and the countless phone calls I'd made for both Pizza Adventure ad space and the upcoming Salonquility commercial. I'd tried to stay focused, to be excited about the out-of-the-ballpark home run I'd hit with the Palettis, but my thoughts kept returning to the phone call with Rachel.

She'd sounded okay, even said she understood my decision to use Carter's coworker for the salon commercial, but I still felt awful. I hadn't had time to dwell on it once the Palettis showed up, but now that they were gone and I was alone with my thoughts (and my conscience), it was torturing me.

I tapped my pencil on the desk and stared down at the nonsensical doodling on the pad in front of me. There would be other commercials, other chances. I'd make sure of it. Heck, I could use her in a Pizza Adventure commercial once the print work was done.

Yes, that's exactly what I'd do.

Feeling a wee bit better, I picked up the phone and dialed Carter's number.

"Hey there, Sunshine."

I knew Carter had caller ID. Knew it every time I called. But it still freaked me out when he knew it was me.

"Uh, hi." I felt the knots in my stomach ease as I anticipated his reaction to my idea. "I didn't think I'd catch you at home."

"I'm due in Renoir's office at five o'clock. For a powwow. Complete with a hatchet, no doubt."

His attempt at a laugh was useless with me. I knew Carter better than anyone. "What would you say if I told you that I had a way to get Fiona off your back?"

"I'd say your excessive sugar intake has finally affected your brain."

I grinned. "Not possible."

"Says you."

"Let's go at this another way then. Remember that miracle you said you needed to keep your job?"

"Sadly, yes."

I twirled the phone cord around my index finger and leaned back in my chair. "Well, consider it done."

Carter crunched something in my ear and guffawed. "So what are you trying to tell me, Sunshine? You're a miracle worker now?"

"If the shoe fits . . . Which, in case you're wondering, does, indeed, fit in this particular case." I turned my head, looked out the window, and waited. Knowledge was indeed power.

"Suspense does not become you, you know."

I grinned but said nothing, determined to wait him out.

"Tobi, you still there?"

I nodded. A futile gesture when you considered the phone and all. "If you got Fiona a real live commercial gig, do you think your job would be safe?"

His snicker morphed into something that sounded a lot like a snort, which, of course, I couldn't let pass. "Did you just snort, Mr. McDade?"

"No."

"Yes, you did. I, for one, know what a snort sounds like."

"I forgot who I was talking to. Yeah, okay, I snorted. But c'mon, I know I'm multi-talented, but even *I* couldn't get that girl a commercial."

"I can."

"Huh?"

"You said she could handle an acting gig that didn't require a lot of depth, right?"

"I'm listening . . ."

"Well, I've got the perfect role for her."

Silence.

Man, this was fun.

"I'm filming a commercial for Salonquility on Friday, and I need an actress on short notice. I thought maybe you'd like to offer the role to Fiona."

Again with the silence.

"The part isn't terribly challenging, but it will require the actress to undergo several of the salon services," I explained.

A childlike voice emerged in my ear. "Did you say *salon services*? As in, um, like a *hair coloring*, perhaps?"

I laughed. "Yup."

"You have room for a male hairdresser in that commercial?"

"But of course I do."

"You're serious?"

"Completely."

"Oh my God, Sunshine, you are the best. The absolute best."

My lip trembled at the return of the Carter I knew and loved. I'd made the right decision. I really had. "After the way you stood by me through the whole Zander slogan thing, it's the least I can do."

"I won't forget this, Sunshine. Not ever."

"Of course you won't. I won't let you."

"Wow, I-I don't know what to say. This is incredible."

I sat up in my chair and looked at the Friday square on my desk calendar. "Have Fiona at Starwood Studios on Market Street at seven o'clock Friday morning, okay?"

"Roger that."

"I'll get her lines to you tonight so she can learn those between now and then. There's not a ton, but she needs to have them down cold."

"Okay."

I closed my eyes and mentally ran through a typical commercial shoot so I wouldn't forget a thing. "Oh. We'll start off first thing with a meeting of the minds. That's when we'll walk through the shoot so everyone's clear on what we're doing."

"Got it. And can I decide on the color she's gonna get?"

"Absolutely. Hairdresser's discretion."

I pulled the phone away from my ear for a moment as Carter whooped—loudly. When it was safe, I said, "Okay, Carter, I've got to stop by the pet shop on the way home. I need to line Sam up for a photo shoot next week and check on Mary Fran. JoAnna says she's stressed."

"Okeydoke. Give her a kiss for me. And so I'll see you tonight? When you drop off Fiona's lines?"

"Right." I pushed back my chair and stood. "Have fun tonight."

"Oh, I will. Believe me." He cleared his throat, his voice softening. "Thanks, Sunshine. For everything."

Chapter Four

Walking into Mary Fran's pet shop was like walking into a meeting at the United Nations. Only instead of a host of different languages, I was greeted by a medley of hellos ranging from dogs barking and cats meowing, to mice squeaking, birds singing, and, of course, Rudder snorting.

"Tobi, is that you?"

"Thanks, Rudder," I mumbled under my breath as I peeled off my coat and hung it on the coatrack beside the door. "Yeah, Mary Fran, it's me."

Mary Fran Wazoli emerged from the back room balancing a cup of cage fluff atop a scoop of cat food, her forehead creased in a series of uncharacteristic lines. "How'd the pitch go today?"

"Awesome." I took the cup of fluff from her hands and walked over to Max's cage. "In here, right?"

"Where else? I swear I don't know what he does with his fluff. He goes through it faster than any other hamster in here. But then again, what can you expect? He is, after all, *a male*."

At forty-three, Mary Fran was stunning. Her copper-colored hair was long and sleek, her eyes a charcoal gray. About five-foot-ten and model slender, she made more heads turn than should be legal. But she had little use for men. Except, of course, her son, Sam.

Sam was the apple of her eye and, according to Mary Fran, the only worthwhile thing a man ever gave her.

Mary Fran was thrice divorced, a concept that still surprised me. Sure, she would argue with the devil if she felt it was a worthy point, but she also had an amazing capacity for love. Like her son.

The funny part? She didn't think twice about trying to fix me up with men of all shapes and sizes. I'd had dates with lawyers, bankers, construction workers, computer geeks, and even a guy with a serious foot fetish. Some had gone well, others had been a disaster. All were an experience.

I think her determination to make sure my love life turned out better than hers was spurred on by my broken engagement to Nick Harmon. She'd been there when we met, watched us fall in love, toasted our engagement, and then dried my tears when I caught him cheating on me with the waitress from our favorite restaurant.

"You okay, Mary Fran?"

She stopped in front of the open kennels and poured a handful of food into three small dishes, clicking her tongue against her teeth. Like a shot, three furry tails appeared out of nowhere and descended on the freshly poured cat food. I still looked for Sadie in the mix, my mouth drooping downward at her absence.

I knew she'd gone to a good home. And I knew I was still able to see her thanks to Andy—correction, I *had* been able to see her PB (pre-Brenna). But I still missed seeing her here, with all the other animals.

I shook my head against the thoughts that instantly stung my eyes and forced my attention onto Mary Fran and the fact that she had yet to answer my question.

"Mary Fran. Is everything okay? JoAnna said you called a few times."

She wiped her hands on the front of her apron and grabbed the broom perched against the wall. "The cops were here this morning."

"The cops? Wait. Why?" I asked, instinctively reaching for the dustpan to collect Mary Fran's dirt.

"We have a new neighbor."

"O-kay . . ."

"He's filed a peace disturbance complaint." Mary Fran swept the pile of cage scraps and stray food morsels into the pan.

I stood and dumped the trash into the container underneath Rudder's cage. "You having wild parties again, Mary Fran?"

She shrugged her shoulders at my playful retort, sadness playing at the corners of her eyes.

"I'm sorry, Mary Fran. You're serious about this?"

She nodded. "Yeah. Apparently, the animals are being too loud at night."

I squatted down once more to retrieve the final sweep of dirt. "And this guy couldn't talk to you about it first?"

Mary Fran placed her left hand on her hip and stared at me as I stood. "He's a *man*, Tobi."

Ah.

I smacked the pan against the trash can and then placed it on its hook beside the counter. "So what the heck are these guys doing in here that they're making so much noise?"

Mary Fran shrugged. "I have no idea. I mean, I know Rudder and Baboo converse at night, but I can't believe they're raising the roof *that* much."

I walked over to Rudder's cage and peered in. "Hey, mister. Are you causing trouble again?"

"Snort! Snort! S-nort!"

Mary Fran laughed. I didn't.

Rudder, in his infinite African grey parrot wisdom, imitates repetitive sounds. You know, creaky doors, throats clearing, the other animals, and . . . yes . . . my snort-accompanied laughs (with an emphasis on the snort portion, of course). It was my biggest bone of contention with the otherwise amusing, albeit obnoxious bird.

"So what are you going to do?" I asked as I made faces at Rudder.

"We're going on a stakeout."

"Come again?"

Mary Fran clapped a hand on my shoulder and batted her long eyelashes at me. "We're going on a stakeout."

"Who, exactly, constitutes this we?"

"You and me."

"Um, okay. And what does this stakeout entail?"

"A sleepover. Here. Saturday night."

"And that's going to do what exactly?" I closed my eyes for a moment and envisioned Rudder in a nightcap and slippers, a bird-sized pillow in his beak.

"It'll give us an idea what these guys are doing at night. Once I figure that out, I can try to fix it before we get evicted." Mary Fran walked behind the counter and opened the refrigerator. Rudder started squawking. "It's coming, big guy."

I leaned against the counter and watched as she pulled Rudder's Tupperware container from the top shelf and popped the lid. The smell of ripe kiwi filled the room in mere seconds.

"It's com-coming. It's coming, big-big guy."

Mary Fran lowered her voice and moved her mouth close to my ear. "Typical male—worried about his needs first."

"Typ-typical male. Typical male."

Mary Fran rolled her eyes upward, mumbled something under her breath, and then started chopping kiwi at breakneck speed.

As obnoxious as Rudder Malone was, he had us all wrapped around his finger—I mean, talon.

"Any chance we can have some chocolate at this sleepover?" I asked, looking around at the limited floor space in the small shop.

"Of course. And popcorn. But no boys."

"No boys," I repeated.

"Unless, of course, you want to invite Andy. He's allowed."

"No! No boys."

"Uh-oh." Mary Fran stopped chopping and pointed her knife at me. "Spill it. What gives?"

"It's com-coming, big guy. Big guy."

Saved by the starving bird.

Mary Fran picked up the cutting board with her left hand, pushed the chopped kiwi onto the container lid, and headed toward Rudder's cage, muttering, once again, under her breath. Something about impatience, weakness, and pathetic males.

The door swung open behind me, bringing with it the sound of its bell (and, therefore, Rudder) and Sam's feet as he headed toward the counter. He stopped when he saw me. "Oh, hey, Tobes, I didn't know you were here. How's it going?"

I raised my face upward and grinned as the fifteen-year-old planted a kiss on my cheek before heading over to his mom for more of the same.

"I'm good, and you?"

"Don't listen to her, Sam," Mary Fran interjected. "There's trouble in paradise."

Sam flashed a quizzical look at his mom and mouthed a single word. *Andy?*

"Hello? I'm right here, people."

"Sorry, Tobes." Sam repeated his quizzical look and spoke his question aloud this time. "Andy?"

I held my hands upward in surrender. "Okay, you two. Paradise is fine. I mean, I *think* it's fine. *Hope* it's fine. I just don't know. And I really don't want to talk about it right now."

Sam looked at me and pointed to his mom. "You realize my mom is standing right here, right?"

I had to laugh as Mary Fran gave her son a playful shove. "I brought you into this world, son, and—"

"I can take you out of it," Sam and I said in unison.

"Take-take you. Take you out."

"Oh, good grief, now you've got Rudder ganging up on me, too?" Mary Fran pulled her apron from around her neck and tossed it onto the counter. "I think I'll make some of my reunion calls from the phone in back while you three have your fun in here."

"No matter how many times I've heard you reference your reunion the past few months, I still can't quite wrap my head around the fact that it's been twenty-five years since you graduated from high school. That makes you sound kind of *old*, you know?"

Mary Fran stuck her tongue out at me. "Gee, thanks."

I traded grins with Sam before focusing again on his mother. "So? Have you spoken to Mr. Wonderful yet?" I asked.

"Would you knock off the Mr. Wonderful stuff, please? Mr. Wonder—I mean, Evan, is just some guy I dated for a while my senior year. Really, you're making far too big a deal out of this, don't you think?"

"I think you doth protest too much, that's what I think."

Mary Fran rolled her eyes. "Whatever. As for your question—if I can even remember it with your mouth constantly moving—no, I've not spoken to Evan. In fact, if he's moved back to the area like his registration card said he would be doing, there have been no sightings reported."

"You'll find him. And if you don't, the reunion is little more than a week away, right?" I picked a tiny piece of kiwi up off the counter and offered it to Sam, who mockingly pointed back at me.

I say mockingly because I don't *do* fruit. And everyone knows that. Unfortunately, Rudder, being Rudder, had absolutely zero interest in a chocolate chip or tasty Rolo.

Mary Fran rolled her eyes a second time, reached into her apron, and handed me a Kiss.

"Thanks, Mary Fran." I unwrapped the silver foil, tossed the little white flag into the trash, and popped the candy into my mouth. "Has *anyone* from your class been in touch with him at all in the last twenty-five years?"

"Kelly Flannigan told me that Sherry Rhodes is in touch with his older brother, Drew."

The women's names meant nothing to me. But that last name rattled around in my brain while I worked the Kiss over with my tongue. "Drew? Drew? Why does that sound familiar?"

"I probably mentioned him at some point. He was two years older than I was. Sweet guy. Had a crush on me. But he never did curl my toes the way his brother did."

I swallowed my Kiss and reached into Mary Fran's apron pocket for seconds. She smacked my hand away.

"You know, if I didn't know any better, I'd think you were showing interest in a"—I lowered my voice to a dramatic whisper—"male."

"Male-male."

I flashed Rudder a thumbs-up. Sam laughed.

Mary Fran turned on her heel and headed toward the doorway that led to the back room.

"We love you, Mary Fran," I quipped.

"I know." She disappeared through the opening and slammed the door shut.

"Uh-oh. Do you think I made her mad?" I nibbled my lower lip inward and looked at Sam.

"Nah, Mom loves the teasing. Besides, she knows she can't deny the fact that she's *dying* to find Mr. Evan Murran, former letterman-of-every-sport and total hunk. *Hunk* being Mom's word, not mine." Sam hoisted himself onto the counter and gave me that look. The one that made him irresistible to everyone around him. "So, is it real bad?"

"What?"

"This stuff with Andy?"

I sighed. "I don't know, Sam, I really don't. I was really starting to fall for him, as you clearly already figured out. But I just don't want to get hurt again."

"Andy isn't Nick, Tobes. You know that."

It never ceased to amaze me how perceptive a teenager could be.

Though, in all fairness, Sam was wise beyond his years and not your typical teenager, by any stretch of the imagination.

"I know. But that doesn't mean he won't hurt me."

Sam twisted his mouth to the side. "True."

I grabbed the stool in front of Baboo's cage and pulled it closer to the counter. And Sam.

"But we need to talk about something else right now."

"Oh?"

"Up for another job?" I asked.

Sam's face lit up. "You bet I am! Who? When? Where?"

Sam Wazoli was probably the only kid his age who wouldn't throw in the more typical "How much?" inquiry. But that was Sam for you. His passion for photography was a part of who he was, just as advertising had always been for me.

"A new client. Dominic and Regina Paletti and their new restaurant, Pizza Adventure."

"Hmmm. A pizza place, huh?"

"Trust me, this place is as far from your typical pizza joint as you can possibly imagine. You're gonna have a field day shooting this."

Sam clapped his hands together and slid off the counter to his feet. "When do we get started?"

I stepped off my stool and headed over to the coatrack. "You have off Monday for Martin Luther King, right?"

"Sure do."

"Will that work for you?"

"Absolutely."

I pulled my coat off the top limb and shoved my left arm inside. "Great. It's a date then."

"Where is this place?" he asked as he helped me into my coat.

"South County."

"I'll get Mom's car."

I felt the smile spread across my face as I turned to face him. "Not sure that'll be necessary."

"Why's that?" Sam's eyes searched my face closely.

When I said nothing, he leaned in. "Tobes, are you holding out on me?"

"I'm going car shopping this weekend. Want to come?"

"You're buying a car?"

I nodded.

He held his hand up for a high five. "That's awesome, Tobes. Way to go."

"Way-way to go. Snort! Snort! S-nort!"

Unless I was mistaken, Carter was skipping down the stairs on the other side of the door. And, based on the big, goofy smile on his face when he opened it, I was right.

"Hey, Sunshine. I was hoping you hadn't forgotten about me."

I reached my gloved hand outward and gently pinched his left cheek. "How could I forget *you*?"

"My sentiments exactly." He stepped aside and waved me into the tiny vestibule that constituted his foyer. "C'mon up."

I waited as he locked the door before leading me up the steps into his neat-as-a-pin living room. My home décor was old by financial necessity. Carter's was old by choice, down to the television with the rabbit-ear antennae on top.

I dropped the script onto the coffee table and sank into the sofa. "So, how'd it go with Princess Fiona?"

Carter's face—already boasting a 60-watt glow—shone even brighter as he picked up the stapled pages and quickly flipped through them. "Would you believe, she hugged me? Said she always knew I was the smartest one at the theater. Next to her, of course."

Sincerity at its finest.

"Good. So she's game? She's going to let you color her hair?"

Carter disappeared into his kitchen and returned with a plate of broccoli, carrots, celery, and some god-awful-smelling dip in a small bowl.

My stomach flopped in disgust. "Where's the chocolate?"

"Pee-shaw. Chocolate at your place. Real food at mine."

My nostril flared. "*Real* food? You call this real food?" I picked up the dip bowl and sniffed, my face crinkling on the initial inhale. "Ugh, Carter. Did you get this stuff at that Booler place?"

Carter took the bowl from my hand and shook his head in mock disgust. "Boulier. Boo. Yay. You don't pronounce the 'l' or the 'r'."

"Silly me," I muttered.

"Yes, I got it there. It's the only place in this town where one can find many of the world's finer delicacies in their pure, unprocessed form. *Pure* being the keyword."

"*Yuck* being the key response." I reached into my backpack for the 100 Grand Bar I'd bought on the way past Ted's Grocery Store. "I bet they don't carry Cocoa Puffs at Booooooyay."

"Shorten your 'oo' sound and you're golden, Sunshine. And no, no Cocoa Puffs. What kind of classless operation do you think they're running?"

I shook my head and unwrapped my candy bar. "Hey, you never said what Fiona thought of the whole hair-coloring caveat."

Carter crunched down on a raw carrot, chewed for a moment, and then looked at me sheepishly. "Technically, I sorta left that part out. For now. Figured I'd spring it on her at the studio. I wanted her to enjoy the moment."

"You wanted her to enjoy the moment? Or you wanted to wait and put her on the spot in front of a studio full of professionals? Geez, Carter, what happens if she pitches a fit and refuses to do it? Then what?" I bit into the candy bar and watched as little flecks of chocolate dropped onto my lap.

"Oh, she'll pitch a fit, there's no doubt of that. But she won't refuse to go on. This is her"—he shot his fingers into the air, air-quote style— "big break, her ticket to the big-time."

"She said that?"

Carter grinned around a celery stalk. "Verbatim."

"You're gonna love every minute of this, aren't you?" I knew it was a rhetorical question, but I asked it anyway. Call me slow.

"Oh, trust me, I already am. And, Sunshine, it's only going to get better come Friday."

Chapter Five

If I hadn't just gawked at the freshly painted Starwood Studios sign hanging over the front door, I would have sworn I'd crossed the threshold of an upscale (read: overpriced) day spa and hair salon out in Ladue or Clayton somewhere.

Gone were the neutral-colored walls we'd used last week for the Zander Closet Company commercial. In their place were three-sided rooms of soothing greens and muted purples, with elegant floor-to-ceiling pillars trimmed in miniature white bulbs designed to add dimension.

Gone was the state-of-the-art closet system Andy's cousin Blake had erected as the focal point of their shoot—the spotlight now divided between a massage table in one room, a hairdresser's chair in another, and a pedicure tub in the last.

Gone were the varying-height clothes racks and multi-tiered shelves that had held some of the most exquisite gowns, suits, shoes, and purses I'd ever seen. Instead, a single luxurious robe now hung from the back of an incredibly real-looking door, a pair of open-toed slippers placed beside it.

My mouth dropped open as I stood there, in utter awe, absorbing the magic of Rachel Clark. Magic being the operative word, since anyone who could execute such a stunning transformation had to be a three-inch-tall fairy with an endless supply of pixie dust.

"Do you like it?"

I turned around and stared into the face of the young woman responsible for creating the illusion behind me. And, truth be told, I was more than a little surprised to see her golden wand was nothing more than a clipboard. "*Like it*? Are you kidding me? Rachel, it's amazing. When did you do this?"

The art director's mouth spread into a tentative smile that stopped short of her pale blue eyes. "I planned it out over the weekend but really started putting it together after we talked on the phone Monday morning."

My throat tightened with guilt. "Look, I'm sorry about rescinding the offer to act in this shoot, but my friend was in a really bad place, and this was something I could do to help." Without thinking, I reached out and touched her, the muscles in her forearm surprisingly tense. "I hope you understand."

"I do. Really. Don't worry. Besides, this is what I'm supposed to do. Create the sets. This whole acting thing is nothing more than a pipe dream anyway."

Ah geez. Nothing like twisting the knife . . .

"If acting is where your heart is, Rachel, then it's not just a pipe dream. You'll get a chance soon, I promise. Once we get the print campaign in motion for my newest client, I'm sure we'll be looking at doing a commercial. And maybe that'll work even better."

"That'd be great, Tobi, but," Rachel splayed her palms outward, shrugging her shoulders as she continued, "I'll be okay if it doesn't. Really."

"Oh. Okay, sure." I stood there for one of those never-ending awkward moments, then pulled back my coat sleeve and peered at my watch. "Well, Carter and Fiona should be here any minute. Once they show, we'll give you all a few minutes to get acquainted, and then we—"

"We already met . . . the actress," came a voice from my left.

I looked over and smiled at Sara Gooden. Sara was the studio intern, though jack-of-all-trades was a more fitting term. She'd earned enough credits to graduate from St. Louis University in December, but chose instead to spend one more semester accumulating on-the-job experience. She was a go-getter in every sense of the word, learning everyone's job—sometimes too well. She had no shortage of confidence and seemed to have her hand in all studio pies (aka conversations) at one time. Like right now.

"Wait. You already met Fiona? When?"

Rachel pulled her pen from the clipboard and scribbled something on the nearly full paper. "Last night. Your friend, Carter, brought her by to see the studio."

Sara grunted.

"Um, did something go wrong?" I was sensing an issue but wasn't sure how much was still emanating from Rachel and how much was new.

"Fiona is kind of, well—"

"Oh, just say it, Rachel. She's a bitch."

Uh-oh.

"Sara!"

I pulled my jaw off the ground and held my palm up in Rachel's direction. "No, Rachel, I want to hear what happened." I looked at Sara and waited for her to bring the picture into focus in a way only Sara could. With brutal honesty.

Instead, she called Jeff Meyer over to the fray. "Jeff, what'd you think of Fiona last night?"

"That's easy. She's a bitch."

I was beginning to sense a trend . . .

"What did she do?" I asked, my stomach beginning its initial things-aren't-good flip.

"What *didn't* she do?" piped in Rocky Jazaray, one of the key grips.

"See? I'm not the only one who found Fiona Renoir totally insufferable." Sara tugged her fitted jacket closer to her waist bone and pointed at the massage table. "I think we need the lights to be lower in this room, and a few of those massage rocks should be lying on the counter. It looks too sterile right now."

I shot a glance in Rachel's direction to gauge her reaction to Sara's criticism but saw nothing. She was probably as used to it as the rest of us were.

"I think the set looks perfect just the way it is," I said with a quiet firmness. "Anyway, would someone please tell me what happened last night?"

"That chick? Fiona? She came in here to see the set and to try out her lines. She stood out there," Rocky said, pointing at the pedicure room, "and told me exactly how she wanted the light to hit her, and how Jeff should position the camera."

"You can't be serious," I squeaked, sounding much more like a freaked-out mouse than president of my own advertising company.

"Oh, he's serious," Jeff said as he fiddled with some buttons on the side of his camera. "She told Rachel how to arrange things, and Sara to hush up and be quiet."

I gulped. "Oh, Sara, I'm sorry."

Sara shrugged, her cheeks reddening at the memory.

"And that's not the best part. I was eating my dinner—a peanut butter and jelly sandwich that Tasha packed for me—and the dame went wild." Jeff stopped fiddling, his eyes widening at the memory. "And I mean *wild*. She started shrieking at me to toss it in the trash. *Outside*."

"She's allergic to—"

"Peanuts," Rachel, Sara, Jeff, and Rocky said in unison. "We know."

Suddenly, helping Carter didn't seem like such a bright idea after all. *Lord, please get me through this day with my sanity intact.*

It didn't take long to realize God wasn't listening. If he was, he wasn't responding.

Fiona Renoir was everything Carter had described and more.

Sure, I'd seen her in a few of the theater productions over the past six months. But that was always from a safe distance and when she was on her best behavior. Or, rather, the best behavior of whichever character she was playing at the time.

In other words, if this tyrant sitting across the table from me wasn't the *real* Fiona Renoir, then she had the infamous role of the Wicked Witch of the West down to an art form. An Academy-Award-winning art form.

I looked down at my glass of water and back up at Fiona.

"Trust me, Sunshine, it won't work."

Lifting my hand to my mouth, I feigned a yawn. "It worked for Dorothy."

"It did. But we're not in Kansas, my dear."

"But it's only one state away." I dropped my hand into my lap and shifted my focus farther down the table—to Rachel, Sara, Jeff, and Rocky, their expressions unified by one common emotion.

Irritation.

"My best side is my right side," Fiona continued, "so all close-ups must be handled accordingly. That said, I have a slight scratch above my right ear, so you'll need to work around that."

"A scratch?" Rocky echoed.

"Yes, a scratch. See?" Fiona pushed back her hair and pointed to an angry red mark. "My uncle's cat is nasty."

Jeff met my gaze and held it, waiting.

I sucked in a breath and, in the process, choked myself with the butterscotch candy I'd pilfered off Rachel's desk. More than anything, I wanted to stand up, tell Fiona she was out, and make good on my original promise to Rachel. But to do so would put Carter's beloved job at the theater in jeopardy once again, and I couldn't do that.

Still, I had to work with Starwood Studios in the future, and burning bridges wasn't wise. So once I was done choking, I wiped my eyes, cleared my throat, and adopted the same voice I used when trying to placate another trying figure in my life.

"Rud—I mean, *Fiona*, I'm sure you understand that our main priority with this shoot is to showcase Salonquility and its services. Because without them, there wouldn't be a need for this commercial, if you get my drift. So while I'm sure Jeff will do his best to keep your right-side preference in mind, he will have to go for the shot that works best for what we're trying to achieve on a grander scale."

Carter's nemesis turned fiery green eyes in my direction. "I'm not asking for the moon and the stars here, Ms. Tobias. I'm just talking about close-ups."

Before I could respond, Jeff shot up his hand. "Noted. Now, can we please move on?"

"Of course." I opened the folder in front of me and removed the stapled pages JoAnna had set inside for me that morning. "Now let's walk through the script and make sure everything feels okay before we take it out to the amazing set Rachel has created for today's shoot."

A snicker-like sound drew my attention to the far end of the table, but not in enough time for a positive identification. What I did note, however, was Rachel's strained smile, Sara's tightened mouth, and the completing arc of Fiona's bored eye roll. Before I could investigate, though, Carter began to read from his script.

Line by line, we made our way from the first sentence to the last, stopping from time to time to pencil in a direction made by either Jeff or Rachel. When they reached the end, Fiona took in the props assembled on the nearby set and then looked back at me.

"So where's my wig?"

I felt Carter stir beside me. "You won't be wearing a wig." I slipped my copy of the script back into the folder and stood.

"But my hair is red," Fiona protested as she too pushed back her chair and stood. "And that whole line about being the envy of Rapunzel won't make any sense if my hair is red."

"That's why your hair will be the color of spun gold at the end of the commercial. So our viewers can see a Salonquility transformation right in front of their own eyes." I sensed Carter's eyes following me as I moved toward the set, but I refused to meet them lest I should start to laugh.

If Fiona noticed my struggle, she didn't let on. Instead, she caught up to me next to the hair-styling station that would be Carter's for the next eight to ten hours. "Right. So shouldn't I try on the wig to make sure it works?"

"You won't be wearing a wig," I repeated.

"But—"

I grabbed a color bowl from the shelf and waved it between us. "Salonquility is a salon, Fiona. We want to show actual services being performed. It's why you'll get a real pedicure on set one, an actual massage—albeit a quick one—on set two, and a real cut and color right here on set three. From Carter."

"*Carter?*" she hissed.

And I mean, hissed. Like a cat. With narrowed eyes and everything.

Before I could even begin a nod, Fiona whirled around, marched over to the door where Carter was now standing, and shoved him backward into Jeff, who in turn toppled into Rocky. "You jerk! You knew this all along, didn't you?"

Carter righted himself against the door frame, helped Jeff and Rocky to their respective feet, and then turned back to Fiona, his normally jovial face twisted tight and ready to pop. Sensing the explosion that was mere seconds from going off, I stepped between them to face Fiona. "Carter knew nothing about this. This was *my* decision."

I know, I know. Lying is frowned upon. But so is war. I just picked the lesser of two evils at that moment and ran with it. "If you have an issue with following the script, I'd be happy to release you from your contract in light of the fact that I have someone who can step in and fill your role right here and right now."

I didn't mean to look at Rachel, but I did, and she was grinning— the kind of smile that reached her eyes. Satisfied, I swung my attention back to Fiona.

"You're serious?" Fiona said, sans hiss.

"I have to think of my client, Fiona."

"They can't just pretend . . . or show a before and"—Fiona threw up a set of air quotes—"*after* that happens to be a wig?"

"Not if we're going to claim actual results—which we are."

Seconds turned to minutes as Fiona wandered from set to set, running her hand across the massage table, inspecting the pyramid of nail polish colors, and finally dropping onto the leather salon chair with a sigh to end all sighs. "Okay. I'll do it. But if Carter screws this up, he's done in this town. And I do mean *done*."

Chapter Six

I think it was around the third exasperated sigh from Rachel, the fourth gritted *ugh* from Sara, and the umpteenth murmured curse word from Rocky that I finally had to admit to myself that involving Fiona Renoir in the Salonquility commercial wasn't one of my better ideas.

And if I hadn't admitted it, Jeff was more than willing to drive the point home—again, and again, and again.

Not that I could blame him, of course. Quite the contrary. If I'd had someone snapping her fingers in my face every time I so much as breathed, I'd be doing a little lamenting myself.

Which, I kind of was. To Carter.

"Is she this bad at the theater?" I whispered as I sidled up alongside my upstairs neighbor as he readied set three for the final phase of the shoot. "Because I can't understand why anyone would keep her around. She's horrible."

"It's called nepotism, Sunshine, remember? Her uncle has a soft spot for the demon."

I watched Rocky huff his way over to a corner of set two, mouth yet another curse word, and then return to his starting place in time to move a cable from Jeff's path. "I get that, to a point. But this chick is over the top. She could be my twin sister and I swear I'd kill her."

Carter squirted Fiona's agreed-upon hair color into a small black bowl and then grabbed a spoon-like utensil from the pile of props Rachel had placed inside a nearby drawer. "Welcome to my world the past few months, Sunshine. Maybe now you'll understand my lapse of judgment last weekend."

"Your lapse of judgment?"

He stopped stirring. "You know, with the Cocoa Puffs. That shrew could drive a nun to drink."

"Or, in your case, drive a food snob to break bread with the unwashed masses?" At Carter's guilt-powered nod, I looked down at my clipboard (at what, I don't know) and exhaled so hard the paper actually moved. "I get it. I really do. I just hope I haven't made it so Starwood Studios tells me to take a hike when it comes time to film a spot for Dom and Gina."

"Dom and Gina?"

"The Pizza Adventure couple."

"Ahhhh." Carter finished stirring the concoction that would transform the tresses of the wicked witch of the Central West End from red to blond and then set the bowl down with a thud. "You said they're still working on some of the adventure rooms, right?"

Grateful for the momentary distraction, I nodded.

"Think they could make a black hole we could shove Fiona into?"

"If only we could be so lucky." I pulled the clipboard against my nonexistent bosom and studied my friend, the smile he'd so easily worn that morning now gone. In its place was something that, at first glance, resembled tension. The worry in his eyes as he met mine only served as confirmation of the thoughts going through his head at that exact moment. Reaching out, I grabbed his hand and squeezed. "Hey . . . we've only got what? Maybe another two hours of her? We can do this. Especially knowing I've got a brand-new, unopened box of puffs waiting for us at my place when we're all done."

Carter covered his mouth to hide his answering retch, but I saw it, and I was not amused. Before I could settle on one of my tried-and-true responses, though, Rachel peeked around the corner.

"Tobi? I know we're going to give everyone a break before we go into the actual shoot for this last scene, but Fiona requested a quick break now, as well."

"You mean *demanded* a break," Sara corrected as she pushed past Rachel on her way toward the Salonquility smock draped across the back of the hairdresser chair. When she reached it, she ran her hand across the client's elegantly written logo on the upper right side and then folded her arms across her chest. "I'm telling you, Tobi, Rocky showed amazing restraint just now."

I felt the groan rising up in my throat a full second before it echoed around the former warehouse. "Uh-oh. What did I miss?"

"She asked him if he'd learned his job from a baboon." Sara pursed her lips, held them for what seemed like a count of eight (with Mississippis included) and then plucked the smock off the chair and unfolded it across her arm. "A baboon . . . can you believe it?"

Rachel stiffened. "When did she say that?"

Sara stopped messing with the smock long enough to sweep her gaze across her boss before landing it back on me. "I mean, don't get me wrong. I understand the frustration that comes with mediocrity, but to take a below-the-belt shot *like that*? It was too much."

I tried to trade glances with Carter, but since his guilt had driven his field of vision down to his shoes, it did me no good. Instead, I resorted to the only response I could come up with at that moment. "What happened—exactly?"

"Jeff moved in for a close-up of Fiona's face as she gazed down at her completed toes, but as he did, he must have realized it was her left side because he backed up and went left." Sara looked around, spotted the color cart off to the side, and wheeled it into position next to the chair. "As he did, Rocky reached for the cable so Jeff wouldn't trip, and when he lifted it up to reposition it, he knocked over a half dozen or so nail polish bottles."

Since I've never been known for my poker face, Sara held up her hand like she was getting ready to address the crowd outside St. Peter's Basilica. "I know what you're thinking, but *I* made sure to tighten the tops on all the prop bottles just in case something like that were to happen. And it's a good thing I did, because there would have been nail polish everywhere if I wasn't so accustomed to dotting all the 'i's' and 't's' around this place."

"When did this happen?" Rachel repeated as first Jeff and then Rocky stepped onto the set, looked around, and then respectively slumped against the closest set wall they could find.

Jeff ran his fingers through his already disheveled hair. "When did what happen?"

"This thing with the nail polish."

Rocky muttered a few choice words under his breath before crossing to Rachel. "Look, I'm sorry. I should have noted the cable's proximity to the cart, but I didn't."

"I told you, man, it wasn't a huge deal." Jeff dropped his hand at his side and then pushed off the wall to walk the latest set. "I could've shot through it if Fiona hadn't gone all ballistic the way she did."

Sara slipped a pile of foils from the drawer and set them on the cart next to Carter's color bowl. "Things fell down. She reacted. Can't pin that one on Fiona."

"Where was I when this happened?" Rachel persisted, varying up her still unanswered question. "How did I not hear this?"

"Because it wasn't that loud." Jeff crossed to Rocky and placed what appeared to be a calming hand on the key grip's shoulder. Then, when the man stopped glaring at Sara, he got to the heart of Rachel's question. "Really, it wasn't a big deal. Your call lasted what? Five minutes at the most, right? So trust me when I say this wasn't a big deal for anyone except Fiona."

"Au contraire," Carter whispered, just loud enough for me to hear.

I lifted the clipboard in line with my mouth in the hopes I could question his choice of words without anyone being the wiser, but just as I went there, Fiona breezed onto the set and stopped less than an inch from Carter's face.

"Remember. If you screw this up, McDade, you'll be looking for a new job. In a new town far, far from here."

Carter tried to play it off as if he wasn't nervous, but I saw it, and it unsettled me. Carter was amazing at what he did. Heck, he'd even managed to make Ms. Rapple look decent when my Grandpa Stu insisted on taking her to dinner the last time he was in town. If Carter could perform a never-before-seen miracle like that, changing Fiona Renoir from a redhead to a golden blonde should be a piece of cake, shouldn't it?

I opened my mouth to point that out but closed it as Rachel began her usual flit around the set, making sure everything we'd noted during our run-through was in place and ready to go. When she was satisfied, she motioned Jeff and Rocky into position, reminded them of the mirror they needed to avoid being seen in in the footage, and then turned to Carter.

"You've mixed the color already?" she asked, peering into the bowl on the cart.

"I have. But I intentionally went one drop shy so I can add that for the camera the way we discussed."

"And where is the bottle?"

Carter opened up the cabinet to the left of the mirror and pulled out two bottles. He held up first the larger of the two bottles, and then the smaller one. "This is the one I used, as discussed at the meeting. And this is the one you said we were to use specifically for camera purposes."

It was a detail I wouldn't have thought of, but now, as I looked at it in Carter's hand, I had to agree with Rachel. It didn't matter how careful Carter was, color dripped onto the label. Having him use a new one for the shoot afforded yet another opportunity for Jeff to pan in on something with the Salonquility name and logo.

We stepped back so Jeff could take his continuity shot—a shot that was interrupted by Sara, who insisted on refolding the Salonquility smock Rachel had just folded. I looked at Rachel to gauge her reaction, but other than a super quick eye roll, there was nothing.

When the smock was back in place, Jeff resumed his shot and then shut off the camera. "We're good."

I took one last look around the set and then, at everyone's nod, looked at Rachel. "Break time?"

Rachel nodded. "Let's take fifteen, everyone."

I'd just spied the sleeve of Rolos behind the last bag of animal crackers on the second-to-last shelf of the vending machine when I heard the thud. I didn't really pay it much mind in that initial second because, well, thuds happen. People bump into things, drop things, throw things. It's life.

But when the aforementioned thud was followed by a cacophony of shrieks and screams, I took off in a sprint, all thoughts (okay, maybe not all) of the nice-girl points I'd get for buying the crew a bag of animal crackers falling by the wayside.

It wasn't that I hadn't heard a few shrieks and screams already that day. I had. But this one was different namely because it wasn't Fiona who was screaming.

It was Carter.

And I'd never heard Carter scream quite like that before.

I ran toward the sounds, aware of my heart beating wildly in my chest as my head began to plug in possible reasons for the scream— he'd cut himself with his scissors, he'd tripped and hit his head on the counter, Ms. Rapple had stumbled onto the set, he'd accidentally turned Fiona's hair green—

I pushed the answering image of Carter and a one-way ticket to Siberia from my mind's eye and kept running, my brain circling back to the notion of Ms. Rapple. It would explain a lot . . .

Picking up the pace, I rounded the corner and pulled to a stop at the sight of Carter staring down at the floor, practically pulling his hair out at the roots. Confused, I followed his gaze and that of everyone else in the room down to the floor and the lifeless body of Fiona Renoir slumped atop his shoes.

Chapter Seven

I was sitting at the kitchen table, staring at the mounting pile of dishes in my sink, when I heard the bathroom door open. It was a sound I'd heard often over the past eight hours, thanks to Carter's unsettled stomach and my own inability to sleep.

"Feeling any better?"

Carter wandered into the room and dropped down onto the chair across from mine, his eyes bloodshot. "Any word yet?"

I opened my mouth to remind him of the bazillion times he'd asked the same question since we'd left Starwood Studios the previous evening, but I resisted. After all, Carter was simply voicing the very reason I kept checking the phone to make sure it was working.

"No."

Propping his elbows atop the table, he caught his head with his hands and released a very un-Carter like sigh. "I just don't get it. She went from bitching about Jeff being on her left and snapping her fingers at Rachel over an unflattering wrinkle in her smock, to getting eerily quiet and then . . . boom—she was face down at my feet. How does that *happen*?"

It was, essentially, the same thing I'd been wondering since the moment it first registered in my head that Fiona Renoir, the star of my Salonquility commercial, was dead. I'd voiced the sentiment to the parade of police officers who'd come and gone from the studio over the next several hours, snapping photos, collecting things in bags, and separating us for the purpose of gathering information.

I'd told the short, stocky officer who had isolated me in Rachel's office everything I knew, which wasn't much. The same officer had rotated Jeff, Rocky, Rachel, Sara, and Carter in and out of the room. And while I hadn't been present for their q and a, I suspected the q part had followed the same basic formula—where were you when the victim began to scream . . . did you see anything . . . is there anything you think we should know . . . and on and on it went.

By the time we'd been released, at approximately ten o'clock (some fifteen hours after our day began), everyone was pretty wiped.

Carter, however, had been nearly catatonic by the time it was all over, which is why I got behind the wheel of his 1975 Ford Granada. I'd tried to talk to him on the way home, but when I say nearly catatonic, I'm not exaggerating. By the time I reached our shared house at 46 McPherson Road, I knew I couldn't send him upstairs to his apartment alone. So, instead, I'd led him into my place, handed him a pillow and a blanket, and pointed him toward the couch, with the reminder that I was just one room away in the event he needed anything during the night.

He took me up on the couch, but his nonstop pacing throughout the night never quite led him to my room. Which meant I was left to wonder what was going on in his head as I listened to his footsteps moving between the couch and the window, the couch and the kitchen, and finally the couch and the bathroom before starting the cycle all over again.

Which brings me to now and the fact I was watching him in much the same way a scientist watches a test subject. I took note of his disheveled Rapunzel-colored hair, the way his jaw tightened and released, and the mixture of shock and fear etched into the part of his face I could just make out around his hands. "So what happened, exactly?"

Slowly, he lifted his face from his hands and leaned back against the chair. "I've played it over and over in my head, and I don't know. I mean short of wish fulfillment being an actual thing, I'm at a complete loss."

"Meaning?"

For a moment, he said nothing, his eyes trained on something just beyond my shoulder. After a quick check to be sure I wasn't in danger of being eaten by a spider, I repeated the question in the event he hadn't heard me.

"I hated her, Sunshine, you know that. I hated her like-like . . . you hate vegetables."

"Okay . . ."

"I *hated* her."

"That's been established."

"I'm going to be a suspect if Fiona's death ends up being hinky."

I stared at him. "Hinky? Hinky how?"

"She was twenty-eight, Sunshine. People that age don't just up and die for no reason."

"It happens." But even as the words left my mouth, I knew it was rare. But still, in order for someone to have caused her demise, someone else would have had to notice, right? I mean, one minute she was—

I stopped when I realized I really didn't know anything about what had transpired before I heard the screams. I'd been too intent on the sleeve of Rolos I was salivating over at the time to know much of anything. And then, afterward, St. Louis's finest had been so busy separating us that I hadn't really gotten the lowdown.

"Did you walk off the set for some reason and then return to find her on the floor like that?"

"No."

"So you just watched her fall out of the chair and onto the floor?"

"I'd just dipped my brush back into the bowl when I heard a funny noise—like a gurgle. I looked at Rachel to see if she was okay, but she had her face buried in her notes. I looked at Jeff in the event he was trying to cue me to move, but he was consulting with Rocky about something. And Sara? She must've heard the gurgle too, because she pointed my attention back to Fiona."

"And?"

"I saw Ms. Princess wave her hands in front of her face and then drop them to the armrests of her chair a nanosecond before her whole body pitched forward and she hit the floor."

"And that's when you started screaming?" I asked, although I pretty much knew the answer.

Carter closed his eyes against what I imagined was the visual accompaniment of his blow-by-blow and shook his head. "No. I screamed when she convulsed twice and then went limp."

"So the gurgle you'd heard was from Fiona?"

He shrugged without opening his eyes. "I guess—yeah."

I tried to process what I was hearing, but it was weird. Carter was right—how many twenty-eight-year-olds let out a gurgle and then just up and die?

Reaching across the table, I grabbed hold of his hand and gently squeezed until his focus (albeit dazed) was back on me. "Look, if we haven't heard anything by lunchtime, I'll call the police station and see what they can tell us. I mean, I'm sure they can understand we're all a little freaked out by what happened and could use some closure."

"You really think it's going to be okay?" he asked in an almost childlike voice.

"There were four other people on that set besides you, right? If something was hinky, don't you think someone would have seen something?"

He cocked his head ever so slightly as if pondering my words. "Four other people," he repeated. "Hmmm . . ."

Unsure of what to make of his expression, I got back to my point. "I don't see how this can be anything but a nonissue. A tragedy? Sure. But anything more than that? No."

A flash of something that looked an awful lot like hope flitted across his face, only to be shoved to the side by resignation. "I probably should stop by the theater. I have close to three dozen text messages from Colton in the box office thanks to this"—he held up a copy of the *Post-Dispatch* and then dropped it back onto the table— "the last of which said Billy—Rapunzel's prince—is about to start binge-eating if I don't tell them what I know. And from what Jenny in costuming says, Billy is already straining his buttons as it is."

"Does it matter?" I asked as he pushed back his chair and stood. "I mean, Rapunzel is dead."

He mouthed the word *understudy*, and then motioned for me to follow him into the living room. When he reached the couch, he slipped his feet into his favorite pair of moccasins and grabbed his coat off the armrest. "Besides, I kind of feel like I should be there in the event the Frankster stops by. After all, with the exception of the Starwood Studios crew, I'm the last person who saw his niece alive. He might want to talk, you know?"

I followed him out into our shared vestibule and then planted a kiss on his cheek as he disengaged the lock on the outer door and opened it to the elements. "You're a good egg, Carter McDade, you know that?"

Draping his accessory scarf around his throat, he offered me an uncharacteristic shrug. "I'm not sure all those thoughts I had about Fiona disappearing off the face of the earth qualify me for good-egg status. Especially now that she's actually gone."

"After watching Fiona in action yesterday, I'm quite sure you're not the only one to have ever had those thoughts. Everyone hated her, Carter—Rachel, Sara, Jeff, Rocky. She was difficult under the best of circumstances."

"What about you, Sunshine?"

I peeked past Carter for any sign our next-door neighbor was within eavesdropping distance, but there was nothing. "What *about* me?"

"Did you hate Fiona too?"

I tried to ignore thoughts of the heat I was losing with each passing second we stood there at the open door and focus, instead, on my memories of the previous day. "Hate might be a bit strong, considering I really didn't have any run-ins with Fiona. I mean, other than that moment when she realized she had to let you color her hair if she wanted to be in the commercial, she seemed to be well aware of the fact that her fate on that set rested in my hands."

"Her fate on that set," Carter echoed. "Little did any of us know, huh?"

There was nothing to say, so I just nodded.

"Things really can change in the blink of an eye, can't they?"

I shivered as the outdoor temperature began to affect my surroundings and took a step back. "Well, you better get down to the theater before Billy eats himself right out of his costume."

Carter dug his hands into the pockets of his jacket but remained in the same spot, making it impossible for me to actually shut the door. "You'll call me after you talk to the police, right? You know, just in case they're prepping a cell for me?"

"I'll call you."

"And you won't forget, right?"

"I won't forget."

"You promise?"

"I promise."

He bent his little finger and shoved it through the doorway. "Pinky swear?"

"Carter, I'm losing heat here. And I'm trying to buy a car, remember?"

"Pinky swear?" he repeated.

When it became apparent he wasn't going anywhere until I played along, I hooked my pinky inside his. "Okay, okay, I pinky swear. Now go!"

He stepped out onto the front walkway and then turned back, the first sign of a smile I'd seen since sometime yesterday morning tugging at the corners of his mouth. "Thanks for being there for me last night. You're the best."

"I didn't really do much except give you my couch."

"It was enough." Lifting his shoulders, he shielded his cheeks from winter's cold. "Maybe, if we're not too tired, you can come up to my place tonight and we can order takeout Chinese and watch *Singin' in the Rain*."

I was mid-nod/mid-door shut when the fact that it was Saturday hit me like a two-by-four. "Wait. I can't."

Carter's shoulders slumped. "Why not?"

I didn't mean to sigh, I really didn't. But after the sleepless night I'd just had, the promise of another was hardly intriguing. "Mary Fran invited me for a stakeout sleepover."

"A stakeout sleepover?"

"Rudder and Baboo have apparently become quite the nighttime rabble-rousers, from what I've been told. In fact, the pet store's new neighbor actually called the cops with a peace disturbance complaint."

"Are you serious?"

"That's what Mary Fran said. Anyway, that's why we're staying there tonight—so we can see what they do at night when the shop is closed."

The sound of Carter's laugh warmed me from the inside out. Almost.

"I could bring a sleeping bag *and* some Chinese food . . ."

I was just about to nod when I remembered the rule Mary Fran had imposed upon our evening. "Sorry, Carter. No boys allowed."

In hindsight, I probably should have called Carter the second I got off the phone with JoAnna later that afternoon, but my head was reeling. To borrow his word, I'd been down this hinky death route before, and I wasn't exactly stoked for an encore.

I mean, really, wasn't there an expression about lightning not striking the same place twice? And if so, why did my otherwise nondescript life have to be the exception to that rule?

It was a question that certainly called for a little soul-searching, but that would have to wait for another day. Right now, all I could really think about was Fiona and the fact that the police were treating her death as a murder.

More than anything, I wanted to believe my secretary had simply misunderstood the conversation she'd been privy to while eating lunch with her best friend, Theresa. But I knew better. JoAnna could hear a pin hit the floor three states over, which is why I tended to leave my office building when I was in danger of saying something I didn't want her to overhear.

It's not that I was afraid JoAnna would divulge my secrets to the world, because I wasn't. Yes, she had amazing hearing, but she was also incredibly loyal to the people she cared about—an inner circle I considered myself extremely fortunate to be part of after little more than eight months.

So, to make a long, roundabout thought a little less roundabout, if JoAnna said she overhead two cops calling Fiona's death a homicide, it was true. And the fact that she shared that news with me on Saturday evening rather than waiting until Monday morning certainly had my personal antennae pinging.

Yet no matter how hard I tried to wrap my head around what JoAnna had said, it just didn't make sense. Fiona fell out of her chair and onto the floor in front of five people. That meant there were five witnesses. There was simply no way some masked killer could run onto the set, stick a knife in Fiona's back, and run away with no one noticing . . .

Then again, whoever killed her hadn't used a knife.

Or a gun.

In fact, now that I was revisiting the scene in my head, there hadn't been any—

"There wasn't any blood." I pushed off the wall on which I'd been leaning and wandered over to the couch, my mind's eye walking through the moment I came around the corner and saw Fiona on the ground. Nope, no blood.

Shaking my head, I leaned forward, retrieved my phone from the top of the coffee table, and dialed Carter's number.

One ring . . .

Two rings . . .

Three rings . . .

"Hey, this is Carter, and it's your unlucky day as I'm away from my phone. But I'll do my best to make things right if you leave your name and number. Toodles!"

I took a deep breath as I waited for the tone. When I was clear to speak, I worked to keep my voice as calm as possible. "Hey, it's me. Sorry I didn't get back to you earlier, but I got a little busy working on some stuff and forgot to make that call I told you I was going to make. But, um, now I have something I need to tell you, so if I've already left for the pet store by the time you get home from the theater, give me a call on my cell, okay?"

I ended the call and stared at the screen for a few moments, my thoughts running in a million different directions.

A quick knock-thud from the vicinity of my front door brought an end to my worry, and I hurried over to see who it was. I assumed it was Carter but hoped it was Andy.

I was wrong on both counts.

"You're not going to believe what I bought for our sleepover," Mary Fran gushed as she breezed past me and into the apartment. "I mean, I knew they existed and all, but I'd never seen one."

I followed her across my living room and into my bedroom, narrowly missing a collision with her back as she stopped without warning.

"Where's your stuff?"

"My stuff?"

Mary Fran gestured around my room. "Your sleeping bag, your jammies, Twister . . ."

"Twister?"

"It's not a sleepover without Twister." Spying my empty overnight bag in the corner of the room, Mary Fran marched over to it, flung it on top of my bed, and pointed inside. "Do you want to pick your clothes, or should I?"

"What's the rush?" I asked, shooing her away from my pajama drawer.

"Saving my pet store, for starters. And secondly, if what I read in the paper this morning is true, you could use a little sleepover fun right about now."

"I'm fine. A little weirded out? Sure. But fine." I plucked out my clothes and turned back to my friend. "As for the pet store stuff, it was just one complaint, wasn't it?"

"For now, yes. But Rudder had that look in his eye when I was leaving today."

"Look? What look?"

Mary Fran disappeared into my bathroom and returned with my toothbrush, toothpaste, and a lavender hair scrunchie I'd forgotten I had. "*The* look."

Chapter Eight

It didn't take a rocket scientist to know our after-hours presence was neither wanted nor appreciated by Rudder Malone. Baboo, the quieter, more appreciative of the two birds, didn't seem to mind, but Rudder—well, he was a different story.

In fact, I swear the eyebrow he didn't have was raised to the heavens when we came through the door and then dipped down to his beak when it became apparent that Mary Fran and I were going to stay.

"Did you see that glare, just now?" I asked as I set my sleeping bag down on top of the counter.

Mary Fran crossed to the refrigerator, removed a container of kiwi from the top shelf, and carried it over to the cutting board. "I'm pretty sure Rudder isn't capable of glaring."

"Oh, no? Have you ever dropped one of his kiwi pieces on the ground and had to throw it away while he watched?" I poked around in a jar containing some sort of treat, lifted one to my nose for a quick smell check, and then, at Mary Fran's shrug, popped it in my mouth. "Mmmm . . ."

"It's a new recipe I've been trying out, and it's definitely a hit with the customers."

I helped myself to another. "What is it?"

"A doggy treat."

"A—" I stopped chewing and rushed over to the trash can. When I was pretty sure I'd cleared my mouth, I turned and faced my friend. "Why didn't you stop me?"

"I was curious, I guess."

"*Curious?*"

"About what you'd think." Mary Fran removed a few chunks of

kiwi from the container and began to cut them into tiny, Rudder-sized pieces. "The fact that you wanted a second was encouraging. Anyway, they're homemade, and there's nothing in them that could hurt you."

"Gee, thanks. I feel so much better now." I leaned against the counter and darted my gaze between my friend and my feathered nemesis. "Isn't it going to mess up his routine if you feed him now?"

Mary Fran looked up, winked at Rudder, and then returned to her task. "He'll be fine."

"Don't they say you shouldn't reward bad behavior?"

"Bad behavior?"

"The glaring."

She picked up the cutting board and carried the chopped kiwi pieces over to Rudder's cage. "He wasn't glaring, Tobi. He was just surprised to see us, is all."

I followed her over to the cage and watched as she held the first piece of kiwi between the bars for Rudder to take from her hand. "I know surprise, Mary Fran. And that look he gave us when we came through the door definitely wasn't surprise."

With the help of her knife, Mary Fran pushed the rest of Rudder's kiwi pieces through the trapdoor of the cage and then moved on to Baboo. "Have you and Carter been watching slasher movies again? Because you're acting a little paranoid."

"*Para-para . . . noid!*"

I shook my finger at Rudder. "Don't start, mister. I've had a really long day, and I don't need grief from you."

"*Don't-don't start. Para-para . . . noid!*"

Mary Fran's laugh echoed around the room, stealing my attention from Rudder for a split second. When I looked back at him, he was glaring. "See? Look! He's doing it again!"

Mary Fran said something softly to Baboo and then turned back to me and Rudder. "Can you two find a way to get along? Please?"

"*Snort! Snort! S-nort!*"

It was official. Rudder was deliberately trying to get to me. Which meant I had two choices. I could ignore him, or I could continue to let him humiliate me. After some mental hemming and hawing, I chose the former—but not before exacting a little retribution by returning to my sleeping bag and brandishing it in the air. "It's going to be sooo much fun staying here. All. Night. Long."

The glare was back, and this time it included a little rocking and cage pecking.

I pulled the sleeping bag to my chest and raised Rudder's glare with one of my own. "Lose the 'tude, okay, pal? We're here to try and keep your feathered backside from being carted off to the pokey on peace disturbance charges, remember?"

"*Snort! Snort! S-nort!*"

"Why does he keep doing that? I haven't snorted even once since we walked through the door."

"I don't think that matters at this point. Rudder associates that sound with you." Mary Fran took one last look at Baboo and then carried the now-empty cutting board toward the sink in the back left corner of the shop.

"Fabulous, just fabulous." I heard the sarcasm in my voice and tried to soften it, but not before sticking my tongue out at Rudder. "So, have you met this sound-sensitive neighbor yet?" I asked as I joined Mary Fran by the sink.

The lighthearted set to Mary Fran's expression disappeared, only to be replaced by a tension that expanded out to her hands and the cutting board she was now scrubbing with a ferociousness that didn't fit the woman or the task.

"Mary Fran?"

With a flick of her hand, Mary Fran turned off the water and closed her eyes. "It's like you said the other day. If there was a sound problem, why couldn't this guy talk to me about it before involving the police? I mean, it's obvious I'm trying to run a business here—a business that was very obviously here when he decided to rent the apartment upstairs in the first place. Yet he's bothered by Rudder talking?"

I opened my mouth to weigh in (and, possibly, point out the fact that Rudder didn't just talk, he squawked), but closed it as the forty-three-year-old continued, her eyes open again and pinning mine. "Seriously, if you wanted peace and quiet, wouldn't you look for an apartment someplace other than above a pet store?"

She had a point . . .

"Heck, there are apartments all over the Central West End, and if none of them happen to be up for rent at this exact moment, there are scads more one exit south and one exit north. But noooo, this guy has to rent the place above my pet store."

"Have you tried to talk to him? Maybe introduce him to the crew so he has a bit more patience?"

"The day I learned about the complaint, I tried to talk to him. I went up the back steps to his door and knocked. But he opted to ignore me."

"Maybe he wasn't home when you tried," I offered as I scanned the assorted pet cages and shelving units that dotted the floor. "Actually, before you address that, can I ask a question?"

"Sure, but he was home. I'm certain of it."

I swept my hands outward. "Where, exactly, are we going find space to roll out two sleeping bags?"

"And the Twister mat—you can't forget the Twister mat."

If left to my own devices, I was pretty sure I could. But since Mary Fran was part of the mix, I knew I would never be so lucky. "Do you have a plan?"

Mary Fran made her way over to the hamster condo and peeked in on Max. "We're going to sleep in my office. Sam helped me push all the furniture aside before we left this afternoon." She scooped up some fluff and added it to Max's bedding. "There's not a ton of space, but we'll fit."

"But I thought the whole point of this sleepover is to see what Rudder and Baboo do at night, when they should be sleeping."

I watched as she moved on to the cat cages and the trio of middle-aged females waiting for homes. "It is. And we will. From the safety of my office."

"I don't—"

"I'm hoping Rudder will forget we're here." Cage by cage, Mary Fran reached her fingers through the slats and rubbed each cat behind the ears, earning herself a thank-you purr—times three—in return. "Which is what we really need in order to have a better understanding of what has Mr. Crankypants all worked up."

"Mr. Crankypants?" I echoed, mid-laugh (aka snort).

Mary Fran retrieved her hand from the last of the three cat cages and turned to face me. "If the pants fit . . ."

"*Snort! Snort! S-nort!*"

I shot what I hoped was a beak-trembling glare at Rudder only to find him glaring back at me. "See! He's glaring! Right now! Look!"

Mary Fran humored me, of course.

So too did Rudder.

Which meant that when Mary Fran did as I asked, Rudder sent his gaze up to the ceiling all innocent-like. The only thing missing from his act was a tap of his foot and the ability to whistle Dixie.

"Moving right along." I stuck my tongue out at the bird one more time and then went in search of the sleepover snacks Mary Fran had mentioned on the drive over.

I checked the drawer under the register—nothing.

I checked the cabinet behind the register—nothing.

I peeked inside Mary Fran's tote and—bingo! "Wait. You brought marshmallows?"

"Of course."

"You didn't mention that on the way here."

"We were talking about a dead body, remember?"

"Your point?" I rummaged further into her bag. "Hey! You have graham crackers in here, too!"

"I know."

I shoved aside the sleeve of crackers and swallowed down the drool I felt forming at the sight of the chocolate bars at the bottom of the bag. "Chocolate!"

"Have you ever had a s'more without it?"

I stopped rummaging. "You brought stuff to make s'mores?"

"I did," Mary Fran said around her wide-mouthed grin.

I looked from the contents of the bag to Rudder and, finally, Mary Fran. "Are we building a campfire in your office, too? Because if we are, might I suggest using Rudder as firewood?"

"*Snort! Snort! S-nort!*"

Mary Fran's laugh echoed around the room. "You can try to hide it all you want, Tobi, but we're all wise to you, aren't we, guys?" Mary Fran paused as if she expected the assorted animals to offer their assent. "You adore Rudder. We all know this. If you didn't, you wouldn't have given up a night with that handsome man of yours to spend it here with us."

I felt my throat constrict at the mention of Andy. "I think *tolerate* is a far more accurate word choice than adore."

There was no mistaking the knowing look Mary Fran traded with Rudder. So instead, I ignored them both and changed topics completely. "You never said how you plan on making s'mores . . ."

Mary Fran rose up on the balls of her feet, pivoted toward the counter, and hurried over to the second of two bags. "It's what I wanted to tell you when I got to your house. But since you weren't packed, I didn't."

I rolled my eyes.

"Anyway, guess what? I. Bought. A. S'more. Maker." Mary Fran clapped her hands and then dug them into the bag. "See?"

I stepped closer and noted each component of said s'more maker as it was placed on the counter alongside the necessary ingredients I'd already uncovered. "That's kinda cool."

"I know, right?"

"So let's get to it then." I grabbed the graham crackers off the counter and pointed toward the back hallway and the office beyond. "Shall we?"

"Not until you tell me what's up with you and Andy."

"Do I haaave to?"

"Would you like a little cheese to go with that whine?"

I rolled my eyes again, though really, Mary Fran was right. I was whining. And while Mary Fran couldn't wave a wand and make Andy's ex-girlfriend disappear, maybe talking to her about it would make my insecurities disappear.

Or at least lessen.

Okay, maybe just placate them for a little while . . .

I took a deep breath, held it for a silent count of ten, and then released it, along with the pertinent facts. Or, rather, fact—as in singular. "Brenna is back in the picture."

The right side of Mary Fran's upper lip curled nearly to her nose. "Brenna? Who on earth is Brenna?"

Slumping back against the counter, I stared at the crackers and the chocolate and the marshmallows. "Andy's old girlfriend."

"And you're letting this be more than a blip because?"

"They dated for four years. He wanted to marry her."

Mary Fran's lip returned to its normal position. "Oh."

"Oh? Oh? That's all you've got?" I squawked, Rudder-like. "Where's the *It doesn't matter*? Where's the *He's with you now*? Or, better yet, the *They broke up for a reason, yes*?"

Reaching behind the counter, Mary Fran extracted two stools and slid one over to me. "Sit."

I did as I was told.

"So why didn't they get married? Do you know?"

"She wanted to chase her career."

"And now?"

I traced my finger along the exposed edge of the counter and then shrugged. "I don't know. I haven't really talked to him since last weekend."

"Did she call or something?"

"No. She walked up to our table at Lewis and Clark's."

Mary Fran nibbled her lower lip, scanned the faces of the shop's residents, and then looked back at me. "How did Andy react?"

"You mean after he got over the initial shock?" At her nod, I shrugged again. "There was hurt, that's for sure."

"Where?"

"In his eyes."

"Oh."

I waited for the rise in her voice indicating the presence of a question mark, but it didn't come. Somehow, the lack thereof made me feel worse.

"And you said he hasn't been in touch since then?" Mary Fran asked.

"That big home show in L.A. is this week, remember?"

"Oh!"

Finally, a verbal punctuation I could get behind. "Is that a good thing?"

"Of course! It means he has a real reason for not getting in touch—a reason you knew about in advance."

I'd be lying to myself if I didn't acknowledge the sudden lift in my mood at the notion that Brenna was a nonfactor. But I'd also be lying if I ignored the little voice in my head that countered the sudden lift with *but still* . . .

"I still thought he'd call, though. Just to say hi . . ."

Mary Fran's fight to keep her shoulders from slumping was valiant, if not entirely successful. "Maybe the time zone difference has something to do with that?"

"Maybe." But even as the word left my mouth, I knew I was grasping at straws. Andy and I were still relatively new, yes. But he'd seen me in action enough to know that I tended to stay up late.

"So what's she like?" Mary Fran asked while trying to look like she was concentrating on anything other than the question at hand.

"She's gorgeous."

Mary Fran's gaze flew to mine. "Gorgeous? Gorgeous how?"

"She's tall—not like you, but still tall. Like maybe five-seven. Seventy-five percent of that is probably legs." I closed my eyes for the mental field trip back to my last date with Andy—a field trip I'd taken at least a dozen times since. "Dark hair. Green eyes. Not a freckle to be found anywhere on her face. And boobs—she has boobs."

Folding her arms in front of her chest, Mary Fran cocked her head in true *I'm waiting* style.

I, in turn, blew a renegade wisp of hair off my cheek. "Must I go on?"

"Yes. Because I've not heard one thing that you don't have."

"You mean besides the height, the legs, the coloring, the lack of freckles, and the boobs?" I knew I was being a bit snarky, but really, was Mary Fran trying to deepen the puddle in which I was already wallowing?

"Please. You can achieve that height with heels, without towering over Andy . . . you're no slouch in the leg department, yourself . . . you are the epitome of every man's California girl fantasy with your blond hair and blue eyes . . . your freckles give you that girl-next-door edge . . . and not all men have a thing about boobs. Some actually find big-breasted women intimidating."

"Then why hasn't he called?" Yup, the whine was back in all its nasally glory.

Mary Fran broke open the package of chocolate bars and handed one to me. "I don't know."

"What if he wants her more than me, just like Nick wanted that waitress more than he did me?" I hated the way my voice broke when I mentioned my lying, cheating ex-fiancé, but I was powerless to stop it. Instead, I unwrapped the chocolate bar and willed my unhealthy eating habits to kick in.

They didn't.

"You can't live your life on *what ifs*, Tobi." Mary Fran reached across the space between our stools and pushed the aforementioned wisp of hair behind my ear. "You just can't, sweetie."

"Why? You do."

Mary Fran shrugged. "Because I'm me . . . and you're you."

"That's a lousy answer."

We sat there for a while, each lost in our own thoughts, our own regrets, our own past hurts. Eventually, though, I shook my head free of Rudder, cranky neighbors, Fiona, Brenna, and Andy and, instead, pointed toward the s'more maker. "You know what? I think it's time we try that thing out and then follow it up with—I can't believe I'm saying this—Twister. So what do you say?"

"I say you're—"

The sound of someone pounding on the front door stole the rest of Mary Fran's sentence and left us staring at one another, wide-eyed.

"If that's the guy upstairs, he has some real issues," I said, bypassing Mary Fran in favor of the door.

Mary Fran followed close on my heels. "If that's the guy upstairs, he's about to have an entirely new set of even realer issues."

When I reached the door, I pulled back the OPEN/CLOSED sign and peeked out into the night, my body sagging with relief at the familiar face staring back at me. "Okay, phew . . . It's just Carter. We're good."

Chapter Nine

"Carter?" Mary Fran said, as she exchanged a few worried glances with me. "Is something wrong? You seem a bit . . . tense."

"Tense! Bit tense!"

I shot a warning look in Rudder's direction and then moved in beside Carter, who kept peeking out the front door for God knows what. "Trust me, the ice cream truck hasn't come down this road in months. So, unless you plan on standing there until May, how about you step away from the door and tell us what's going on."

Carter motioned toward the road with his chin. "See that car across the street? The dark one?"

"No, not"—I bobbed my head left and then right until I had a clear visual of said car—"wait. Yup. I see it. But I'm picturing something smaller, more fuel-efficient, you know?"

Carter turned to me, his mouth open.

"The car," I said. "You're thinking I should go for one of those, right? But it's all wrong for me. I mean, yes, I want something nice, but I also need whatever I get to be practical—aka cheap. And I don't want to be pressured by salesmen until I know what I want. Which is why Sam and I are going to do a little poking around tomorrow when the car places are all closed. So I'm in a position of strength when I finally do sit down with them."

I met Carter's wide eyes with what I was pretty sure was one of my more winning smiles. "See? I'm always thinking."

"Snort! Snort! S-nort!"

"And snorting, according to Rudder." Mary Fran tried to hold back her grin, but she was wholly unsuccessful.

I, of course, revved back, ready to chastise my fine feathered headache but stopped as Carter swung his attention back to the window. "I'm pretty sure they followed me here."

"Followed you?" Mary Fran echoed.

"It's like in that movie we watched the other night, Tobi, remember? The one where the cops kept following Roger White's character around waiting for him to slip up?" Carter wiped his forehead with the back of his hand and sighed. "They're waiting for me to do the same. So they can swoop in, cuff my hands behind my back, and order me to don orange—*orange*, for God's sake."

I laughed at the sheer torture that was Carter's at that moment, only to have the joy disappear as something about his diatribe took root. "Wait a minute. This has something to do with Fiona's death being investigated as a homicide, doesn't it?"

This time, when Carter looked at me, it wasn't with the wide eyes of the confused but, rather, the narrowed eyes of the perturbed.

I swallowed.

"You knew, and you didn't warn me?" he asked.

"I left you a voice mail telling you to call me, but you didn't. So I figured I'd just fill you in when I next saw you."

He clutched a hand to the base of his neck. "Did they come to the house? Did they pepper you with questions designed to make you break?"

"Make me break?" I slid a glance in Mary Fran's direction to see if she was following any of this, but based on the way she was staring at Carter, I knew she was as perplexed as I was. "Make me break about what? I didn't do anything wrong."

Slowly, he lowered his hand back down to his side as he took one last look at the parked car on the other side of the road and then, finally, turned and headed toward the now vacant pair of stools. "You didn't, but I'm pretty sure they think *I* did."

I took one last look at the car myself and then trailed Carter over to the counter. "You're pretty sure they think you did what, exactly?"

"Murdered Fiona."

I'm not sure who gasped louder—me, Mary Fran, or, subsequently, Rudder.

When I got myself under control, I sat down next to Carter and grabbed his hand. "Look, I know that whole scene yesterday was hard on you—it was hard on everyone there. But no one thinks you're responsible, Carter."

"I'm not so sure about that, Sunshine."

My confusion must have been etched across my face because he continued, his voice a curious mixture of calm and fear. "*I* was the one coloring her hair. And I'm the one who mixed it."

"Okay . . ."

"So I get why they're out there, why they came to the house to try and get to me through you."

I teed my hands between us. "No one came to the house, Carter. Not unless you count Mary Fran here"—I gestured over my shoulder—"and she only came to make sure I'd packed for tonight."

"She hadn't, by the way," Mary Fran inserted with a touch of irritation.

Carter rolled his eyes in a show of solidarity as I took control of the conversation again. "What does Fiona's hair color and the fact that you mixed it have to do with any of this?"

Seconds turned to minutes as Carter closed his eyes and took a few deep breaths. "That's how she died, Sunshine."

I looked for any tells that Carter was kidding, but there was nothing. Then I looked at Mary Fran to see if maybe she was grinning, but she wasn't.

"I'm not following," I said when it was clear this was no gag.

"She had a reaction."

"To?"

"Peanuts." Carter extricated his hands from mine and splayed them upward. "I'm guessing it was that cut on the very top of her ear."

I mentally chastised myself for not choosing tongues as my foreign language in school and then leaned forward, my gaze locked on Carter's. "What does Fiona's allergy to peanuts have to do with a cat scratch and your hair—"

I sat up tall as the reality Carter had been dancing around hit me like a two-by-four to the head. "Someone put *peanuts* in Fiona's hair color?"

"Peanut *oil*, I imagine, but yeah . . . that's what they're saying." Carter set his left elbow on the counter and dropped his forehead into his hand.

"That's what *who* is saying?" Mary Fran asked as my brain worked to absorb everything my ears had just heard.

"The cops. They came to the theater in the late afternoon and stayed until just before I came here."

"What did they say, exactly?" I asked when I was fairly certain my brain had caught up.

"They asked questions more than anything else."

"*Asked-asked questions!*"

I turned, pelted Rudder with a glare to end all glares, and trained my focus back on Carter. "What kind of questions?"

"They wanted to know if I knew about Fiona's allergy."

"And?"

"I said of course I did. Everyone and anyone who knew Fiona knew about her allergy."

"What did they say to that?"

Slowly, and with much effort, he lifted his head off his hand and shrugged. "One of them—the tall, dark, and dreamy one—walked over to my color cubbies and started asking questions about my work. How long I've been doing it . . . how long I've been at the theater . . . how I got involved in the Salonquility commercial shoot . . . how Fiona got involved . . . that sort of stuff."

"And? What did you say?"

"I told him I've been enamored with hair color since I was in elementary school. I told him that when I was fifteen, I got a job answering phones at my local salon. I told him that once I graduated from high school, I worked at the salon during the day and went to beauty school in the evenings. I told him how I knew, even then, I wanted to combine my work with my love of the stage and how I got hired on to do hair for the theater here."

"Okay, good. And the rest?"

"You mean the questions about the shoot?"

"Yes."

"I told him that we're friends—you and me—and how you were doing me a favor by hiring Fiona to work on the commercial."

Uh-oh.

The yucky taste was back. "Did he ask you why?"

Carter's nod was slow, labored. "He did. I tried to leave my answer a little vague as I didn't want to take the chance Frank would walk in and hear me talking ill of his now-dead niece, but it was an exercise in futility, thanks to Mimi."

I knew, from my near daily chats with Carter, that Mimi was the theater's jack-of-all-trades. If a secretary was needed to take calls, she took calls. If an extra body was needed in the box office, she provided the extra body. If one of the actors needed someone to run lines with, she ran lines. And on and on it went. Which meant Mimi knew just about everything that happened inside the walls of Carter's beloved theater—including the moment Carter had hit his limit regarding Fiona Renoir and had called her out in front of everyone during one of the initial reads for Rapunzel.

"Mimi was there when you told Fiona off?" I squeaked out.

"*Everyone* was there."

"Okay, and everyone knows what it's like to have a bad day."

"They also know I despised Fiona like I'"—he stopped, breathed through his nose—"despise over-the-counter hair color."

I cast about for something to say to soften the impact of what I was hearing. "From what I saw at the studio yesterday, I find it hard to believe you were the only one who felt that way about her."

"I wasn't. But I'm the only one who stood to lose his job over her."

Crap. I'd forgotten that part . . .

"But Mimi didn't know about that, right?" I asked, crossing my fingers atop my lap.

"She's the one who called to tell me Frank wanted a powwow with me in his office."

Uh-oh times two.

"Did she tell the cops that?"

The answering shift of his eyes told me all I needed to know. And it wasn't looking good.

I took a deep, cleansing breath and waited a few beats as Rudder did the same. When he was done, I moved on. "Okay, so you were temporarily afraid for your job following a verbal altercation with Fiona a week or so ago . . ."

"*Six days* ago."

"But you kissed and made up via the commercial," I reminded him. "So everything was fine. Or as fine as anything could be with a shrew like that."

"Except for one thing."

"One thing?"

"Fiona is dead now."

"Yes, but that doesn't mean you did it!" I protested

"*You! You did it!*"

Clearly affected by Rudder's words, Carter dropped his gaze to the floor. "It's no secret—especially across the Northern Hemisphere—

that I despised Fiona Renoir. I was always plotting ways to get rid of her."

"I know. I remember." And I did. "But really? Who doesn't do that on occasion when there's someone they really don't like."

"You don't," he countered.

"You don't know me as well as you think you do then."

He narrowed his eyes on mine. "Nick doesn't count."

"Sure he does."

Carter looked to Mary Fran for assistance—assistance she offered readily. "No. He doesn't."

"That still doesn't mean—"

"I was the one who mixed the color, Sunshine. I'm the one who was putting it on her hair when she fell on the floor and died."

"Semantics." But even as I uttered the retort, I knew it wasn't that simple. If peanuts had, indeed, found their way into Fiona's hair color, the only natural questions were how . . . and why.

And the only natural answer to both those questions was Carter.

As in *my* Carter—Carter McDade.

So if I, as Carter's best friend, could come to that conclusion, it made all the sense in the world that the two cops he was convinced were sitting outside the pet shop watching his every move could as well.

Unsure of what to do or say, I took advantage of Carter's fascination with the floor to glance back over my shoulder at Mary Fran. But the second I saw the expression on her face, I wished I'd never looked her way.

Chapter Ten

If our pet shop sleepover had gone according to plan, I'd have been able to get to the bottom of Mary Fran's sudden mood shift over s'mores or, heaven forbid, Twister. But since the obvious reason for her discomfort ended up bedding down with us, I'd been left to my own imagination on the subject.

In all fairness though, I'd only given it a passing thought during the night as my focus had been on trying to keep Carter calm.

But now that I was back home and Carter was upstairs showering, I couldn't help but try to come up with an explanation that would quiet a growing sense of dread I couldn't seem to shake off.

It made no sense, really. I mean, why *wouldn't* Mary Fran have been quiet? Our girls-only night had been altered. Instead of girl talk, we'd spent virtually the entire night trying to keep Carter away from the window. And the whole reason we'd even had the sleepover was to see what Rudder and Baboo did at night when they thought they were alone—another bust thanks to Carter's incessant need to keep tabs on the cops, who obviously felt the need to keep tabs on him.

I let loose a groan and wandered into the kitchen, my destination unclear. The bagels Mary Fran had brought along for breakfast had been, more or less, filling. Yet I was stressed, and when I was stressed there wasn't a bag of chips or a piece of junk food that was safe.

The easy answer would be to take advantage of Carter's absence to call Mary Fran and assure her Carter would be okay, but she'd looked really beat when we arrived back home, and I didn't have the heart to wake her in the event she'd actually managed to fall asleep. Besides, her son, Sam, and I had plans to walk around closed car lots sometime after dinner, and maybe, just maybe, Mary Fran would agree to come along.

I headed straight for the cabinet tasked with housing most of my chocolate, yanked it open, and studied the contents. There were, of course, my go-to Cocoa Puffs, but for once, they didn't call to me. The next shelf held a package of chocolate-chip cookies (meh), a bowl of loose candy (meh), and a box of Charleston Chews that gave me pause (meh).

I stood there, considering my options, for nearly five minutes before I gave up and walked away. Whatever the hole was that I was trying to fill, junk food wasn't the answer.

Disgusted at myself, I wandered back into the living room and over to the front window. A quick peek from behind the curtain revealed two things—Ms. Rapple and her annoying little kick-me dog, Gertrude, were still nowhere to be found, and the cops who had followed Carter's Grenada all the way home from the pet store were looking mighty bored.

I let the curtain swish back into place and made my way over to the couch—the answer to my internal twisting suddenly so clear I was surprised I hadn't put it together sooner.

I didn't need chocolate, I needed Grandpa Stu.

For as long as I could remember, my Grandpa Stu and I had had an unbreakable bond. He loved my siblings, of course, but there was something different between us from the get-go.

My mom knew it.

My dad knew it.

Heck, even my brother and sister knew it.

It simply was. And for that I was eternally grateful.

Storytime on his lap when I was really little had slowly evolved into conversations (where my "why?" was always answered), life tips (the majority of which I still use today), and laughter, always laughter. He was, in a nutshell, the most treasured part of my growing-up years.

I took in the time on the screen of my phone and tried to imagine what he was doing at that exact moment. My guess was either watching reruns of his favorite detective show or hustling a little vending machine money out of the man who lived in the apartment next to my grandfather's.

If it was the former, I hated to interrupt, but I also knew Grandpa

Stu would drop anything if I needed him. Even if all I needed was to simply hear his voice, as I did at that moment.

I hit number one on my speed-dial settings and lifted the phone to my ear, the answering rings giving me a chance to catch my breath as I settled into my favorite corner of the couch.

Halfway through the third ring, he picked up.

"If you're selling, I'm not buying. If you're preaching, I've already got religion. And no, I'm not going to give you my bank account number."

"Darn. I was hoping for the last one."

I heard his smile as it spread across his face and matched it with one of my own as the sound of his voice warmed me from the inside out. "Tobi! Why, I was just talking about you not more than five minutes ago."

"Please tell me your neighbor isn't still falling for your animal cracker routine . . ."

"Works like a champ every time," he quipped. "I keep wondering when he's going to notice the empty bag in my trash can, but so far, he hasn't."

I know I shouldn't have laughed, but the image of my grandfather using me as a way to land his favorite snack out of the vending machine each morning never grew old. "You're too much, you know that?"

"That's just want your grandma used to say to me."

"I know. It's where I got it." I heard the twinge of sadness in his voice and rushed to head it off at the pass with the one thing I knew would perk him up. "Are you busy?"

"When it comes to you—never."

I closed my eyes and allowed myself a moment to savor the certainty that was my Grandpa Stu. Then, when I felt my mental hole starting to fill up, I grabbed the closest throw pillow with my free hand and hugged it to my chest. "I need to bounce some stuff off you."

His smile was back, its effect on my grandfather's mood audible. "Shoot."

So I told him.

I told him about Andy and Brenna.

I told him about Mary Fran and the not-so-nice tenant living above the pet store.

I told him about Fiona and Carter.

And I told him about the commercial shoot and Fiona's death.

He listened the way he always did when I needed to talk, letting me speak without interruption. Until, of course, I mentioned the part about the pair of cops sitting in an unmarked car across the street from the duplex-style home I shared with Carter.

"They're wasting time," he said.

"Who? The cops?"

I heard him swallow what I imagined was one of the animal crackers he'd swindled out of his neighbor under the ruse I was coming for a visit. How his neighbor continued to miss the fact I hadn't been there in several months was beyond me.

"Anyone with a brain in their noggin knows that young man couldn't hurt a flea. Unless, maybe, that flea was biting you."

It was true. Carter was, in a word, easygoing. His glass was always half full. His door was always open. And happy was his mood of choice.

The only time his smile ever really faltered was when I was upset. When that happened, his first instinct was to try to cheer me up. But if that failed, he'd move heaven and earth to find the source of my unhappiness and fix it.

He was kind of the big brother I actually had but rarely saw.

I churned my grandfather's words around in my thoughts and shrugged. "That's just it. They don't *know* Carter."

"Not to mention the easy math right in front of them."

"Easy math?" I echoed. "You lost me."

"At first glance, Carter has the only things that matter in a homicide."

"What's that?"

"The means to do it *and* a motive."

I resisted the urge to tease him about watching too much TV and, instead, mulled the facts. Grandpa Stu was right. Carter was in the process of coloring Fiona's hair when she fell over. According to what Carter learned from the police, Fiona died of a reaction to peanuts—in the bowl of color Carter was using.

As for motive, Carter had that too. He, who had no ill feelings for anyone, openly despised Fiona—an emotion that only deepened when she held the fate of his beloved job in her hands.

I lolled my head back against the couch. "He's in trouble, isn't he?"

"If they take everything at face value, he is. But if they pull their magnifying glass back just a little, they'll realize they need to move their car or find themselves some clones."

"Meaning?"

"Correct me if I'm wrong, but I'm thinking someone as unlikeable as this Fiona person likely had enemies everywhere she went."

"Grandpa Stu, you have no idea." I looked up at the ceiling and tried to imagine how nice it would look if my landlord actually gave a darn about his properties. I couldn't, so I gave up. "I don't think I've ever met someone so prickly—so rude—in my entire life. You should have seen the way she talked down to the studio people on Friday. If you listened to her, they were all buffoons when it came to doing their respective jobs. And she took great delight in making them *look* like buffoons in front of their coworkers every chance she got."

"How'd they take that?"

"It varied. Jeff, the cameraman, was clearly agitated, but he kept his cool when he was filming. I think he just wanted to get the whole thing done and over with. Rocky, the key grip, taught me a few curse words I'm not sure I've ever heard before, but in all fairness, he was pretty good about stepping away when he needed to vent."

"Do you know anything about their standing at that studio?"

I swear I could hear the mental gears in my grandfather's brain shifting across the miles, and I wasn't sure what to make of it or his question. "No, not really."

"Anyone else?" he asked.

I told him about Rachel and Sara—how I'd promised Rachel she could be in the commercial but had to recant in order to help Carter; how Rachel was ever the professional during the shoot; and how Sara, the intern-on-the-rise, vacillated between being fed up with Fiona and being almost giddy when Rachel was on the receiving end of Fiona's diva-like behavior.

"See, it's just like I said. Them fellas outside need to find themselves some clones."

"I don't understand."

"Revenge is a powerful motive, Tobi."

"I know that. It's why Carter makes such a good suspect."

"True. But it's also why the four folks you just mentioned do as well. If someone has enough screws loose, they'll seek revenge for all sorts of things. Humiliation included."

"I don't know, Grandpa Stu. I can't imagine killing someone because they humiliated me, you know?"

"Most people wouldn't, Tobi. We just need to figure out who *would*."

I blinked rapidly against the tears I felt forming. Sure enough, my grandfather had settled my heart in a way only he could. He'd listened as I needed him to, and he'd left me with food for thought, just like he had since I was a little girl.

"Thank you, Grandpa Stu."

"It was my pleasure. I've grown mighty fond of Carter since you two became neighbors."

"He feels the same about you."

I was just about ready to end the call when I heard the telltale throat clear that meant more was coming.

I waited.

"As for that young fella of yours? Andy? You didn't learn this wait-and-see thing from me. Quite the contrary, in fact."

Grandpa Stu was right.

Sitting in the wings, waiting, did nothing.

I knew this.

Tossing the pillow onto the other end of the couch, I squared my shoulders. "You're right. I'll call him."

After I said good-bye to my grandfather, I looked at the clock on the DVD player and thought back to my last face-to-face with Andy. It had started out so perfectly—dinner together at a great restaurant, fun conversation, the sparkle in his eye when he reached for my hands while we waited for our meals . . .

And then—Wham!

I'm not sure how I'd known the woman walking toward our table was Andy's ex, but I had. Maybe it was the confidence with which she walked in our direction—like she had every right to intrude. Maybe it was the smug smile she flashed at me just before Andy looked up. Or maybe it was the fact that she was drop-dead gorgeous, just as Andy's brother Gary had described (in the kind of detail I hadn't sought yet oddly enough craved as the new girlfriend).

But it was the part Gary had obviously left out that had left me ill prepared for what had come next.

Yes, Andy had tried to hide it, and maybe if I hadn't been watching him like a hawk as he interacted with his former flame, I wouldn't have noticed. But since I was, I did. And what I'd seen had been hurt—

the kind of hurt I knew all too well myself but was happily shedding thanks to Andy and my growing feelings for him.

Yet there was Andy . . . with me . . . and still obviously in pain over his breakup with Brenna.

I looked down at the phone and gave some thought to calling my grandfather back to see if he was sure, but I knew what he'd say without hitting his number on my speed dial.

I knew because he'd been saying the same basic thing my whole life.

Take the bull by the horns, Tobi.

Sometimes you just gotta bite the bullet.

Might as well just jump in with both feet.

No matter how he chose to say it on any given day, he was essentially saying the same thing—just do it.

"Just do it, dummy." I hit the button for contacts and scrolled up until I found Andy's number. Then, drawing in a breath that was more dramatic than I intended, I placed the call.

One ring became two rings became three rings, until just as I was trying to decide whether I should hang up or wait and leave a message, a woman's voice filled my ear.

"Hello?"

Confused, I pulled the phone away from my ear just long enough to make sure I'd called the right number (I had). I swallowed.

"Uhhh, yeah . . . hi. Is, um, Andy available?"

The sound of the woman's answering giggle sent a chill down my spine. "He just stepped out for a moment. Can I take a message?"

I was trying to decide what to say when I heard a funny sound in the background of the call, followed by Andy's voice. "Who are you talking to?"

"I'm not sure." The woman's voice returned to full strength in my ear. "May I ask who is calling?"

"Tobi. Tobi Tobias."

Why I added my last name, I have no idea. Nerves, perhaps? Or maybe just because I had no idea what else to do with myself at that exact moment.

I tried to slow my heart rate as I waited for the giggly woman to relay the information to Andy, but it was hard. That little voice that had kept my heart from further harm in the aftermath of Nick's betrayal was back.

Unsure of what to say or do, I strained to pick out any of the muf-fled conversation playing out on the other end of the phone, but short of a sound I identified as a giggle, I came up empty.

I was trying to decide what to do when Andy finally came on the line.

"Hey, Tobi."

"Hi yourself." I hoped my voice sounded natural, but I knew the likelihood of that was slim to none. Still, I tried. "When did you get back from L.A?"

"Last night."

I considered teasing him about waiting so long to call me, but then I remembered he hadn't called. *I* had. And a woman I'd be will-ing to bet good money was Brenna Adams had answered.

For the first time ever, I found myself questioning my grandfather's advice. But as I did, I realized something.

If I hadn't called, I wouldn't know. And I'd take knowing over not knowing any day of the week.

At the next background giggle, I drew in a breath and stood. "You know what? I'm going to let you go. Take care, Andy."

Chapter Eleven

We were almost in St. Charles County before I realized I hadn't said more than two words to Sam since we'd commandeered his mother's old Beamer for our preliminary car-shopping expedition. I might have grunted at a momentary traffic slowdown as we'd approached Chesterfield Parkway, and I might have mumbled something about being an idiot for not leaving well enough alone, but no real conversation.

Shaking my thoughts into the here and now, I forced my lips into something that felt like a smile and took advantage of a straight stretch of highway to take in the fifteen-year-old in my (correction, Mary Fran's) passenger seat.

"So, what do you think? Lamborghini or Rolls-Royce?"

Sam's answering laugh made my own smile a lot more real. "Both."

I laughed. "As if."

"Okay, so maybe you can't buy even *one* of those now, but you will one day. You're too good at what you do not to."

For a split second, I actually considered pulling over onto the shoulder of the highway just so I could give Sam a hug. But in the interest of time and maintaining my composure, I opted to keep driving. Still, the teenager's words and the sincerity with which he'd said them birthed a lump in my throat I had difficulty clearing. "Don't ever change, Sam, okay? Not in college, not afterward, not ever."

"I promise not to if you promise not to."

I exited onto Highway K in O'Fallon and traveled north, the new hotels to our right and new shopping centers to our left little more than a blur as I glanced back at Sam. "You're afraid *I'm* going to change?"

"I saw your face when I showed up at your door with Mom's keys, Tobes, and it looked like it did before. You know, after"—he looked down at the string he was fiddling with along the seam of his jeans and then back up at me—"*Nick*."

A familiar warmth spread across my face, and I was more than a little grateful for the need to return my attention to the road. It gave me time to process and devise a suitable change in conversation that would lighten the atmosphere until we reached the first of the four dealerships on my list. But just as I was settling on the best diversion, Sam pivoted in his seat so that he was facing me more than the road.

"You're awesome, Tobes. You make people smile, your slogans are like really cool, you make me believe I might actually be able to make it as a photographer, and you're super pretty too. So if Andy is gonna be a big jerk like Nick, then that's his loss. Cut him loose and move on." Sam turned back, rested his forehead against the passenger side window, and gazed out at the strip malls and restaurants whizzing by. "Because there's someone out there for you, just like there's someone out there for Mom if she'd quit stamping her foot and refusing to *see*."

The lump was back, and this time it was accompanied by the all too familiar pinprick of tears. "Sometimes, when you say stuff like that, I have to wonder which one of us is the adult in this relationship, you know that?"

Sam's shoulders rose and fell with a shrug. "I just pay attention is all."

I slowed to a stop at the next traffic light and took advantage of our momentary cessation of movement to really study him. To the casual observer, Sam appeared to be just like any other fifteen-year-old boy. The jeans that had been the perfect length the previous month were a smidge too short now. The braces tasked with straightening his teeth glistened in the sun. And the complexion that only a few years ago had still been rosy was now dotted with a little acne. But as the saying went, looks can be deceiving. And that old adage was alive and well in Sam Wazoli.

A second-semester high school freshman, Sam was a dynamo who had no use for sports or getting into trouble like his peers. His bedroom walls were covered with poster-sized photographs that he, himself, had taken—a waterfall, sunlight glistening across an autumn leaf, a sea lion leaping into the air. His idea of a fun Friday night involved spending time with his mom. And while his mother had married and divorced two more times since his father had walked out on them when he was not quite two and a half, he still hoped and prayed she'd meet a worthy mate.

"Wow. Your mom sure hit the kid jackpot the day she had you."

"Nah. I hit the mom jackpot." Sam directed my attention back onto the now-green traffic light, and I, in turn, shifted my right foot to the gas pedal. "Seriously, Tobes, I don't know what Andy did to make you look so sad this afternoon, but don't let it get you too down."

I considered trying to convince him I was fine, or that whatever he'd sensed in me back at my place was simply a figment of his imagination, but Sam wasn't dumb. Still, I wanted—no, needed—to focus on something different for a little while.

In addition to the whole bull by the horns thing, Grandpa Stu had always taught me the fastest way back to feeling happy was to find something to smile about. "You know what, Sam? You're right. I've been dreaming about this day for months . . . no, *years*. So let's have some fun with it, okay?"

Sam's silver-clad smile spread like wildfire across his face. "That's the spirit!"

I gestured toward the Honda dealership on our right and, at Sam's nod, pulled into the car-strewn lot and parked. A glance at the windowed showroom confirmed my reason for waiting until Sunday to begin looking. No salesman equaled no pressure. "Let's do this, shall we?"

Dealership by dealership, we made our way down Highway K—Honda, Toyota, Chevrolet, Ford, Subaru. I didn't realize I was developing a pattern as we went, but Sam did and became adept at steering me toward smallish, mid-sized cars in white or maroon with a gasp-free sticker price. We talked through the various buzzers and bells offered and narrowed my would-like-to-haves down to radio controls on the steering wheel and heated front seats (aka butt warmers).

Two hours later, with my head only mildly spinning, we headed back toward the highway, exhausted but happy. "I can't believe I'm actually going to be able to buy my own car. No more borrowing wheels from your mom or Carter or JoAnna."

Sam shifted in his seat, coughed, and then shifted again. A peek at his face as I made a left onto the on ramp churned my stomach a smidge. "Sam? What's wrong?"

He looked down at his lap and then back up at the traffic just beyond the merge point. "I guess I'm just having a hard time believing this stuff about Carter. I mean, he's *Carter*, you know? You don't get much more easygoing than him."

"Believing what stuff?" I looked over my left shoulder, merged into the right lane, and slid my gaze back to my favorite teenager. "What did I miss?"

Sam's face drained of all discernable color. "You don't know?"

I heard a faint alarm going off in my head and tried to shake it off. "Know what?"

"That Carter might have killed that crazy lady from his theater? The one that's related to his boss?"

I stopped myself mid-laugh when yet another glance at Sam revealed that he wasn't joking. Elevating my gaze to the rearview mirror, I made sure the coast was clear and pulled onto the shoulder. When we were safely stopped as far to the right as possible, I slid Mary Fran's Beamer into park and turned to face her son. "Yes, a pair of cops might have followed Carter to the pet store last night, and they might have stayed until we left this morning, but that doesn't mean he killed someone, Sam."

"But Mom said . . ." The rest of his sentence disappeared as he stopped, swallowed, and gestured toward the road. "Um, I'm thinking maybe we should head back now."

"Oh no you don't. You don't get to say something like that and then stop."

The sudden crimson hue of his cheeks stood out against the otherwise still pale canvas that was his face at that moment. "I guess I just figured that since you and Mom were together last night, she might have told you. But since she didn't, can we just let this go? I don't want Mom to get mad at me."

"*First*—no, we can't let this go. Because, *second*, your mom doesn't get mad at you. Unless maybe you've eaten your way through the pantry before she's even put the grocery bags away."

His Adam's apple bobbed with a swallow. "She told you about that?"

"Your mom tells me everything, Sam." Yet even as I made that little proclamation, I couldn't help but realize it wasn't true. If it was, I wouldn't be there, sitting on the shoulder of Highway 40/64, trying to get to the bottom of her son's cryptic and unsettling words.

"I was hungry," he said by way of explanation.

I swept my hand atop the center console and tried hard not to roll my eyes. "Get back to the part about your mom and whatever she said about Carter to make you think he had something to do with Fiona Renoir's death."

"Please, Tobes? Let's talk about something else . . . like the shoot we're doing for Pizza Adventure tomorrow. I'm pumped about that."

I considered taking part in his distraction attempts, but before I could fully commit, my mind's eye wandered back to the previous evening. I'd been so busy trying to keep Carter calm and reassure him everything would be fine that Mary Fran and I hadn't had the kind of girl-time we'd planned. Which meant I hadn't had an opportunity to inquire as to why she seemed distracted. Then again, she hadn't appeared that way until after Carter showed up on the doorstep with tales of . . . well, tails, and tainted hair color.

Uh-oh.

The faint alarm I'd shaken from my head in favor of my car-shopping euphoria was back. Only now it wasn't so faint, and it came equipped with the kind of stomach churning that had me gauging the distance between my seat and the grass just beyond the passenger side of the car.

When I was semi-confident I could keep my one meal of the day confined to my stomach, I asked the dreaded yet necessary question. "Are you saying your mom actually thinks Carter killed Fiona?"

His gaze out the window was all the answer I needed.

"But why? And, more importantly, how could she actually think that? She knows Carter every bit as well as we do." I could hear the shrillness of my voice, but I was powerless to make it stop. "She knows he couldn't and wouldn't hurt a flea!"

When he didn't look at me, I felt my body deflate in my seat. "Sam . . . please. Talk to me."

Slowly, he turned, his eyes hooded, his expression pained. "She said she heard him, Tobes."

"Heard who? Carter?"

He nodded once.

"She heard him what?"

Sam raked his fingers down the front of his face, exhaling loudly as he dropped his hand from his chin to his lap. "I told her she must have misunderstood, but I don't know. She was really upset when she got home this morning."

"Upset about what?"

Sam closed his eyes briefly, then opened them as he tilted his chin up toward the ceiling of his mother's car. "Last week, when he had that run-in with Fiona at the theater? Mom had just gotten home from the pet shop when she saw him heading up the walkway to your front door. She could tell he was upset, so she called out to him and asked if he was okay."

I waited as he took a breath and then slowly lowered his attention back to me. "Mom said he looked like a crazy man when he turned in her direction. His eyes were wide, he was fisting his hands at his sides, and—"

"That's because he was angry!" I pulled my right calf onto the seat with me and leaned the left side of my body against the steering wheel. "He'd unleashed a verbal tirade on a woman he despised and got caught doing it. By his boss, no less. A boss who just so happens to be this woman's uncle."

"She heard him *say* something, Tobes."

"Say what?"

He waited a beat and then, leaning his head against the seat back, he blurted it out. "He said something about Fiona making a"—Sam swallowed hard—"catastrophic mistake the day she put him in her crosshairs."

"I repeat: he was angry."

Sam's eyes widened with uncertainty as they met mine. "He said he was going to make her pay . . . that he was going to rid the theater world of Fiona Renoir once and for all."

I searched his face for any indication he was kidding but, once again, there was nothing.

It was my turn to swallow, and swallow I did.

More than anything, I wanted to believe Mary Fran had taken liberties with what she'd overheard for the sake of a good story. But I knew Mary Fran. She was as honest as the day was long. If she said she overheard Carter say something, she did. Which, translated, meant my brain was back to calculating how quickly I could get out of the car and over to the grass. Midway through my calculations, I gave up and simply ran.

Of course, by the time I got there, Sam was out of the car and holding back my hair like the well-trained son of a single mom. A few cars honked as they whizzed by, and I'm pretty sure someone yelled "Cool!" from an open window, but really, all I could think about besides getting sick was the very real sense of dread pressing down on my shoulders.

"Aww, Tobes, I wish I'd kept my mouth shut. But I just figured Mom had said something to you about it last night."

I reached into my pocket for anything resembling a napkin, and when I came up empty, Sam jogged back to the car and returned with one from the glove box. "I remember thinking she seemed weird after Carter got there and told us what was going on, but I just figured it was residual stress over the dumb guy living above the shop."

When I was sure I wasn't going to get sick again, I straightened up and looked out over the highway, my thoughts here, there, and everywhere. But no matter how many times I mentally looped back to what Mary Fran had overheard, I knew Carter could never hurt anyone—even Fiona Renoir.

It just wasn't possible.

Sam looked me over from head to toe, and then, when I passed inspection, he guided me back toward the car and waited as I made my way around to the driver's side and took my place behind the steering wheel. "Mom's afraid the cops will question her on account of her being Carter's neighbor. She doesn't want to have to tell them what she overheard."

I peeked at the approaching traffic in my side-view mirror but didn't budge. "I get that she doesn't want to share that with the cops, but she doesn't actually think he did it, does she?"

The answering silence told me everything I didn't want to know.

"If your mom said she heard Carter say that, I'm sure she did. But I'm equally sure Carter didn't kill Fiona," I said firmly. "Did she get under his skin? Sure. Did he hate her? Yeah, I'm pretty sure he did. But kill her? No. No way."

Sam's whole being sagged with palpable relief. "Thank. You. Tobi. Phew . . . I mean I know what my mom said, and I know what she said this morning about the hair coloring being what killed Fiona, but I've been outside with Carter when an ant has crawled across his foot, and as much as he shrieked and carried on, he refused to kill it. Flat out refused. And when I moved in to do it, he turned away."

I slid the car into drive, checked the side-view mirror, and pulled back onto the highway, Sam's relief matched by mine. Granted, I'd still believe in Carter's innocence if I was the only person on the face of the earth who did, but hearing that Sam felt the same way helped.

A lot.

"So who do you think really did it?" Sam asked as we crossed the Boone Bridge, heading east.

"Logic says it's one of the other four who were on set that day." I moved into the left lane and stepped a little harder on the gas. "Now, don't get me wrong, I don't want any of them to be responsible for someone's death, either . . . but *I know* it wasn't Carter."

"Who else touched the bottle of hair coloring?"

It was a good question. "I don't know . . . Probably Rachel and Sara, but that doesn't mean Jeff and Rocky couldn't have at some point too."

Sam grew quiet as we passed the exit for Chesterfield Mall, and I took the opportunity to assemble everything that had happened in the past forty-eight hours into some sort of workable order. I was just moving on to the point when Carter had arrived at the pet shop when Sam finally spoke again.

"Any chance we could look at the footage that was shot that day? You know, for the commercial?"

I shrugged. "I don't know, why?"

"Maybe we'll see something that'll help."

"I doubt Jeff just happened to be filming when the person who killed Fiona slipped the peanut oil into the hair color." I cringed at my answer and rushed to soften it. "I didn't mean that as rudely as it sounded, kiddo."

Sam waved away my worry. "I doubt it too. But it can't hurt, can it?"

He had a point . . .

"Do you know much about that kind of film?" I asked.

"It comes from a camera, doesn't it?"

Chapter Twelve

I was rummaging through my refrigerator for something that could pass as dinner when I heard the knock at my back door. For four, maybe five glorious seconds, I hoped it was one of the plethora of dinner-delivery guys on my speed dial, but a second, slightly louder knock ushered in my pathetic reality—I hadn't called for takeout anything, and if I had, it would come in via the front door. With a sigh to end all sighs, as my mother loved to say, I pushed the refrigerator door closed and crossed to the back door.

"Mary Fran?" I let the simple curtain panel resume its place in front of my lookout spot and yanked open the door, my friend's worried expression impossible to miss. "Is everything okay?"

Without waiting for an invitation she certainly didn't need, my friend and former weekend boss shuffled into the kitchen and spun around to face me. "Where's Carter?"

"Upstairs. In his own place."

"But it's Oldies Night."

Now, don't get me wrong, I too was a little crushed over Carter's decision to refrain from participating in our newly imposed Sunday night tradition in favor of the sleep he and I both knew he wasn't going to get. But there were times arguing and cajoling weren't the best solution. Besides, by the very nature of Oldies Night, we could simply watch the selected episode of *Family Ties* next Sunday.

I pushed the door closed, shrugged, and made my way back to the refrigerator and my previous quest.

"It's because of me, isn't it?" Mary Fran asked.

"You?" I moved a carton of milk to the other side of the top shelf so I could get a better view of the container in the back left. Flashing back through my week, I tried to remember what I'd put inside the fridge, but when I came up empty-handed (or, rather, empty-brained), I popped open the lid and peered inside.

"Ewwww," I stared down at the piece of molding mozzarella I'd intended to shred for an English muffin pizza the previous week but hadn't, thanks to a last-minute offer for dinner from Mary Fran. "Gross!"

"Sam said he told you about what I overheard. So I imagine that means Carter knows now, as well."

I emptied the moldy cheese into my trash can and flung the container into the sink. "Trust me, I didn't say a word. He'd have been crushed."

A gargled sound from just over my shoulder made me turn and face Mary Fran. "I know my thinking Carter killed that woman has to be a real slap in the face, and I'm sorry. When I step back and focus on *Carter* rather than his words, I know he couldn't have done something like that."

"You're right. He couldn't."

"It's just that"—Mary Fran pressed her knuckles to her mouth— "well, he *said* he was going to rid the theater world of her once and for all."

"I'm sure he did," I said as I made my way over to the pantry and the bag of pretzels I knew was on the middle shelf. "But saying and doing are two very different things. Just ask my former fiancé, Nick the Jerk . . . or-or"—I stopped, swallowed, and held my voice as steady as possible—"Andy. Both those guys said I mattered, but as we well know, their actions didn't always match their words.

"I mean, think about it . . ." I ripped open the bag, poured some pretzels into a bowl, and held it out for Mary Fran. "You know how John, my old boss at Beckler and Stanley, used to make me batty, right? In fact, I'm quite sure I said I wanted to kill him at least a half dozen times each and every week. But just because I said it didn't mean I was actually going to do it. The same holds true with Carter."

"But John didn't die," Mary Fran half whispered, half mumbled. "Fiona did."

"It doesn't matter. I know Carter, and so do you." I hooked my thumb in the direction of the living room and then led the way on foot. When I reached the couch, I dropped into my favorite corner and waited for Mary Fran to claim her usual armchair.

She did—with a sigh that made me question whether my earlier one had really been worthy of my mother's infamous tag.

"I know you're right, Tobi. I really do. I think I'm just overly stressed and maybe a bit punchy." Mary Fran leaned her head back against the chair and stared up at the ceiling. "I know it's not an excuse, but this thing with the pet store has got me on edge, and then all this last-minute hoop jumping for the reunion is taxing whatever sanity I have left."

"Tell me."

Rising to her feet, Mary Fran zigzagged her way across my tiny living room—moving between the front window and the couch, the side window and the armchair, the hallway and the front door, and finally back to a scrap of wall that gave her a better view of me. "I can't believe that guy called and complained about the animals. I mean, I've had that shop in that same spot for coming up on four years. Yes, animals have come and gone in that time, but it's not like I've suddenly added a fleet of howler monkeys."

I smacked myself on the forehead and groaned. "Can you imagine Rudder if there was a howler monkey in the store? He'd *never* shut up."

"Tobi, I can't afford to move the shop—I just can't!"

I dropped my hand back down to first my lap and then the cushion beside me in a pat. "Whoa. Slow down. Come sit."

"I can't. I'm just"—Mary Fran flapped her hands wildly—"oooooh, I'm so angry I could *scream*."

I helped myself to another pretzel and held the bowl in Mary Fran's direction again. She waved me off.

"We were there last night, Tobi. Rudder and Baboo made no more noise during the night than they do during the day. Unless you count Rudder's snoring."

I stopped, mid-nibble, and stared at my friend. "Rudder *snores*? Seriously? I didn't hear that."

"That's because you were sleeping . . . *and snoring*."

Great.

Opting to ignore that last sentence, I finished my pretzel, helped myself to two more, and then steered the conversation into safer waters. "I know you knocked on this guy's door once, and I know you're convinced he was there, but why not try one more time? Maybe you're right, maybe he was inside. But maybe he was on the phone with an employee or a friend or his mom. And then there's the chance you're wrong and he wasn't there, and you're expending all this energy stressing over something that can be fixed with a simple apology and some good old-fashioned conversation."

Mary Fran gave me the first semblance of a smile I'd seen on her face since before Carter showed up at the pet store the previous night. "If I didn't know better, I'd think you did some sort of weird body swap with your grandfather just now."

I laughed at the image her words created in my mind. "Why?"

"Because I could so see him saying that same thing."

"And he probably would. I *am* his granddaughter, after all, and he took great pains to mold me into his mini-me." I contemplated another pretzel but held off in favor of a trip down memory lane. "Although my mother *did* put her foot down when I asked if I could shave my head."

Mary Fran's grin widened a little more. "You wanted to shave your head?"

"Grandpa Stu was bald, so I thought I should be bald too." I shrugged, helped myself to the last pretzel, and stared into the empty bowl, my stomach far from satisfied. "I was six. What did I know?"

She stepped over to her armchair once again and took a seat. "Maybe you're right. Maybe I really should give this jerk one more chance. Maybe invite him into the store so he can meet some of the animals himself. Because really, how can he resist them after that?"

"True. Assuming, of course, you put a gag in Rudder's mouth and drop a black sheet over his cage."

Mary Fran wagged her index finger at me. "I know you like to tell everyone how Rudder is such a pain and how he drives you nuts and all, but I know the truth, Tobi Tobias. And so does Sam."

I pushed off the couch, shooting a sidelong glance at Mary Fran as I did. "And what truth might that be?"

"That you love Rudder."

"*Love?*" I echoed. "Puh-lease. I think you might be going overboard a little."

Mary Fran settled back in her chair, her satisfied (and smug) smirk following me into the kitchen. "Do you really think I fell for that whole *I'll check the locks one more time* thing as we were settling into our sleeping bags last night?"

Although I could feel her mocking gaze through the back of my skull, I was glad I was walking away from Mary Fran at that exact moment. It was really the only way I could keep her from seeing the visual effects of the sudden and not so coincidental heat spike in my cheeks.

"I wanted to make sure they were locked."

Mary Fran's laugh was so deep and so rich I couldn't help but grin too. "You knew they were."

I wanted to protest but knew it was futile. All I could do now was hope Mary Fran hadn't actually heard me singing that lullaby to Rudder and Bab—

"Nice rendition of 'Rock-a-bye Baby,' by the way."

I didn't even bother to look back at the living room. Instead, I skulked over to the pantry, plucked the open box of Cocoa Puffs off their assigned shelf, and dug in. "I on't ow at our alking out."

"You shouldn't talk with your mouth full."

If I wasn't afraid of losing a puff, I'd have stuck my tongue out right then and there. But I was, so I didn't.

Two handfuls later, I peeked my head around the corner so I could gauge whether the coast was clear to return to my couch. Based on the fact that Mary Fran's eyes were closed and she was mumbling something under her breath, I figured I was good.

"Soooo," I said as I returned to the living room with my box of puffs in tow. "Have you hunted him down yet?"

"Him?"

"Ook o's eing oy ow." I waited for her eyebrow to return to its normal position and then repeated myself with an empty mouth. "Look who's being coy now."

When she didn't respond, I gleefully took over the role of tease-ee. "I know you've been hoping to hear something about Mr. Wonderful, your high school heartthrob."

Laying her forearm atop the armrest, Mary Fran began to pluck at a single strand of thread along the seam. She twirled it between her fingers, gave it a slight yank, and then went back to twirling, the almost rhythmic sequence making my eyelids heavy. But just as I thought about actually trading my puffs for a nap, she let go of the string and razzed a slow breath through clamped lips.

"I know it must seem really silly that I'm expending this much energy on a guy I dated when I was eighteen, but I'm curious."

Setting my puffs down (really, I did), I scooted across the couch until I was on the end closest to Mary Fran. When I reached my destination, I leaned forward and guided her hand away from the string (I'm trying to buy a car, not a chair) and back onto her lap. "I don't think it's silly. I think it's kind of encouraging, actually."

"Encouraging?"

"When I was engaged to Nick, you were our biggest champion. When I caught him cheating on me with that waitress, you stood by my side, reminding me I was worth more. Since then, you've been relentless about getting me back into the dating game. Yet, all the while, you've refused to date or even consider dating."

"Because men are"—Mary Fran tilted her head side to side—"well, *men*."

"And that's different for me because . . . wait. It's not different."

"After three failed marriages, *I* can be done. *You* can't be."

I considered a variety of responses designed to point out the hypocrisy in her line of thinking but decided to skip the obvious and get back to my point. "What I find encouraging is the fact that this Evan guy is the first person I've seen you smile over since you and I met. That has to mean something, don't you think?"

"No." Mary Fran looked down at her hands and then back up at me, the hope in her eyes a stark contrast to her words. "It just means I'm curious about someone I once knew is all. Someone I *didn't* marry."

"Someone who—to borrow a phrase of yours from the other day—curled your toes."

Mary Fran grinned. "He did, indeed."

"So what happened? Why did you two break up?"

"I had an extreme reaction to something that, in hindsight, shouldn't have been a big deal. And I guess I wonder, from time to time, what might have been if I hadn't gone all crazy the way I had."

I leaned back, letting my thoughts wander back a week. "Fascinating, really. But I think I'm more curious about his brother. The one who had a crush on you. Was he good looking?"

"Incredibly."

"Did the fact that he had a crush on you irk Evan?"

"Evan didn't know." Mary Fran stood, crossed to the box of puffs, and shoveled a small handful into her mouth.

"Ooooh, do tell."

Looking down at the last puff in her hand, Mary Fran's voice took on a faraway tone. "The week after our graduation, I planned this big elaborate picnic for Evan. I made chicken, baked his favorite brownies, and actually bought a red-and-white checked blanket like you see in the movies. I went to the park, got it all ready, and waited for him to show at the prearranged time. Only he never did.

"I waited, and I waited, and I waited. Being eighteen, I imagined all the reasons he wasn't there—all the girls he may have been with, et cetera. So by the time Drew showed up, I was in tears."

Intrigued, I scooted back to my starting place on the couch and wrestled the box of puffs from her hand. "Go on . . ."

"He saw me there, crying, and when I told him his brother hadn't shown, he told me I deserved better."

Mary Fran threw her head back and let out a laugh that was more heartbreaking than anything resembling happy. "I was so taken aback, I think I just stared at him like he was from another planet. He proceeded to tell me all the things about me he found special and finished by asking if I'd consider letting him take me out."

I sucked in a breath (and a puff). "What did you say?"

"I just cried harder. And that's when Drew got down on the blanket, stretched out on his back, and just started talking. He told me about his week, his classes at the local college, and his dreams for the future. Slowly but surely, I stepped out of my self-imposed pity party and started telling him about my dreams too."

Mary Fran wandered over to the front window but stopped short of moving the curtain to actually see outside to the darkened street. "That was the first time I ever told anyone I wanted to own a pet store and why."

I paused my hand inside the box. "Hmmm . . . I'm not sure *I* even know the why."

"I considered being a vet, but discarded that when I realized I'd have to put animals down. I considered working in a shelter, but nixed that when I remembered visiting a pet store with my mom when I was little. My family didn't have a lot of money, but looking at the puppies and kitties in the store's front window was cheap entertainment. Even after my dad got a better job, that was still my favorite thing to do. We went so often, I started giving the animals names. Every time we went, I'd race to the window to see who was still there and who had found a home. Sometimes I'd get sad if one of my favorites was gone, but when I realized they'd found a family, it made me happy."

With the lone exception of anything related to her son, I'm pretty sure I'd never seen Mary Fran look more beautiful than she did at that moment. Her smile was so pure, so true, I actually had to look away for a moment.

Curiosity made me turn back. "So? What happened after that? With Drew?"

"We ate the food, cleaned up, and because I broke up with Evan later that night, I never saw Drew again."

"Wait. So that was the extreme reaction you mentioned?" I challenged. "You broke up with Evan because he blew you off?"

"He was out with his friend. He forgot about the picnic. It wasn't worth breaking up with him over."

I set the box down, pushed off the couch, and made my way over to the window and Mary Fran. "Unless, deep down inside, you knew Drew was right—that you deserved better."

"That's just it. That stuff with Drew is *why* I got on my high horse and ended it with Evan. But it was stupid."

"Had he blown you off like that before?"

Mary Fran's shoulders rose and fell in a shrug. "A few times, yeah. But he was popular. He had a lot of friends—"

A sudden yet persistent vibration from somewhere in our vicinity interrupted Mary Fran's response and sent me on a search-and-rescue mission. When I located my phone between the cushions, I pulled it out, looked at the screen, and felt my mouth dry.

"Tobi?"

Slowly, I lifted my gaze to Mary Fran's. "It's . . . Andy. What do I do?"

In a flash, she was at my side, planting a good-bye kiss on the side of my head. "You take the call. You get the facts. And you decide from there."

Chapter Thirteen

I heard the door click closed behind Mary Fran and lifted the phone back to my cheek. "Okay, I'm here now."

"I saw the paper. Are you okay?"

I tried to ignore the traitorous pitter-patter in my chest at the concern in Andy's voice, but it was hard. A heart felt what a heart felt. Still, I worked to keep my own tone as even as possible. "Things are a little crazy right now, but I assure you it won't affect my dealings with your company."

If it were possible to hear a person deflate over a phone, I heard it in the heavy silence that followed my verbal assurance. For a moment, I felt a little bad. But that lasted about as long as it took for me to remember the sound of Brenna giggling in the background of our last call.

"Anyway, if that's all, I'll make sure to have JoAnna follow up with you on the specifics of next month's Zander mailing first thing in the morning."

"Whoa, whoa, whoa, Tobi. I'm not calling because I'm worried about Zander. I'm calling because I'm worried about you."

I squeezed my eyes against the tears I felt forming and willed them to remain at bay. Crying changed nothing. "Between JoAnna, Mary Fran, and Sam, I've got all the support I need. And Carter has ours, so really, there's nothing for you to worry about."

"*Carter?*"

"Yes, Carter. Because we know him. And we know he wouldn't hurt anyone—even someone as mean-spirited and difficult as Fiona Renoir." Yup, my tone had officially crossed the line from even (with a side order of cold) to full-fledged bitchy. But I didn't care. Forgetting people who mattered to me wasn't my M.O.

The silence was back. Only this time, instead of coming on the heels of a deflating exhale, it followed a gasp that was so sharp, and so unexpected, I actually had to pull the phone away for a second.

"Are you telling me the cops are looking at *Carter* for this?"

Bitchy ebbed to confusion as I dropped onto the couch and pulled my knees up and under my chin. "They're grasping at straws, that's all. But really, I'm sure it's only a matter of time before they stop chasing their tails in favor of the truth."

"Why didn't you tell me about this when you called this morning?"

I heard the sarcasm in my laugh and let it stand as I cast about for the best answer I could give. When I finally settled on one, I lowered my feet back down to the ground and tightened my hold on the phone. "I'm not in the habit of burdening my clients with tales of my personal life."

"But I'm not just your..." His sentence drifted off as what I imagined was his internal lightbulb turned on.

I held my breath and started a mental count as I waited to see whether his response would take the route of pathetic excuse or arrogance.

"Wait. Is this about earlier? When you called?"

Realizing I'd forgotten to add *feigned ignorance* to the list of potential tactics Andy might take, I corrected my mistake, placed a mental check mark next to it, and then straightened up in preparation for battle.

"You know what? How about we skip the games, shall we?" I took a breath and forged ahead. "Was that Brenna who answered?"

The length of his pause was all the answer I needed. The barely audible confirmation that eventually followed was really just overkill.

I felt my throat starting to tighten and my eyes starting to water, and I detested both. I'd been down this road before. I really should be immune. But then again, I'd thought Andy was different . . .

"I can assure you I will not let this affect our working relationship." I stopped, took a breath, and continued. "I'm a professional, you're a professional, and all that really matters is keeping Zander in front of prospective clients."

"Tobi, I—"

I held up my hand as if Andy was in the room. "Andy, let's not, okay? Let's not prolong the inevitable or dress things up to be something they're not. I've been on the receiving end of that once already, and I'm not interested in being there ever again. I know how you felt about Brenna, and I'm glad you're getting a second chance."

"I'm not sure I want that," Andy finally said, his voice raspy and filled with emotion I prayed wasn't pity.

Not sure . . .

I felt my eyelashes beginning to lose their battle against my tears, and I squeezed them closed. All my internal song and dance about being tough and knowing when to cut my losses was just a bunch of crap. I'd actually been holding out hope he'd balk at the notion of a second chance with Brenna. But he hadn't balked.

It was official. I'd left myself wide open for yet another kick, and, well, here I was.

Again.

"I'll have JoAnna call you in the morning. Good-bye, Andy."

I was still sitting there, more than an hour later, when my phone vibrated in my hand. A check of the screen revealed Carter's smiling face. For a brief moment, I considered letting him go to voice mail, but midway through the third ring, I changed my mind.

"Hey."

"Will you come visit me in prison, Sunshine?"

"Why would I do that?"

"Because you love me. And because"—Carter's voice hitched with his breath—"I'll be lonely locked away in the Big House."

"You're not going to prison, Carter. You didn't kill her."

"You remember *The Shawshank Redemption*, don't you, Sunshine? That movie with Morgan Freeman and Tim Robbins? We watched it one night last spring. With Sam. He ate the veggie sticks I brought, and you didn't."

"I bought double chocolate cupcakes at the bakery for that particular movie night. Sam devoured three, and you ate none," I countered.

"Touché."

"I try."

An audible intake of air in my ear was followed by words so hushed I had to strain to make them out. "Tim Robbins's character didn't kill his wife, remember? But he still spent something like twenty years behind bars."

"He got himself out."

"I'm not that crafty," Carter protested.

"Don't sell yourself short. You've perfected the Army crawl to a point where you've actually made it to Mary Fran's *what—three* or four times without Ms. Rapple catching you? Though, that last time? When you cleared her mums and she was there waiting for you, hands on hips? You have to admit that was funny."

I smiled at the memory.

I was pretty sure Carter didn't.

"Don't you see, Sunshine?" he finally said. "Innocent people go to prison all the time."

He had a point. But since admitting that aloud would be counter-productive to soothing my friend's fears, I kept that thought to my-self. Instead, I reached past my own aching heart for the positive attitude I knew he needed from me. "But they didn't have me . . . and Mary Fran . . . and Sam in *their* corner, now did they?"

I heard a sound I suspected was a swallow, or maybe more of a gulp, followed by a sniffle. "You all are? Truly?"

"We are what?"

"In my corner?"

I looked up at the ceiling and mouthed an apology to my late grandmother. "Yes."

Yes, I know lying is wrong under most circumstances. But I also know Carter. And if I'd shared with him the fact that Mary Fran had expressed some doubt, he'd be inconsolable. Besides, if I hadn't got-ten through to her on the subject earlier that evening, I'd try again and again until I did.

A whoosh of air filled my ear a split second before the first sem-blance of a laugh I'd heard from Carter in days took its place. "You have no idea how much I needed to hear that, Sunshine. I feel like I'm a freak in some sort of traveling circus the way everyone is star-ing at me."

"How can people be staring at you when you haven't left the house all evening?" I stood and made my way around the living room, stopping to lock the front door and each of my three first-floor windows in preparation for the sleep my eyelids were beginning to demand.

"I went back to the theater. Just to have something to do. Every-one there was strangely quiet."

"Maybe because the boss's niece was just *murdered*?" I headed into the kitchen, put the box of Cocoa Puffs back on its shelf, and then shut off the light. "I'm thinking that could dampen a mood."

"But I heard their laughter when I opened the door. And I heard the way it stopped completely the moment they looked up and saw me."

"Maybe they're worried about you."

"Or maybe they thought I was a crazed murderer intent on doing *them* harm, as well."

"Did you?" I asked around my yawn as I made my way into my bedroom.

"Did I what?"

"Kill them."

I pulled the phone from my ear at his gasp and then returned it to its starting place in time to hear the encore that was his wounded indignation. "Tobi Tobias, are you really asking me that?"

"In the interest of making my point, yes." Bypassing the switch for the overhead light above my bed, I flopped onto the mattress and closed my eyes. "So humor me and answer it, okay?"

I was too tired to even crack a smile at his huffing and puffing. But I yawned—twice.

"Of course I didn't kill them!"

"Then maybe that should tell them something."

"Like?"

"Like they're barking up the wrong tree in regard to Fiona's killer."

A beat or two of silence (his) might have been followed by the beginnings of a snore (mine), but it didn't last long thanks to a second, louder gasp that made me sit up tall. "Carter? Are you okay?"

"Someone on that set—or someone connected to that set—killed Fiona . . . and they're trying to pin it on me! That is just *so* not acceptable, Sunshine."

At the sound of my Carter-given nickname, I stood. "You're right, it's not."

Chapter Fourteen

There was no denying the rush I felt when an idea became reality. The fact that the idea responsible for my current rush wasn't mine made no difference. Dom and Gina Paletti were poised to strike gold with Pizza Adventure, and it was impossible to be anything but giddy as Sam and I helped lay the final groundwork.

Sam lowered his camera in line with his chest and looked at me across his shoulder. "Can you believe this place, Tobes? It's incredible."

"Did I not tell you you'd have a field day with this shoot?" I returned my own gaze to the Drive-In Movie room and did a little marveling of my own.

There were no two ways about it, Dom and Gina had outdone themselves. Tables that looked like old cars? Waitresses on roller skates? Black-and-white cartoons projected onto the far wall?

And that was just the main room.

Seven offshoot destination rooms promised to jettison pizza enthusiasts to a tropical island, Batman's cave, a princess's castle, the African jungle, the deep blue sea, Old Hollywood, and Paris—without ever leaving South County. The fact that you got to eat the best pizza in all of St. Louis while visiting said locations was simply the cherry on top.

"Dom and I talked about it. Or, rather, I talked, and he pretended to listen." Gina Paletti sidled up alongside me and brushed a piece of lint off the sleeve of my blouse in very JoAnna-like fashion. "But either way, first pick for next week's soft launch belongs to you, Sweetie."

I did my best to stifle my answering squeal, but judging by Sam's laugh off to my right, I knew I'd been largely unsuccessful. "Seriously?"

Gina nodded.

"I'll take this room," I motioned toward the red car booth that sat front and center. "With Bugs Bunny cartoons, please."

"You want *this* room?" Gina asked, drawing back. "Really?"

I shook myself back into the present and slid my surprise in Gina's direction. "You do know how incredibly cool this room is, yes?"

"Oh, I know it's fun." Gina tapped her index finger to her chin as she took in the room responsible for the scads of pictures Sam was still actively taking. "In fact, this room is a nod to Dom's and my very first date when we were in high school. He likes to pretend he doesn't remember many details from that night, but the minute he picked out that booth over there"—I followed the path forged by Gina's finger to a pale blue car with white trim—"I knew he was full of hooey."

"The car you were in looked like that one?" I asked.

"Right down to the silver trim around the back license plate." Gina's soft laugh echoed around the cavernous room. "I'm not supposed to know this, but the manufacturer told me Dom gave him a picture of the car he drove that night, and it's a perfect match."

Something about the admission made it difficult to breathe for a moment, and I looked away in an attempt to compose myself. But just as I was getting a handle on the unexplained, Gina stepped closer and grabbed my hand. "Now don't get me wrong, Tobi, a night of drive-in cartoons can obviously lead to the same place, but don't you think an evening alone in Paris or on a tropical island would be a better fit for you and your young man?"

"M-my young man?"

"Surely you know we want him here with you that night," Gina offered by way of explanation.

This time, when I looked away, it was as much about buying myself a little time to swallow as it was to find my game face. When I was pretty sure I was good on both accounts, I met her eyes just long enough to offer what I prayed was a carefree smile. "I'm planning on coming by myself that night—unless it would be okay to bring my friend, Carter. He could really use a night out. Especially if it involves cartoons."

"Oh dear."

Something about the inflection in her voice surprised me, and I looked from her, to Sam, and back again. "Gina? Is something wrong?"

"Something's happened, hasn't it?"

I widened my visual field to include the Palettis' goddaughter, who'd been brought in to don waitress attire and a pair of roller skates. When I was sure she was still standing and that Sam showed no indication of any issues, I returned my focus to the woman at my side. "I'm sorry, Gina, but I'm not—"

"Dom and I certainly had our share of spats along the way in our early days, but when it's meant to be, it always has a way of working out. You'll see." Gina gestured her goddaughter over, fussed with the string of the teenager's apron, and then sent her back in front of Sam's camera. "My bones are never wrong, Tobi. They know when storms are coming, they know when it's best to buy a scratch-off, and they know when two people—like you and your young man—are destined to be together for the long haul."

"But you've never even met him," I protested.

"I've been in your office a few times when he's called, and I've seen the way your entire face lights up when JoAnna gives you the message. That's enough for my bones to know."

I bit down on my tongue and held it there between my teeth until the urge to suggest she get her bones checked had passed. After all, while my agency was in better shape than it had been just a few months earlier, I couldn't afford to lose the Palettis from my list of clients. Especially if I was going to pull the trigger and buy that cute white four-door Chevy with the tan-colored seats and power sunroof that had popped into my dreams at least a half dozen times throughout the night . . .

"Well, that's a wrap." Sam pulled his camera away from his face for the last time and dropped down to a squat beside his bag. "I think we've got more than what we need for the mailings and print ads, Tobi. And it's really great stuff."

"Hard to expect anything less when you've got a great subject and a great photographer." I captured Gina's hand with my own and gave it a squeeze. "I have absolutely no doubt that your grand opening is going to be one for the record books."

"Do me a favor and say that to Dom next time you see him." Gina returned my squeeze and then clasped her hands in front of her throat.

"He's been doing so much pacing lately, I swear we're going to need new floors both here and at the house."

"Tell him to quit worrying." I retrieved my clipboard of notes from the front counter and mentally checked off each to-do item on the list. When I reached the bottom, I shoved it into my tote bag and kissed Gina on the cheek. "When I have the ads ready for proofing, I'll send them to you to approve and then get them in the paper."

"That sounds wonderful, dear."

Sam zipped up his camera bag, slung it over his shoulder, and met me en route to the door.

"I'll take my thank-you in the form of an extra-large milk shake," he whispered. "From the Shake Shack right there by Starwood Studios."

I stopped. "Your thank-you?"

"For getting you off the hot seat just now."

"What are you talking about?"

Sam motioned toward Gina and her goddaughter with his chin. "She was grilling you about Andy, so I wrapped the photo shoot."

"You weren't done?" I whispered back.

His cheeks turned crimson a half second before his shrug. "Technically, I was done five minutes earlier."

I followed his less-than-subtle glance back toward the Drive-in Movie room and the teenage girl batting her eyelashes in his direction.

Ahhh . . .

With a quick wave at Gina, I pushed open the door to the parking lot and held it as Sam walked through. "So will that be vanilla or chocolate?"

"Is it just me or did that lady in the office just now seem super stressed?"

I met Sam's wide eyes across the top of his chocolate shake. "That was Rachel, the art director, and no, I picked it up too."

We were crossing one of several sound stages en route to the cutting floor, and other than the occasional ooh-ahh from my teenage assistant, I was pretty sure I could hear the proverbial pin drop if, in fact, someone had dropped one.

"I want a studio just like this," Sam gushed as he stopped at the threshold of yet another set and took in his surroundings much like a child half his age took in the mountain of brightly wrapped packages under the family Christmas tree. "I could do family portraits on one set and baby pictures on another. Of course, I'd be out on location a ton, too, doing ad work for you."

"If you can still fit me in your schedule," I said, only half kidding. Sam and his photographic eye were going places—big places. The only real questions now were where and when.

Sam took one last slurp of his shake, looked around for a wastebasket, and deposited his empty cup inside the nearest one. "I'll always fit you in, Tobes. You were the first person to believe in me as a photographer, remember?"

"Technically, I was the second. Your mom was the first."

"True." Sam crossed back to my side and peeked inside my cup. At my offer, he took it and polished off the last of my shake as well. "Still, when you call with a job, I'm yours. No questions asked, and without fail."

I opened my mouth to challenge him with all the things—like a wife and kids—that might make being at my professional beck and call in the future more difficult than he realized, but I let it go. Sometimes intent was enough.

We fell into step beside each other once again as we continued down the hallway. At the next set, I stopped, the silence of the warehouse-sized building no match for the sudden thumping in my chest. "This is where it happened." I pointed toward the section of flooring right in front of the salon-style chair—a section now singled out by yellow crime-scene tape. "Right there, in fact."

"Did you see her fall?" he asked in a hushed voice.

"No. I just heard Carter's screams, and it was awful."

"Was that lady here, too?"

"You mean Rachel?" I asked. "The one I just introduced you to in the office? Yes, she was here. In fact, unlike me, she *did* see it happen"

"That explains it then."

I shook the image of Fiona's lifeless body from my thoughts and turned to Sam. "Okay, kid, you lost me. What explains what?"

"She's going through what you went through after our first Zander shoot. And just like you, she's having a hard time forgetting."

Sometimes, when Sam spoke, it was hard to believe he was just fifteen years old. Because despite his short time on earth, he had a wisdom that belied his years and an ability to empathize that was rare.

His observation took me back to Rachel's pale face, her wide, almost shell-shocked eyes, and her incessant fidgeting as she half listened to my request to see the footage from my Salonquility commercial. I'd noticed her behavior, of course, but I'd rationalized it via the tried-and-true scapegoat that was a Monday afternoon—especially a Monday afternoon that some folks were lucky enough to have off.

"Crap. You're right. I'll send her some flowers or candy or something when I get back to the office. Just so she knows I'm thinking about her."

Sam nodded and then backed his way off the set, his index finger guiding me toward our ultimate destination.

Once inside the cutting room, and after another chorus or two (or five) of oohs and ahhs from Sam, I located the footage from the Salonquility commercial and handed it to him. "This wasn't shot in order. We were going to piece it together, with the client's requested music, tomorrow. But now, on account of our actress being dead, not only will the commercial not be ready for release on the intended date, it will have to be reshot in its entirety."

Sam pressed a few things, turned a few dials, grunted something that sounded like a response to my ramblings, and then sat back as a long sweeping shot of an empty pedicure tub was followed by one of an empty massage table. He hit the PAUSE button and looked back at me. "Taken for continuity, yes?"

"How'd you know that?" I slipped into the chair next to Sam's and looked from him to the frozen image on the screen and back again.

"I do the same thing with my photographs. It's a way to make sure any necessary reshoots don't look like reshoots."

He turned back to the screen and hit PLAY. The empty massage table morphed into a sweeping shot of the set from which we'd just come—same mirrored booth, same salon chair, and same product bottles on the makeshift shelves. The only difference between the scene playing out in front of us and the one we'd just left was the color bowl on the cart. In real time, it was no longer there, its scrutinized contents the sole reason Sam and I were here in the first place.

I shuddered so hard, Sam shot me an odd look. "You okay, Tobes?"

"I guess. It's just kind of eerie looking at that bowl and its contents now and realizing it was used as a murder weapon less than twenty minutes later."

I followed his gaze back to the screen and watched as he rewound, and moved forward, and rewound again. "What are you doing?" I asked as he did the same thing a few more times.

"The guy who shot this didn't shoot these all at one time." Sam pointed at the time stamp on the bottom right hand corner of the screen. "See? This first set was recorded at ten o'clock. And this one"—he fast forwarded ahead to the massage room—"was recorded at eleven-thirty."

I compared his find to what I remembered from Friday and realized it made sense. It had taken just under ninety minutes to shoot the pedicure scene. After that, we'd moved onto the massage shoot. I shared that detail with Sam.

"That actually makes sense. If he'd shot all the sets in the beginning, someone might have changed something along the way. This way, he's frozen the set moments before actual shooting began." He fast-forwarded to the final set and again directed my attention to the time stamp in the corner. "And this shoot began in the neighborhood of two o'clock?"

"That's right."

Sam leaned to the side, unzipped his camera bag, and retrieved his camera. With practiced and efficient hands, he stripped his camera down to its original lens and pointed it at the scene on the screen. A few clicks later, he lowered the camera down to his lap and removed the continuity footage from the editing machine.

"Why'd you do that?" I asked.

"So we can show it to Carter."

"Show it to Carter?"

Shrugging, Sam inserted the commercial footage into the machine and rewound it back to the beginning. "Maybe something will jump out at him that we might not necessarily notice."

Damn, this kid was smart . . .

I couldn't help but beam at Mary Fran's son with pride as the click indicating he'd reached the beginning of the tape echoed around us.

"Ready, Tobes?"

"Yep."

The second he hit PLAY and the pedicure scene came to life in front of us, any and all lightheartedness I'd managed to muster was gone, replaced by a sudden dryness in my mouth as the camera zoomed in on Fiona.

"Wow. She's pretty."

"*Was* pretty," I corrected.

Sam glanced over at me. "She's the one?"

I nodded.

"Oh. Wow. She doesn't look like a . . ." The rest of his sentence trailed off as Fiona suddenly pointed at the camera.

"I told you," Fiona hissed through clenched teeth. "If you want a side shot, take it of my right side!"

"And *I* told *you* I would do my best, but no guarantees."

Sam and I leaned forward in unison just before some sort of plinking noise threw the camera angle off Fiona and over to the red-faced key grip.

"Who's that?" Sam asked.

"That's Rocky. The key grip." I kept my focus on the screen as Rocky lunged forward, scooping up bottles of nail polish from the floor while Fiona's voice berated him for his stupidity and carelessness. "Sara told me about this shortly after it happened. Rocky was moving one of the cables so Jeff could try to accommodate Fiona's angle request, and he knocked over a few of the nail polish bottles."

"Man," Sam muttered under his breath, "nothing like embarrassing a guy even more than he already was."

"Classic Fiona behavior, according to Carter. She was always doing that to him at the theater."

"No wonder he wanted to—" Sam stopped, cleared his throat, and tried again. "No wonder he wasn't a fan."

I knew where he'd been going, and it was probably best he'd stopped. Even though I was certain Sam knew Carter was innocent, a verbal reminder of some of the things that had passed through our neighbor's lips in regards to Fiona were best left in the past. Where no one could overhear them and make a mountain out of a molehill.

Sam pulled his phone from his back pocket, checked the time, and then set it on the table next to the screen. "I promised Mom I'd be back in time to help her feed all the animals before closing time, so we probably should move on if we can."

"Sure. Yeah. Of course." I leaned back and then forward as he hit PLAY again and we found ourselves in the massage room as Fiona—clad in a white robe and white slippers—walked in.

For the first time, I actually really looked at Fiona—Fiona the person, not Fiona the thorn in Carter's side. I noted that her shoulder-length red hair was pulled into a messy bun but actually looked soft and flattering alongside her high cheekbones and slender nose. Her posture was perfection beneath her robe, and I self-consciously straightened in my seat.

The next shot moved to Fiona facedown on the massage table with hot rocks on her delicate, shapely back. A third shot that I knew would have found its way between the first two had Fiona on her back, her eyes closed, a peaceful expression on her face.

As I watched, I was aware of a nearly insatiable need to feel the same peaceful calm Jeff had managed to capture on Fiona's face. The effect left me wanting to get a massage sooner rather than later.

Yup, my vision for the commercial had been spot-on. And if we'd been able to finish it and get it on the local television stations as I'd planned, Salonquility would have surely seen a hefty spike in appointments. But things hadn't gone as planned, which is why I was watching the footage with Sam instead of the Starwood Studio folks.

"You can always find someone else to play the customer, Tobes."

I glanced over at Sam to find him eyeing me with a worry he shouldn't have at fifteen. "I know that, kiddo. In fact, Fiona wasn't even my first choice—Rachel was."

"The AD?"

"She went to school to be an actress, but when she hadn't landed any parts after six months, she got involved behind the scenes." I pulled my braid across my shoulder and fiddled with its end. "I figured I could give her something for her résumé by letting her do this commercial."

"So why didn't you?"

"Because Carter needed me to hire Fiona—so her uncle wouldn't fire him." I pushed my braid back in place and slumped back against my chair. "So, instead, I reneged on my word to Rachel and gave the gig to Fiona."

"You were trying to help."

"Considering Carter is now a suspect in Fiona's death because of something that happened on *this* shoot, I'm thinking it's safe to say I failed in the whole help-Carter thing."

I'd be lying if I didn't admit I was waiting for Sam to disagree with me, but even if he had, I would have known it wasn't genuine.

By trying to help Carter, I'd hurt him. Pretending otherwise might make me feel better for all of about a half second, but it wouldn't last.

"Carter didn't do it. We know this." Sam removed his hand from the editing machine just long enough to give my arm a quick pat. "That's why we're here. So we can prove it to anyone who believes otherwise.

"And once we do, you can reshoot the commercial with Rachel and everything will be A-okay, as Mom likes to say."

I gave him the smile I knew he was waiting for and then followed his attention back to the screen. Sure enough, the massage scene was fading into the first shot on the hair-styling set.

There, standing beside the chair, was Carter, the smile on his face as he greeted Fiona pretty convincing for someone whose job at the theater was simply to make the actors and actresses look good. Fiona smiled back, sat down in the chair, and allowed Carter to cover her clothes with a Salonquility smock. They smiled, exchanged a bit of chitchat that would have been dubbed over by music in the final cut, and then Carter grabbed the color bowl off the cart and gave its contents a quick stir

"Whoa."

Sam glanced back at me. "What?"

"The bowl. It was on the far side of the cart with the brush already inside it." I scooted forward on my chair as Carter began to brush the agreed-upon color onto Fiona's long locks. "Rewind, rewind, rewind!"

Sam did as I asked and then pressed PLAY again.

"See?" I practically shouted. "The bowl's on the right . . . with the brush inside."

"Okay . . ."

"That's not the way it was in the continuity shot." I grabbed the first tape and held it out for Sam.

He took it from my hand, stood, and headed for a second editing machine with me close on his heels. Popping it into place, he fast-forwarded through the first two sets and stopped on Carter's set. Sure enough, the color bowl was on the left side of the cart with the brush neatly positioned beside it, not in it.

Like synchronized swimmers, Sam and I looked from one screen to the next with Sam finally breaking the silence. "Whoa is right."

I felt my mouth begin to dry and my hands begin to sweat as I weighed the possibilities, the most obvious being basic human error. Yes, the whole point in taking continuity shots to begin with was to cut down on mistakes, but they still happened. That said, the Starwood Studio folks were aces. I knew this. I'd seen this firsthand.

Which really left only one other option: we were seeing evidence that someone had, in fact, tampered with Fiona's color.

I took a moment to process things as Sam snapped another picture with his camera and then I reached around him to rewind the continuity footage back to the moment Jeff had started on the hairdresser set. The time stamp on the bottom right corner showed 2:10 P.M.

Armed with that information, I crossed back to the first editing machine, rewound the commercial footage to the start of Carter's scene, and compared times. Jeff had officially started shooting at 2:32—leaving a twenty-two-minute window in which to tamper with Fiona's color.

Twenty-two minutes was a substantial amount of time. Especially when we were talking about a squirt or two of peanut oil and maybe a quick stir.

"We need to find out what happened during that twenty-two-minute window," I said, as much to myself as the teenager now standing behind me. "Like did everyone leave? Did anyone double back? Maybe return to the set under the guise of having forgotten something? You know, that sort of thing . . ."

"You don't remember anything during that time?" Sam slipped into his first seat, glanced up at me, and, at my nod, stopped the tape and returned it to its case.

I closed my eyes and tried my best to piece together the time leading up to Carter's screams, my words serving as a tour guide for Sam and for me. "I remember Jeff going to shoot the continuity clip but waiting as Rachel made sure the Salonquility smock was folded to show the company's logo. And I remember Sara stopping him once he readied the camera so she could refold the smock because she felt Rachel hadn't done a good enough job—though, truth be told, I saw no difference when she was done."

"Did anyone else stop him?"

I paused, gave his question some thought, and then shook my head.

"Then let me check something real quick." Sam returned to the continuity footage one more time and fast-forwarded to the end. "Okay, with that one stop and restart, and the time it took for the smock to be refolded and placed in its proper position, our window shortens to nineteen minutes."

"Nineteen minutes is still long enough to stir in some peanut oil." I watched Sam remove the tape, return it to its proper case, and then cross back to me, his brow furrowed.

"What happened after he finished the continuity shot?"

"Rachel suggested the crew take a break."

"Did they?" Sam asked.

"I remember Jeff putting down the camera like he was going to . . . and Rocky reaching into his pocket for a cigarette, which he would've had to smoke outside."

"And the AD?"

"She said something about a call she wanted to make, and I'm pretty sure she headed toward—yeah, she did! I know, because I was only a few steps behind her as I headed toward the restroom."

"Anyone else?"

"Yeah, Sara. The intern."

"The nitpicky one?"

My thoughts had already skipped ahead (or back, as was the case) to what would surely be Sam's next question. "I don't remember Sara necessarily leaving. I remember her watching Rachel leave . . . I remember her rolling her eyes . . . and I remember her consulting Rachel's clipboard for what I imagine was a rundown of the scene."

Sam stared at me. "So she was alone on the set while everyone else took a break?"

"When I first left, yeah, she was still on the set. But that doesn't mean she didn't leave right after me to get a drink or check her email or even sit outside with Rocky while he smoked his cigarette. In fact, all I know for sure is that when Carter screamed and I went running, they were all there, staring at Fiona's body."

"Even if she left, there's no reason she couldn't have snuck her way back onto the set, right?"

"In nineteen minutes, any one of them could have returned to the set and slipped a few drops of peanut oil into the hair color." I crossed my arms in front of my chest and tried to rub away the chill I felt building. "What doesn't make sense is how a person who is trained on the importance of continuity would have put the bowl in the wrong place. Unless that was all part of the frame-Carter plan."

"Meaning?"

"Meaning putting the hair color on the opposite side of the cart would make sense for a novice like Carter."

Sam's eyes widened. "That would be some serious track-covering if that's the case."

"Which makes sense if someone is trying to get away with murder."

"True." Sam retrieved his camera bag from the floor and then hoisted the strap up and across his shoulder. "Then again, maybe whoever did it heard someone coming and put the bowl back down before they really had a chance to think."

He had a point—a good one.

I tried to stifle my sigh, but I'm not too sure I was successful. Figuring out who killed Fiona wasn't going to be easy. That much was clear. But if I'd learned anything in my twenty-eight years on this planet (beside the fact I was lousy at picking men, of course), it was that I didn't need things to be easy. If I had a reason to make something happen, I would.

"I think it's time to cozy up to the crew. I think that's the only way, short of a surveillance camera the studio doesn't have, to figure out who really killed Fiona."

"Makes sense, I guess." Sam triple checked the POWER button on both machines and then gestured toward the door and the hallway beyond. "So how do you plan to do that, exactly?"

"Honestly? I haven't a clue—yet. But I will. You can count on that."

Chapter Fifteen

Part one of my plan came to me within minutes of dropping off Sam and the car outside To Know Them Is to Love Them. I'd walked no more than two blocks in the direction of home when it practically leapt out at me from the front window of Tara's Tasty Treats—the local bakery where everyone (and by everyone, I mean *everyone*) knew my name.

You see, instead of bellying up to a bar after work hours, I tended to cap off my day with a shot or two of sugar. Cupcakes and brownies were my preferred delivery system, although I certainly didn't scoff at cookies or candy.

It had become such a habit during the past year that Tara had instructed her legions of high-school-aged employees to refrain from hanging the shop's CLOSED sign until after I'd exited with one of her drool-worthy treats clutched in my hand and part of my paycheck tucked inside her cash register.

So it was while I was standing at the window, ogling the plate of white chocolate brownies that seemed to be whispering my name, when it hit me.

Chocolate. Cures. All. Ills.

It was a known fact.

Across every country on every continent.

With the lone exception, of course, of Carter McDade—who'd surely been dropped on his head as a baby (I mean, really, what other possible explanation could there be for not liking chocolate).

I made a mental note to thank my mom for never dropping me on my head the next time we spoke on the phone and then looked back at the delectable display featuring all my faithful friends—chocolate-chip cookies, chocolate layer cake, chocolate-covered caramel candy, and triple-chocolate brownies.

Surely Rachel—assuming her mother had had a tight grip as well—would welcome a bag of Tara's Tasty Treats after the hellish few days she'd had . . .

My mind made up, I went inside, ordered a little of this and a little of that, and made the half mile or so trek back to Starwood Studios. I knew I was taking a gamble that Rachel would even still be there at—I checked my phone—four-forty-five on a Monday afternoon (a holiday Monday, at that), but the woman was a self-proclaimed workaholic. And workaholics tended to have a hard time calling it a day.

When I reached the warehouse-style building, I was pleased to see a light coming from the general vicinity of Rachel's office. I was downright giddy when a peek through her open doorway gave me confirmation that my gamble had paid off.

I rapped my right fist on the trim around the door and then waved as the AD spun her desk chair around to face me. "Hey," I whispered so as not to interrupt her call.

Rachel spun back around, mumbled something into her phone before ending her call, and then turned back to me with questioning eyes. "Did you forget something?"

"No. And I didn't mean to interrupt your call. I just"—I lifted the baby-pink bag up for Rachel to see and gave it a little shake—"wanted to stop by and bring you a little pick-me-up gift."

"A pick-me-up gift? Why?"

I inched my way into her office and over to her desk, holding out the bag as I did. "A few months ago, I was where you are now. I remember it vividly. And I guess I want you to know that I get it."

Rachel took the bag from my hands, opened it, and then held it to her chest. "Oh. Wow. Thank you. I could really use something like this right now."

"Good." I set my purse on a nearby chair and dug around until I found the stack of napkins I'd picked up on the way out of the bakery. Keeping one for myself, I handed the rest to Rachel. "I wasn't sure if you were as into chocolate as I am, so I got some cheesecake bites just in case."

"Not into chocolate?" Rachel reached into the bag, extracted one of the white-chocolate brownies that had first caught my eye out on the sidewalk, and placed it on her napkin, the faintest hint of a smile twitching at the corners of her mouth. "Is that even a thing?"

I removed my backpack from the chair and, at her nod, sat down. "In some bizarre parallel universe known only to my friend, Carter, apparently." After she'd tried a few bites, I rested my elbows on her desk and dropped my chin into my hands. "Do you like?"

"Oh my gosh, it's fantastic. Just what I needed."

"I stop there"—I pointed at the bag—"pretty much every single day on the way home from work."

Rachel took another bite. "I can see why."

"Anyway, so how are you holding up?"

All chewing stopped. "About . . ."

"You know, with Friday and everything." I watched as her confusion morphed into discomfort, and I rushed to head it off before it resulted in my dismissal. "I don't know if you remember much about it or not, but a few months ago, while on a job, a man's body fell out of a closet right in front of me."

Rachel swallowed, set her remaining brownie down on her napkin, and stared at me. "Seriously?"

"I think I replayed that moment in my head a bazillion times those next few days. Every time I tried to go to sleep, I saw him. And when I finally did manage to drift off to sleep, it was the first thing I saw when I opened my eyes again. It was awful." I contemplated reaching across the desk and helping myself to a piece of her brownie, but I resisted. "Even now, after everything has been resolved and the person who did it is sitting in jail awaiting trial, I still see that man's face staring up at me."

"So this man you saw . . . he was murdered then?" Rachel asked.

My chin bumped against my hand as I nodded. "I still can't believe it some days." And it was true. I couldn't.

"I guess the one saving grace for me, then, is the fact that Fiona fell facedown onto the floor. No eyes to haunt *me*." Rachel picked at the edge of her brownie and then gathered it up in her napkin and deposited it back into the bag.

I held my breath as her gaze settled on the trash basket beside her desk. Fortunately, any thought she might have had about discarding the remains went unfulfilled. Instead, Rachel thrust back against her chair with a heavy sigh. "I suppose it would be normal for me to be stuck on what happened—and I am, to an extent. But I can't wallow. If I do, that little tyrant will surely find a way to use it to her advantage."

Little tyrant?

Slowly and quietly, I too leaned back in my chair, my focus squarely on the woman now staring up at the ceiling as if the dot pattern on the tiles was some sort of secret code capable of solving life's biggest mysteries. I considered my various response options but remained mum as she started back up again.

"I swear this new generation is a real piece of work. They seem to think that working somewhere for five days entitles them to a raise, a promotion, and a corner office. And if it doesn't work that way, they have no qualms about trying to get it by being dishonest."

"I know!" But, honestly, I didn't. When I'd been employed at Beckler and Stanley, I'd been the fresh-faced newbie in a sea of suits who were more than happy to remind me of my place. And now, with my own company, there were no newbies and no suits. It was just me and JoAnna.

Rachel's groan snapped me out of my own thoughts and back into the conversation.

"Everyone knows she's gunning for my job. She's hardly subtle about it." Rachel flicked her fingers at the air. "You know what I'm talking about—you saw it too."

It took me a moment to attach her words to reality, but once I did, a single image popped into my head. "You're talking about your assistant, Sara, aren't you?"

At Rachel's half shrug, half nod, I dove in. "I know she was always following behind you, adjusting things you did even when the adjustment she made was negligible at best."

"Thank you." The chair squeaked as Rachel rocked forward and onto her feet. "Unfortunately, I'm not too sure the studio execs have paid attention enough to notice that. They just hear her criticize and think I'm not doing my job."

I remained in my chair but followed Rachel across the office and over to the industrial-sized window with my eyes. "I noticed her doing it the first time about three weeks ago," Rachel said. "My immediate boss was spending the day here at this studio, and he asked me to give him a tour of some of the sets we were working on for an upcoming shoot with national reach potential. Halfway through the tour, he came across something I'd done that he wasn't crazy about. When Sara suggested an alternative, he ate it up. She, in turn, ate up his response and proceeded to find a way to alter something I'd done on each subsequent set during the rest of the tour."

Unsure of my best response, I went with simple. With a side order of empathy. "Oh. Wow. That wasn't too cool."

Even from the back, I could tell Rachel's shrug was labored. "It bothered me, of course. I work hard. I'm always the first one here and the last one to leave. And our clients are always happy with my work. So for my boss to see—or, rather, be *led* to see something different—was a hard pill to swallow. But I was able to shake it off because I was already dreaming of . . ."

Her words trailed off into a sudden and unsettling silence that made me shiver.

"Anyway, as you are well aware, I'm no longer in a position to shake it off." Rachel spun around, returned to the desk, grabbed the bag with her remaining brownie, and tossed it into the trash. "I need this job. Period."

I slid my hands beneath my thighs and pressed down against the urge to conduct a search-and-rescue mission for what would probably amount to two—maybe three bites. "You sound worried."

"Because I am." Rachel opened her top drawer and shifted a few papers around, and then when she didn't find whatever it was she seemed to be looking for, she pushed it closed with a thud. "And I swear, if that little tyrant actually takes my job before I . . ."

I waited for her to continue, but she didn't.

"You think they'd fire you because of a few differences of opinion on some quick studio tour a few weeks ago?"

"No. But couple that with the fact that someone just died on my set, and yeah . . . It's safe to say my boss is less than pleased with me at the moment."

"Okay, so Fiona died here, but that doesn't mean it's your fault."

Rachel picked up her phone, checked the screen for something I couldn't see from my vantage point, and then tossed it onto her chair. "It happened on my watch. That's all that matters."

"Wow."

"It's a business, Tobi. They're afraid something like this will scare off clients."

"It didn't scare me off, and it happened during *my* shoot. And going a step further, I fully intend to reshoot once it is appropriate to do so—with you as our actress, if you're willing."

Rachel's gaze lifted to mine and held it. "I was willing the first time, if you'll recall."

This time my shift was more of a squirm. "I know. And I'm sorry about that."

Something about her expression had me bracing for a not-so-nice retort, but instead she lowered herself to the edge of her chair and fixated on something just over my head. When I turned to see what it was, there was nothing there except maybe a spiderweb.

Seconds turned to minutes before she finally looked back at me, but still she said nothing.

I cleared my throat. "If it would help, I'll talk to your boss."

"I'll keep that in mind." A few more seconds of silence led to more shifting (mine) and more phone checking (hers). Eventually, though, she gestured toward the trash can and gave me a half smile. "Thanks for checking in on me, and for the treats. That was . . . nice."

"I'm glad you liked it." I made a show of picking my backpack off the ground and tightening straps that didn't need to be tightened. When I felt as if I'd played the casual card just long enough, I leaned forward. "Hey, before I go, what can you tell me about Jeff and Rocky? They seem like really nice guys."

Rachel reached up, captured her hair into a ponytail, and secured it with a clip she plucked from her top drawer. "They're nice enough, but I wouldn't date them, that's for sure."

I started to wave off her incorrect conclusion as to why I was asking, but decided against it. "Oh?"

"First, Jeff is married. But even if he wasn't, he's kind of moody. One minute he's the life of the party; the next he's snapping at you for reasons you can't figure out." She swiped her fingers across her bangs a few times, and then, when she was satisfied with what she saw in the mirror on the wall behind my chair, she closed her drawer and stood. "Sometimes, he's the embodiment of Dr. Jekyll and Mr. Hyde. Seriously."

I tried to conceal my surprise, but I suspected I wasn't too successful when Rachel began to nod. "Trust me, I couldn't have imagined it, either, if I hadn't seen it myself—at least a half dozen times."

"Are there triggers that set him off?" I reached into my backpack for a notebook and pen, but left them inside when I thought about how it might look if I actually began taking notes. Instead, I did my best to keep my ears engaged.

"Being told how to do his job is a big one. So is asking him to reshoot something." Rachel checked her phone again and then pointed toward the hallway. "I'll be back in a second. I just have to make sure the back door is secured before I head out for the evening."

For a moment, I stayed where I was, waiting for her return. But as her footsteps faded away, I took stock of the opportunity her temporary absence afforded. Jumping to my feet, I lunged for her phone only to realize she'd taken it with her.

Drat . . .

I cocked my ear toward the hallway and strained to make out anything that might indicate how long I had to snoop. The answering echo of dead bolts in the distance put it at about forty-five seconds— a minute if I was lucky.

Unsure of what, exactly, I was looking for, I yanked open Rachel's top desk drawer and shifted aside a few items. But other than the standard stapler, box of staples, pens, rubber bands, and other office supplies, there was nothing worthy of a raised eyebrow, let alone a murder conviction.

The sound of the final dead bolt was followed by Rachel's returning footsteps, each muted click of her sensible heels against the studio floor growing louder. The good voice in my head told me to give up and sit down. The not-so-good voice, however, convinced me to keep going just a little longer.

I peeked under the calendar blotter, inside the desktop pen holder, and quietly slid open the bottom left drawer. There, sitting atop a stack of clipboards, was the pad of paper I'd given her with my company's logo emblazoned across the top in the eye-catching teal green color JoAnna and I had fallen in love with at first sight. Only the logo had been scribbled over with such intensity, my name was no longer recognizable beside *Advertising Agency*.

A warning bell sounded in my head as Rachel's footsteps grew closer, but I was so fixated on the mutilated pad of paper, I turned a deaf ear. Swooping down, I started to scoop up the pad but stopped as my gaze fell on a single word peeking out from the outermost edge of one of those scribbles.

A single word that made me stumble back a step.

Hate.

I swallowed back the hint of bile I tasted in my throat and glanced up at the door. Based on the sound, I had no more than five seconds if I was lucky. Five seconds to close the drawer and return to my chair . . .

Lunging forward one more time, I scooped up the notepad, shoved it inside my back pocket, and practically dove back into my chair a half second before Rachel appeared in the doorway.

"Everything locked up?" I asked, while simultaneously hiking the strap of my backpack up my arm.

"It is."

"Okay, well, I'd probably better head out. I need to rustle up something for dinner and get in a little more work before I call it a night." I heard the shake in my voice and tried like hell to stop it, but judging by the look Rachel gave me as I headed out the door, I hadn't succeeded.

Chapter Sixteen

The first thing I noticed when I started walking was the temperature. The January thaw forecasted by the Channel Two weatherman the previous evening had been grossly overstated to the tune of about thirty degrees.

Unfortunately, my chattering teeth and runny nose made nary a dent in my single-minded focus (or paranoia, if you will).

Rachel Clark hated me.

She hated me so much, in fact, that she couldn't stand the sight of my name in a logo on a pad of sticky notes—a pad of *complimentary* sticky notes, by the way.

And just in case I tried to chalk the scribbling up to distracted doodling, there was the handwritten one-word note above it to remind me I was a naïve idiot.

I tugged the flaps of my jacket collar up around my neck and chin and bowed my head against the frigid winds that had also apparently misread the weather memo. Like a turtle seeking solace inside its shell, I raised my shoulders practically to my ears and tried to focus on the car I hoped to have by this time next week.

But try as I did to lose myself in the whole sunroof/no-sunroof debate, I couldn't get the image of that one word scrawled above the place where my name had been.

Hate.

I tried to tell myself it didn't matter. That it was just a word. But the second I felt the tension in my body starting to lessen, my mind's eye served up the unsettling reality.

Rachel had written that word in the same heavy hand responsible for scribbling a hole clear through the next three or four notes on the pad.

I didn't need a magnifying glass and a detective hat to know Rachel had clearly been livid when she'd picked up that pen. And since it was my name she'd defaced, it wasn't hard to deduce that her anger had been directed at me.

At the next block, I turned right, my feet moving fast. Until I had reneged on my offer to let her star in the Salonquility commercial, Rachel and I had always gotten along. In fact, I'd actually considered asking Andy if he had any single friends who might be a good match for the super-sweet art director.

Two blocks down, I turned left, my eyes seeking and then settling on my street.

"Just three more blocks . . . Just. Three. More. Blocks."

I felt around in my jacket pocket for a tissue and used it to wipe my nose. Let's face it, I was well versed in the whole "life can change in an instant" thing. I'd lost my grandmother in one of those instants, and I'd lost my fiancé in one too (though, technically, Nick had been fooling around with the waitress for months before I walked in on them). Yet even with that kind of experience, I still found it hard to wrap my head around the fact that Rachel and I had gone from a budding friendship to such blatant and volatile hatred.

For *me*, of all people.

When I reached McPherson Road, I turned right and froze.

There, sitting (outside!) on the front porch she shared with Mary Fran and Sam, was Ms. Rapple, giggling like a school girl with an elderly man . . .

A *bald* elderly man . . .

A bald elderly man with *a suitcase* beside his feet . . .

"G-G-Gran-Grandpa S-S-Stu?" I swiped the tissue across my nose one more time and then took advantage of the remaining distance to let loose the groan befitting the nightmare playing out in front of my eyes.

Now don't get me wrong. I couldn't love my Grandpa Stu any more than I did. He'd been my life coach, my confidante, my therapist, and my best friend since I was no taller than his knees. And his being here, on the front porch next door to mine, with his suitcase in tow, was a fabulous surprise. But seeing him cozying up to my personal thorn was nothing short of terrifying. Especially when you factored in the way Ms. Rapple was gazing up at him . . . and the way he was smiling back at her.

I contemplated turning around and heading for Duke's Tavern on the other side of Euclid, but drinking had never been my thing (unless you counted Nesquik). The problem with that plan, however, was that my running the other way gave Ms. Rapple even more time to make goo-goo eyes at Grandpa Stu.

Shaking the traumatizing image from my thoughts, I took a deep breath, made one final swipe at my nose, and marched myself up the walkway with purpose.

"Grandpa Stu!" I ran up the steps, dropped my backpack on the porch floor, and threw myself into the same arms that had held me in the hospital when I was little more than a few hours old.

As I buried my face in his chest, I swear I heard my mother's cluck in my ear—a sound she always made when she saw Grandpa Stu and me together.

With his arms around me and his breath warm against the top of my head, I forgot all about Fiona and Carter, Rachel and her anger, Andy and Brenna, and even Ms. Rapple.

Ms. Rapple, however, didn't go quietly.

She cleared her throat.

She tapped her foot.

She pretended to call for her annoying little dog even though she knew damn well the little rat was pooping in my bushes.

And, finally, she put her hand on my grandfather's shoulder and gave it a (God, please no) seductive squeeze.

Ms. Rapple.

A seductive squeeze.

On my grandfather's shoulder.

I shivered. Which, in turn, earned me a worried look from Grandpa Stu as he stepped back for one of his famous head-to-toe visual inspections.

"Did you just get off the bus?" Grandpa Stu bookended my arms with his weathered hands and gave me a vigorous rub.

Now that I was standing in one spot, I couldn't ignore the clatter of my teeth any longer. Nor could I see anything but the plume of smoke escaping my lips with each and every exhale. "N-N-No. I w-w-walked the wh-whole w-w-way fr-from St-Starwood St-Studios."

"Then we need to get you inside before your mother rings me up and tells me I'm the reason you have pneumonia." Pulling my hand through the crook of his left arm, he reached down for his suitcase with his right. When all was secure, he winked (I cringed) at Ms. Rapple and softened his voice. "Thanks for fetching me at the bus stop, Martha. Seeing your face when I came down those steps was a real treat. One I will repay in my own special way very soon."

I was mid-second shiver when he gave my (okay, the whole neighborhood's) nemesis a once-over, followed by the kind of approving nod he usually saved for bikini-clad models on the cover of men's magazines.

My shiver morphed into what might best be described as a violent shudder. In turn, my grandfather, who thought my reaction was to the cold rather than the nightmare playing out in front of my eyes, guided me next door and into my first-floor apartment.

Before I could protest or even request a handful of Cocoa Puffs, I was on my couch with an afghan draped around my shoulders and another across my legs. "There. That should warm you up."

I pulled my legs up to my chest and cocooned myself inside the blankets until my teeth finally stopped clacking. When I was sure I could speak in a complete sentence, I looked up at my grandfather. "I can't believe you're really here."

"I believe it." He rubbed his backside. "My seatmate was a gargantuan fella who fell asleep the second the bus started moving. Since he was on the aisle, I was trapped."

"What? No flirting with the women on the bus? No dancing in the aisles? No impromptu comedy routines?"

"Gargantuan."

Laughing, I patted the cushion next to mine and then snuggled my head against his shoulder when he acquiesced. "Sooo, why didn't you tell me you were coming? If you had, I could have saved you from having to call Ms. Rapple."

"Maybe I *wanted* Martha to pick me up."

I felt another violent shudder building and did my best to hold it at bay, lest I knock my grandfather off the couch. "You *wanted* her to pick you up?"

His chin left the top of my head a split second before he exhaled a dreamy sigh. "I never knew the scent of lilacs could be so alluring . . ."

"Lilacs?"

"Or that housecoats could be so sexy."

"H-Housecoats?" I dropped my feet back down to the ground with a thud, the urge to run straight for the bathroom almost as strong as it had been that one time I succumbed to Carter's peer pressure and actually tried eating something leafy and green.

That foray into healthy eating had been a disaster.

This thing with my grandfather and Ms. Rapple was poised to be ten times worse.

Before I could mount a protest, though, he pointed up at the ceiling. "How's our boy holding up?"

It took me a moment to follow the shift, but I finally caught up. "Carter? He's pretty freaked out." I pivoted myself until I could see my grandfather straight on. "That's why you're here, isn't it? You came to help clear Carter."

"He'd do the same for me."

I gave in to the relief coursing through my body and let it power my embrace of the nearest throw pillow.

He came because of *Carter.*

"Hallelujah."

Grandpa Stu's bushy white eyebrows shot upward. "You didn't think I'd come?"

"No, I thought you'd come because of . . ." Some instinct I was not eager to explore kept me from completing my sentence.

I shuddered.

"Still cold?" my grandfather asked.

I held off the addition of a third afghan with my hand and, instead, tossed off the first two and stood. "Have you eaten dinner yet?"

"Martha and I stopped for shakes on the way here, but that's it. I figured we'd want to talk suspects and strategy over pizza or some of that Kung Pao chicken Carter likes so much."

"*We?*"

"You, me, and Carter."

"Oh, thank God!" I sank against the wall. "I actually thought you were going to"—I waved away the ludicrous thought that had Ms. Rapple sitting at my kitchen table glaring at me one minute and making moon eyes at my grandfather the next—"oh, never mind."

My grandfather studied me for a few moments before extricating himself from my couch. "Do you want to call him, or should I?"

"You mean Carter?"

"No, Daffy Duck."

It felt good to laugh. So, so good. But it was short-lived, thanks to my grandfather's toe tapping. "What?"

"Do you want me to call him?"

"You don't have his number."

Grandpa Stu slipped a hand into his bulging front pocket, pulled out his flip phone, scrolled through his contacts, and then held the phone out for me to see.

Sure enough, Carter's name and number was front and center on his phone.

"You two talk?" I asked.

"A couple times a week."

I knew I was staring at my grandfather as if he'd grown a second head. But I couldn't help myself. "About what?"

His narrow shoulders rose and fell with a shrug. "His theater, my seniors' group, and . . . you."

"Me?"

"Oh, and we watch *Celebrity Dance-a-thon* together on Tuesday nights. He's pulling for Mark Brubaker, and I'm pulling for that cute, perky little actress, Sally Rourke."

I stared at my grandfather, waiting for the first sign of a *gotcha* smile, but it never came. Instead, he made his way around me and into the kitchen, his recently polished loafers making a soft squeaking sound against my linoleum floor. "Now that I'm thinking about it, maybe we should hold off on telling Carter I'm here until I'm up to date on everything I need to solve this case."

My smile was back. So too was my laugh. But neither lasted thanks to my decision to slip my hands into the back pocket of my jeans at that exact moment. Slowly, I pulled out the pad of sticky notes and stared down at the hole where my name had once been.

"What's that?" Grandpa Stu moved in beside me, peered down at the paper, and then took it from my hands. "Bad day at work?"

"I didn't do that."

I felt his eyes as they left the notepad and looked at me. "JoAnna?"

"Nope."

"*Carter?*"

"Nope."

He shifted the pad to his left hand and used his right to guide me toward the kitchen table. When I was seated, he tossed the offending object in front of me and sank into the chair across from mine. "Who did this?"

I filled my lungs with air and then let it out through pursed lips. "Her name is Rachel Clark, and she's the art director at Starwood Studios."

Recognition fired behind my grandfather's eyes. "Ain't that the place where you were filming your commercial when Ms. Princess was killed?"

"How do you know Carter calls Fiona . . ." I stopped, shook my head, and then transitioned the motion to a nod. "It is."

He picked up the notepad and wiggled it at me. "Clearly, this Rachel Clark has a lot on her mind."

"Like her hatred for me." I took the pad from his hand, set it on the table in front of him, and pointed at the word written atop the hole that had, at one time, been my name. "See?"

He picked up the pad, squinted his eyes at the place where my finger had just been, and then placed it back down again in favor of retrieving his glasses from the breast pocket of his black-and-gray flannel shirt. Once his second pair of eyes was in place, he took a second, closer look, his face paling as he did.

"Unsettling, isn't it?"

After a beat or two of silence, he pushed the pad back into the center of the table. "Do you remember when you went off to school and that nasty little redhead cut your braid off during art class that one year?"

"Her name was Karen, and we were in first grade. I cried all the way home from school that day."

"Do you remember what I said when your mom brought you over to see me?"

"You told me you loved my new haircut."

"And?"

"You told me I looked even prettier than Tinker Bell."

"And?"

"You told me not to let the bastards get me down."

His eyes twinkled. "Before that. But after the Tinker Bell part."

"You said people are only jealous of something they wish they had or wish they were."

"That's right. And it still holds true today. With"—he gestured toward the notepad—"this."

"Rachel didn't do this out of jealousy, Grandpa Stu. She did it out of anger. At me."

"*That*"—again, he motioned toward the mutilated pad—"angry?"

"Apparently." I ran my finger around the outer edge of the pad and then looked up at my grandfather. "Rachel went to school to be an actress. She took the job at Starwood so she could pay the rent and eat. Weeks turned into months, and months turned into a year of her setting up shoots so other people could do what she wanted to do. She's so busy doing her job, she rarely has time to audition for anything."

Grandpa Stu rolled his finger in the universal get-to-the-point way.

"So, since we were becoming friends through my work with her and Starwood, I told her she could be in the Salonquility commercial."

"Isn't that the one you just did? With Carter and the dead woman?"

"Yes, that's the one."

"Then why'd you tell this Rachel woman she could have the part?"

"Because when I said it, Carter wasn't in danger of losing his job."

"Not because of Fiona, no."

"When I realized how genuinely worried he was in light of what he'd said to Fiona, I knew I could help smooth some feathers by casting her for the commercial." I planted my elbows on the table and dropped my chin into my palms. "So I called Rachel, explained my situation, and apologized."

Grandpa Stu leaned forward in much the same way my childhood dog used to wait beside my chair during dinner. "And? Did she get all crazy?"

"No. She didn't." I drew back, lowering my hands to my lap as I did. "I mean, could I tell she was disappointed? Sure. How could she not be? But other than a little standoffishness during the run-through Friday morning, I think she handled herself quite well."

"Didn't you find that odd?"

"No, why would I? Rachel has the job at Starwood because of her professionalism and her work ethic. And besides, I told her I'd make good on my promise the next time I needed to do a shoot with some-one her age." I rose to my feet and crossed to the drawer of takeout menus to the right of the refrigerator. A quick check of the pile turned up one for my favorite Chinese place. "So, what sounds good to you tonight, Grandpa? Green pepper steak? Sweet-and-sour chicken? General Tso's? Or Kung Pao chicken?

"Kung Pao."

I picked up the phone, dialed the restaurant's number, and or-dered. When I was sure the man who'd answered the phone had my correct address, I hung up. "It'll be here in thirty minutes."

At my grandfather's answering silence, I peeked at him over my shoulder. His attention was still fixated on the notepad.

"Grandpa Stu? Did you hear me? Dinner will be here in thirty minutes."

"I think this"—he shook the pad at me again—"makes it clear Rachel isn't as okay with your casting decision as you'd thought."

I sagged under the weight of a reality I hadn't wanted to face—a reality that upped my guilt and seemed to solidify the whole notion that Rachel had known exactly what she was doing when she defaced my name the way that she had. "Sadly, I think you're right. The only question now is whether her anger was confined to that pad of paper or if it spilled over into the unthinkable."

"You thinking she may have killed Fiona as a way to get the part back?"

"It's possible." I turned back to the cabinet and removed two glasses and two plates before moving on to the silverware drawer for the forks we'd invariably need when we gave up on the chopsticks.

"But why frame Carter?" he asked.

"Because he's my friend, and what better way to get back at me than hurting him?" I hated that I even had to think this way, but, really, it made sense. In a creepy, surreal kind of way.

"So that's it? I've been here less than"—he squinted down at his wristwatch—"an hour, and the case is already solved?"

I carried the plates and silverware to the table, set them in front of our respective spots, and then returned to the cabinet for glasses. "Rachel is one suspect out of four. I think discarding the others at this point might be a bit premature."

Grandpa Stu looked from me to the refrigerator and back again. "Got any of that chocolate milk?"

"You have to ask?"

Flashing the grin I'd loved my whole life, he reached into the front pocket of his flannel shirt once again and pulled out a magnifying glass. "I made sure to bring this as I was heading out the door."

"For . . ."

"Crime solving, of course." Grandpa Stu pushed his shoulders back against the chair, puffing out his chest in the process. "All the great detectives had one, you know."

Chapter Seventeen

I set the white paper bag on top of JoAnna's keyboard and tried not to dwell on the discrepancy between our two desks. "We got you a blueberry bagel and a coffee on the way in."

JoAnna's eyebrows lifted a split second before my brain caught up with my mouth.

Uh-oh.

"*We*—as in you and *Andy*?" she whispered. Then, without waiting for a reply, JoAnna clasped her hands—prayer-like—in front of her chin and released a satisfied sigh. "See? I told you everything would work out just—"

"Good morning, JoAnna. Don't you look absolutely stunning this morning."

I watched with amusement as JoAnna's hands slipped back down to her desk and her gaze moved back to me. "No. *We*—as in me and *Grandpa Stu*."

JoAnna mouthed an apology at me, stood, and made her way around the desk to greet my grandfather.

"Stu! It's so good to see you." JoAnna returned a cheek kiss for a cheek kiss and then spread her arms in surprise. "Tobi didn't tell me you were coming for a visit!"

"That's because *Tobi* didn't know." I pointed at her workstation. "I will never understand how you can keep everything so neat while you're working. It boggles my mind."

JoAnna made her way back around to her chair and sat. "I put things back after I use them. It's really very simple." She reached into the tray marked INBOX, removed a pink sticky note, and held it out to me. "Gary called. He said he'd like to speak to you this morning."

I tried to keep my reaction in check, but it was hard. Ever since

Andy and I had moved from client to client-dating, my dealings with Gary, his brother and partner, had been minimal. If Andy needed me to do something for the company, he'd call me himself. The fact that Gary was now calling on behalf of the company could only mean one thing—Andy and Brenna were officially back together again.

Lifting my chin, I looked up at the ceiling until I was sure I could breathe. When I had myself together, I took the note, nodded, and hooked my thumb in the direction of my grandfather. "When you get a sec, can you get him settled in with the computer in the spare office? He wants to look up a few things this morning."

I saw JoAnna winding up to say something about the note, but I shook her off. The last thing I wanted at that moment was to talk about Andy. The *last* last thing I wanted to do was talk about him in front of my grandfather.

"I'm doing some real-live investigating," Grandpa Stu boasted.

JoAnna pulled her focus off me and fixed it, instead, on the wiry bald man behind me. "Are you helping Tobi pick out a car?"

"No. He wants to help clear Carter." I gestured my grandfather down the hallway and toward the second door on the right. When he was safely out of hearing range, I turned back to JoAnna. "He doesn't really know that much about computers, so you might be in and out a lot."

"We'll be fine."

"Thank you."

"Oh. One more thing before you go." JoAnna reached into her inbox one more time and removed the only other item in the tray. "Sam brought these by on his way to school this morning. They're the pictures from yesterday's shoot at *Pizza Adventure*, and they're dynamite!"

I took the envelope, reached inside, and pulled out a stack of photos. One by one, I peeked at each, my awe over the teen's talent growing exponentially with each passing picture. "Wow."

"He's one talented young man."

"He is, indeed." When I came to the pictures he'd snapped of the editing machines at Starwood, I slid them back into the envelope and tucked it under my arm. Later, after work, I would run them by Carter. "Dom and Gina are coming in today at eleven, right?"

"I confirmed with them not more than two minutes before you got here."

"Thank you. For that, for"—I jerked my chin in the direction of the room that had swallowed my grandfather—"*that*, and for just being you."

JoAnna came all the way out from behind her desk and pulled me in for a power hug. "Everything is going to be fine, Tobi. One way or the other."

"Everything?"

"Carter. Andy. Everything." JoAnna gave me one final squeeze and then released me so she could take care of my grandfather.

"I wish I had your faith," I mumbled as I followed her down the hallway. When she turned into the spare office, I continued on to my own, the note from Gary uppermost in my thoughts, despite my best efforts to the contrary.

Part of me wanted to ignore the request to call, maybe blame it on a busy schedule or an error on JoAnna's part. But as appealing as that was, I couldn't do it. JoAnna didn't make errors. And like it or not, Gary was a client—a bill-paying client. If I wanted to stop borrowing cars and walking home in sub-zero temperatures, I needed to do my job.

I stuffed my backpack under the desk, deposited Sam's pictures into my own slightly (okay, *way*) messier inbox, and dropped onto my chair, reaching for my desk phone as I did.

Maybe, with any luck, my call would go to voice mail, and I could put the ball back in Gary's court . . .

He picked up on the first ring.

"Gary, here."

I swallowed.

His initial greeting turned icy. "Hello? Is anyone there?"

"Hi Gary. It's Tobi."

"Oh. Hey. I was afraid you were a solicitor there for a minute." He paused (and, likely, flexed). "So how's it going, gorgeous? Ready to abandon my straightlaced, boring brother in favor of a little fun and excitement with me yet?"

I rolled my eyes like I always did when Gary went from client to skeeze-oid in the blink of an eye, but this time, I might have smiled a little too. Because well, let's face it, it was nice to know I was capable of turning a head or two in my direction every once in a while.

"Things didn't work out with Mitzi, I take it?" I asked.

"Eh."

"Sorry to hear that."

"I'm not," he said, his quick response belying his words to anyone with an ounce of observation skills. "Because now I'm available for you."

"You're my client, Gary."

"That hasn't stopped you where my brother is concerned."

I tightened my hold on the phone, squeezing my eyes shut as I did. "And that was a mistake."

A momentary silence was soon followed by something that sounded a lot like a knee slap. "Ahhh, okay, now I get it."

"Get what?"

"The reason Andy asked me to call you. I mean, I thought it was weird, but I actually took him at his word when he said he was busy."

I counted to ten in my head and then opened my eyes, determined to get to the point and get back to my day. "So what can I do for you this—"

"It's Brenna, isn't it?"

His words may as well have been a punch to the gut the way they left me struggling to breathe, unable to speak and unable to move.

"He's a fool, Tobi. A world-class fool."

I covered my mouth to try to stop my answering gasp, but I was a little too slow.

"Aww, Tobi, I'm sorry. I really am. I mean, I'd be lying if I didn't admit I've been jealous as hell over what you and my brother have—"

"*Had*," I corrected.

"Okay, had. But that said, you two really seemed to be building something special."

"I thought so too." I forced myself to inhale, to exhale, and to straighten upright in my chair. "Anyway, enough of that. We both have businesses to run. So what can I do to help run yours?"

"Tobi, I—"

"Do you want to move up the next direct-to-home mailing? Run another radio spot? Talk about a new commercial?" I drummed my fingers against the top of my desk and tried to keep the impatience out of my voice. "Those things I can do, Gary. This other stuff? No."

"Other stuff?"

"Andy—talking about him, thinking about him, whatever." I swiveled my chair to the side and looked out over the alleyway between my building and the dry cleaner next door. "I-I've got other things on my personal plate right now. *Important* things."

I braced myself for an argument, but after what seemed like an eternity of silence, he let me off the hook. "We've got a new system we're rolling out—one specifically designed for children's rooms. With cubbies, and drawers, and folding play stations and stuff, and we're thinking maybe we should put a picture or two of it in the next mailing. Assuming we can get Sam out here to the office to shoot the demo sometime in the next week or so?"

Pushing aside a mound of paperwork awaiting my signature, I located my desk calendar and a pen. "Absolutely. I'll speak with Sam about that later today and then get back to you on a time and date ASAP. I'm thinking too that a few catchy words to appeal to moms and dads will round it out perfectly."

"And that's why we love working with you, Tobi."

"I'll be in touch." I returned the phone to its cradle, made a note to myself to reach out to Sam, and then turned my attention to the papers now scattered across my desk. One by one, I added my signature to the bottom of several invoices and a handful of checks. When I was sure I had them all, I stacked them into a neat pile, carried them out to JoAnna's desk, and deposited them in her otherwise empty inbox.

Feeling accomplished, I headed back toward my office, carefully avoiding the spare office lest I get sucked into a conversation. Still, as I passed by, I sneaked a look inside.

Grandpa Stu was at the computer, pointing at something on the screen, while JoAnna wrote something down in his favorite marble notebook. I gave in to the smile the sight of them birthed and returned to my office. A glance at the clock showed I had just over an hour to draw up a mock brochure for Pizza Adventure utilizing my slogans and Sam's photographs.

I spent that hour hunched over the draft table in the corner of my office, moving pictures, changing angles, and experimenting with fonts, grateful for the distraction the design work provided.

This was when I was at peace—when I was working with words and pictures, trying to find the best way to reach a reader or a viewer or a listener. It was as if I was putting together a puzzle of sorts. With just the right pieces in just the right places, I could motivate a person to attend an event, make a call, purchase an item, et cetera, et cetera.

Pizza Adventure was the first multi-destination restaurant of its kind in the St. Louis area, if not the entire country. It was up to Gina and Dom to make the experience one their customers wouldn't forget. It was up to me to make sure Gina and Dom had that chance.

When the mock-up was exactly what I wanted, I tossed my pencil onto the table and stretched my arms above my head, the stiffness in my back and shoulders my punishment for sitting in one place for too long. I slipped off the stool and wandered into the hallway, the familiar tapping of JoAnna's keyboard (and the image of the candy jar to its right) calling me for a visit.

"Well, I think the Palettis are going to be very, very happy." I stopped in front of JoAnna's desk and stretched again. "Oh. Wow. I was at it a long time."

"If you're happy, then it was worth it, yes?" JoAnna paused her fingers long enough to give me a once-over. "You might want to run a brush through your hair before your meeting. You're looking a wee bit disheveled."

"Lack of sugar."

JoAnna made a face. "That's a new one."

"Gotta keep things fresh around here." I pointed at the candy jar. "May I?"

I think she nodded, though I'm not entirely sure. The second I spied the bag of red jellybeans through the side of the glass jar, I was a goner. But as I pulled off the lid and reached inside, it hit me that the spare room had been empty as I'd walked by.

"Where's my grandfather?"

JoAnna began typing again. "He went out."

"Did he say where he was going?"

"No." JoAnna stopped, hit the RETURN button a few times, and then looked up. "I just know he rushed out of the office and made a beeline for the front door. When I asked him if everything was okay, he said he'd be in touch."

"He'd be in touch?"

"That's what he said." JoAnna started to type but stopped before she'd tapped out more than a handful of words. "Oh, and he has his magnifying glass with him."

"His magnifying glass?"

"That's what he said."

"Hmmm . . ." I fished out the bag of jelly beans, ripped open the top, and popped three or four (okay, more like six) into my mouth. "E ound omething, idn't e?"

JoAnna's fingers continued to fly across the keyboard even as she looked up at me with a semi-amused eye roll. "Swallow and then try again."

I did. "He found something, didn't he?"

"Excuse me?"

"He found something when he was snooping around on the computer, didn't he?"

She stopped typing, replaced the candy jar lid I'd left on her desk, and shrugged. "I was out here, he was in there, so I can't say for sure. But he had his notebook with him."

Yup. Grandpa Stu was on the hunt.

I reached a finger between my neck and the collar of my blouse and tugged. "Is it getting hot in here?"

"I'm sure he's fine, Tobi."

I waited for JoAnna's calm to become mine, but it wasn't happening. "Maybe I should give him a call and make sure he isn't doing something that'll get him—"

"Hello, hello, sorry we're late." Gina Paletti breezed into JoAnna's office, her fingers making short work of the buttons on her coat. "Dom forgot to fill the quarter slot in the car, so I had to dump out my purse to find enough to feed the meter out front."

Dom ambled up behind her, shaking his head with each step. "And if you've ever looked inside my wife's purse, you can imagine the undertaking it was to put everything back inside when she was done."

"Oh, quit your belly achin', would you?" Gina slipped out of her coat, hung it on the coatrack across from JoAnna's desk, and then clapped her hands together. "Oooh, I am so excited to see what you've come up with, Tobi!"

I saw the smile on JoAnna's face and knew it was mirrored on my own. Dom and Gina were the quintessential dream clients. The fact that they had deep pockets was simply the icing on the proverbial cake.

JoAnna rose to her feet, came around her desk, and held her hands out for Dom's coat. "I'll hang that up so you can get started. In the meantime, can I get you both something to drink? Some coffee? Tea? Water?"

The quintessential dream clients being fawned over by the quintessential dream secretary . . .

Really, could I get any luckier?

Wait. Yes, yes I could. I could know specifics of my grandfather's whereabouts.

The sudden silence in the room startled me back into the present just in time to find Gina eying me curiously.

Uh-oh.

"Shall we get to it?" I asked. At Gina's emphatic nod and Dom's shrug, I gestured them down the hall toward my office. When they were safely past, I glanced back at JoAnna. "Can you see if you can reach him? Maybe try to get him to tell you where he is and what he's doing?"

"As soon as I get their coffee taken care of, tracking down Stu is top on my list."

"Thank you, JoAnna."

"I take it that went well?"

I swiveled back around to my desk and motioned JoAnna over to the chair most recently inhabited by Gina Paletti. "They loved it— and by loved it, I mean *loved* it."

"Congratulations."

"Thank you." My chair squeaked as I leaned forward against my desk. "So? Did you track him down?"

"I did."

Something inside my stomach flipped and then flopped. "And?"

"He is—or was—at Starwood Studios."

I forced my lower jaw back into place. "You're kidding, right?"

"No."

"Why?"

"He didn't say." JoAnna, being JoAnna, matched my lean. Only her lean had nothing to do with me and everything to do with the fact my desk was a complete mess. In a flurry of movement, papers were piled, my calendar/blotter was spun around to face me, and the plate of cookies she'd brought in with the coffee at the start of my meeting were unearthed from beneath Gina's scarf.

Oops.

"Can you give Gina a call and let her know I'll get her scarf back to her just as soon as possible?" At JoAnna's nod, I moved on. "So what, exactly, *did* he say?"

"He said he's on the case . . . knocking on doors . . . looking under rocks . . . poking sticks in cages."

I dropped my head into my hand. "Ay yi yi."

"Who knows, maybe he'll turn up something that will actually help."

"Or maybe I'll get a call from the St. Louis PD asking me if I know the bald man tippy-toeing around Starwood Studios with a magnifying glass in one hand and a pilfered donut from the Green Room in the other."

JoAnna held the last remaining cookie out for me to take, and once I took it, she rose to her feet and turned toward the hallway. "I'll be sure to patch the police department through to you if they call."

"You mean *when* they call." I shoved the cookie in my mouth and hurled myself back against my chair with a sigh. I needed a plan. Something that could keep my grandfather occupied during the day while I was at work . . .

What that something was, I had no idea. But even a plan to have a plan was better than no plan at all.

That's what I was trying to convince myself of when a soft tapping at my door broke through my woolgathering and shifted my focus back to my open doorway.

"Gina—hi!" I pushed back my chair and stood. "I guess you're here to get your scarf?"

"That's what I told Dom, yes. But it was all just a ruse to be able to have a little time alone with you." Gina stepped all the way into my office, pointed at the open door, and, at my nod, pushed it closed. "Now we can talk."

I felt my stomach flip again. "Is-is everything okay? Did you decide you don't like the ad?"

"The ad is perfect, dear. Absolutely perfect." Finger by finger, Gina pulled off her right glove and her left glove and then slid them into the pocket of her coat. Once they were safely tucked inside, she removed her coat as well. "But work isn't everything, is it?"

Unsure of what to say, I simply sat there and waited.

Gina lowered herself to the chair, her eyes fixed on mine. "I realize I give Dom a hard time as a matter of routine, but that's just the way we are with each other. But there's nothing I wouldn't do for him. You believe that, right?"

"Gina, all anyone has to do is look at you to know you love your husband. It's written all over your face."

Gina beamed. "That's the way it is when you're with the right person. You're happy, you're at peace, you feel . . . *safe* to be your-self."

I grabbed a pen out of my upper desk drawer and turned it be-tween my fingers. "It sounds lovely."

"You say that like you've never experienced it."

"You mean being with the right person?"

"Yes."

"Then you're right, I haven't."

Gina looked left, right, and then over her shoulder at the closed door before looking back at me. "I couldn't say this when Dom was here. If I had, he'd have told me to mind my own business. And maybe I should. But I'm not wired to stay silent when I see a mistake unfolding right in front of my eyes. I just can't do it."

To say I was confused would be an understatement. To say I wasn't wishing for a brand-new plate of cookies to appear on my desk to help with that confusion would be a fabrication.

I pressed the intercom button on the side of my phone, and when JoAnna responded in her usual cheery way, I requested a refill—stat. When I was confident she understood the gravity of the situation, I left her to the task and turned my attention back to Gina.

"You were saying?" I prompted, despite the warning bells sound-ing in my skull to simply stay quiet.

"You've done so much to help Dom and me with the restaurant these past few weeks that I want to return the favor and help you."

"Gina, you and Dom have a really great thing in this restaurant. It's an honor to be part of it."

"Well, I think you and your young man have a really great thing too. And that's why I want to help make things right for the two of you."

I tried to make sense of what I was hearing through the roar in my ears. JoAnna's knock and subsequent cookie delivery did little to help.

"Now, before you remind me that I've never met him—you're right. I haven't. But I saw your smile before, and I've seen your"—

Gina used her fingers to simulate air quotes—"*smile* since whatever went wrong between the two of you, and it's clear you're hurting."

I shifted my focus to JoAnna and tried my best to send her the universal *Get me out of this* signal, but the rat fink deliberately avoided eye contact with me right up until the moment she started to pull the door shut in her wake. Then and only then did she nod at me and mouth the words, *Gina is right*.

Chapter Eighteen

I checked Starwood Studios—nothing.
I checked Fletcher's Newsstand—nothing.
I checked Central West End Perks—nothing.

I checked all of the other places I thought my grandfather might be (including, I'm horrified to say, Ms. Rapple's place)—nothing.

I knew I shouldn't be worried. My grandfather, after all, was a grown man. But he didn't always make good choices (hello . . . Ms. Rapple). Add in the fact he fancied himself the lead character in the new detective show *Spyglass Escapades*, and, well, I couldn't help but worry at least a little.

Slipping my key into the front lock, I twisted my hand to the right and listened closely for anything resembling a sound—the pop of the toaster, the jingle of a television commercial, the chortle that came from the ever-shrinking comics section in the daily paper. But, once again, there was nothing.

I stepped all the way through the door, tossed my key onto the tiny table that served as my catchall for important things, and then froze. For there, sitting at my surprisingly clean draft table was Grandpa Stu.

"Grandpa, where on earth have you been? I've been looking all over for you!"

His bald head swiveled on his neck as he turned to look at me. I met his eyes and then dropped my own to his hand and the pen clutched tightly between his fingers. "I've been doing my job."

I flung my backpack onto the couch and quickly peeled off my coat. "And what job is that? Making me hunt all over the Central West End for you?"

"Investigating that woman's murder."

"Ahhh, I see. And? Get anything good?" I crossed into the kitchen only to retrace my last few steps in the interest of manners. "Would you like something to eat? Maybe some crackers and cheese?"

I did a mental inventory of my pantry. "Actually, scratch that. I don't have crackers and cheese. Or really much of anything. I'll get to the store sometime this evening, I promise. In the interim though, I do have Cocoa Puffs . . ."

"You ever just get a feeling?" Grandpa Stu returned his attention to whatever held it when I first entered. "Something that don't sit right the second you see a person?"

It was on the tip of my tongue to mention Ms. Rapple, but I refrained. Instead, I ventured all the way into the kitchen and flung open the food cabinet. Sure enough, the cupboard was bare—except, of course, for my old trusty standby. Grabbing the open box, I carried it back into the living room and offered some to my grandfather.

"I got one of them today."

I felt my heart swell with pride. "You got another box of Cocoa Puffs?"

"No. A feeling. I got a feeling about someone today."

My heart sank as my grandfather took three large helpings of puffs and then handed me back the almost-empty box. It was hard to focus on anything besides what was quickly becoming an emergency grocery run, but I tried. It was that or risk hyperventilating.

"Let me guess: *Ms. Rapple?*"

I must have said it more quietly than I realized because Grandpa Stu turned back to the table, pulled his magnifying glass out of his shirt's front pocket, and slowly moved it down the open page of his notebook. "How well do you know the people at that studio?"

I crunched a few puffs and shrugged. "I guess as well as you'd know anyone you've met a few times in a professional environment . . ." The words fell away as my brain narrowed in on the specifics of his question. "Wait. You're talking about Starwood, aren't you? Please, please, please tell me you weren't snooping around."

"I wasn't snooping around."

"Thank God." The chorus of hallelujahs in my head accompanied my buttocks onto the armrest of the couch. "You almost gave me a—"

"Now, do you want me to keep telling you something that isn't true, or would you rather I shoot it straight so we can get to the part that matters most?"

The hallelujahs transitioned to something far less hallelujah-like, and I felt my palms start to sweat. "What made you go there? Alone?"

"It's where she was killed, isn't it?"

I nodded.

"And you knew I was doing a little behind-the-scenes investigating today. It's why I went to the agency with you, remember?"

I started to share the real reason I'd taken him to work with me, but the mere image of my grandfather and Ms. Rapple potentially canoodling in my apartment was bad enough. Putting it out to the universe via the spoken word was downright nauseating (and considering my current food situation, I couldn't afford to lose even so much as a morsel to the porcelain god).

"I know," I finally said. "But I thought you were going to do your snooping over the Internet—you know, looking up background on Fiona, seeing if you could find anything on Rachel, that sort of thing. I had no idea it was going to involve showing up on the doorstep of people I work with."

Grandpa wiggled his bushy eyebrows at me. "If you're worried, Sugar Lump, I kept my clothes on the whole time I was there."

"*Your clothes?* Why on earth would I think otherwise?"

"I thought maybe you'd heard . . . things. From one of my fellow Sexy Seniors, maybe?"

I held up my hands, crossing guard style. "I don't want to know, Grandpa. I really don't."

"You don't want to know I'm kidding?" he teased.

"Are you?"

His eyes twinkled as he slid off his stool and came to sit beside me on the couch. "Wouldn't you like to know . . ."

I looked down at his weathered hand encasing mine and tried not to focus too hard on the fact that his skin grew paler and looser with each passing visit. He was aging, and there was absolutely nothing I could do to stop it.

Pulling my feet up onto the couch next to me, I snuggled the side of my head into my grandfather's shoulder and allowed myself a moment or two to savor the rise and fall of his breath and the way his very presence made me feel safe.

Grandpa Stu was a force to be reckoned with whether he was infiltrating a group of twenty- and thirtysomethings at a bar, entertaining people on a dance floor, or snooping around a studio. Still, it was hard not to let my imagination run away when it came to him and subtlety. The two went together like . . . well, they didn't. And, truth be told, it was one of the things I found most endearing about him, even if I gave him grief for it at times.

After a few minutes, he turned his lips to my temple, held a kiss there for a few seconds, and then smacked his hands down atop his thighs. "I stopped at that studio claiming you forgot something the last time you were there."

I stared at him. "O-kay. And what did you say this seemingly misplaced item was, by chance?"

He squared his shoulders and pretended to straighten the bow tie he wasn't wearing. "A picture. Of me. Told that young lady it must've fallen right out of your pocket during all the chaos on Friday night."

"I was there yesterday, remember? When I found that pad of sticky notes she destroyed?" I swear, if I could have screamed at the top of my lungs, I would have. But, one, that would disturb Carter if he was even home (and now, come to think of it, I hadn't noticed his Grenada when I was popping in and out of the bushes in front of Ms. Rapple's house hoping and praying my grandfather wasn't there), and two, I wasn't entirely sure what I'd be screaming about.

Yes, my grandfather had stuck his nose in where it didn't belong, but if it turned up something that could clear Carter, did it really matter?

Grandpa Stu waved my words away as if they were a bothersome gnat. "I'm old, Sugar Lump. People give leeway for just about everything to old coots like me. It's both a curse and a gift."

"And in *this* case it was aaaa . . ." I rolled my hands.

"Gift. With a great big red bow on top."

"Do tell."

"It's like I told you before, I got a feeling about someone. You mark my words, Sugar Lump, that gopher fella is up to something. Can't figure out why else he's always looking over his shoulder the way he does. That and all his sweating seems mighty suspicious to me."

"I don't know who you're talking about."

"The one who's always following behind that cameraman, picking up wires and resituating them all the time."

"You mean Rocky Jazaray?" I narrowed my eyes on my grandfather. "The Starwood Studio's key grip?"

He clapped his hands. "That's it! Rocky! Strange fella."

"Because he *sweats*?"

"It's January, Sugar Lump. Those folks operate out of a gussied-up warehouse. Heating that place is surely no small task. In fact, today it was so cold in there, you could see your breath on occasion, depending on what set you were on. Yet as frigid as it was, this Rocky fella was sweating up a storm."

"Maybe he has a thyroid condition," I suggested as I dug my hand back into the cereal box and felt around. When I was sure I had puffs rather than just dust, I pulled them out and popped them in my mouth.

Grandpa Stu struggled to his feet and wandered back to my draft table. "He nearly jumped out of his skin when that young lady walked up behind him."

"Rachel?" At my grandfather's vacant expression, I added a few more details. "Dark hair? Blue eyes?"

"Nah, this one had hair the color of that mouse that used to get your grandmother hollerin' after me to set a trap under the kitchen sink, remember?"

I did remember. And it made me smile.

"And her eyes are brown too. Only darker than her hair."

"You're talking about Sara—Sara Gooden. The intern."

I watched my grandfather consult his notebook, nodding as he did. "That's right. Sara. I keep forgetting her name because she doesn't look like a Sara."

I revved up to ask what a Sara looked like but gave up when it became clear my grandfather wasn't done talking. "Sara walked up behind that Rocky fella while he was finishing up his break, and he jumped so hard and so fast he almost broke that fancy camera they use to film all them things. And when he saw how agitated the other camera fella—"

"Jeff," I supplied.

"When he saw how agitated this Jeff fella got over his carelessness, he got even more jumpy."

I looked into the box, accepted it was empty, and set it on the end table to my right. "Sara affects all of them, one way or the other. She's what you might call difficult to work with."

He picked up his notebook and shook it at me. "It's more than that, Sugar Lump. When I was pretending to look for your lost picture, I heard him on the phone. He was trying hard to keep his voice down so no one could hear, but you know me—there's no one slyer than me in these kinds of situations."

Unsure of how an answering laugh might be taken, I hid it behind my hand until I was sure I had it under control. "Did you hide behind a potted plant? Or pick up another extension?"

"I stopped and scratched my knee. And I heard everything this Rocky fella said."

"That's eavesdropping, you know."

"Call it whatever you want, Tobi. But I got us something real good by listening the way I did."

I waited to be filled in, but when it became apparent he was waiting for me to ask, I played along. "What did you get, Grandpa?"

"I reckon I got us a confession."

Chapter Nineteen

I wasn't even halfway through the living room when I heard Carter's footfalls on the stairs outside my front door. Looking down at the still-warm pizza box in my hands, I counted to three. Sure enough, he knocked.

"I'm telling you, he could have an entire chapter in a Psych 101 book all to himself."

"You finally ready to admit that what I heard was a confession, Sugar Lump?"

"Nope." I made my way back to the door and yanked it open. Carter peered back at me beneath eyelids that were half-mast at best. "Don't worry. I'm not here to eat your pizza."

I didn't mean to laugh quite so hard, but once I really took in my best friend's pained posture, my hilarity ceased as quickly as it had started. "Hey . . . my pizza is your pizza. Always. You know this."

He slumped against the edge of the open doorway and stared down somewhere in the vicinity of my feet. "The thought of food right now is like . . . It's like . . ." His voice dropped to a near whisper, "It's just not good, that's all."

My stomach roiled in a way that had nothing to do with the fact I was starving. Carter McDade was the master of the simile. Clever figures of speech rolled off his tongue as easily as most folks said their own name. To see him at a loss for one was unsettling, to say the least.

"C'mon. My grandfather is waiting to eat and—"

Carter's gaze lifted to meet mine. "Stu is here?"

"Yep." Holding the pizza box with my left hand, I tugged Carter through the doorway with my right. "He got here last night. Our favorite neighbor picked him up at the bus station."

I shivered for the both of us.

"I didn't know there was a visit planned."

"There wasn't." I motioned him to follow as I turned back toward the kitchen and the sound of ice being tossed into glasses. "But when he heard what's going on with you, he wanted to help. And, here he is!"

I busied myself with plates and napkins while Carter and my grandfather performed their usual greeting—a routine that included a handshake, something with their elbows, and a lengthy explanation behind whatever color hair Carter was sporting at that moment. Today, though, there was only a handshake.

I saw the surprise on my grandfather's face and knew it was a reflection of my own. I also understood the flash of worry that came next.

From a purely physical standpoint, Carter looked the same as always (unless, of course, you factored in the glassy eyes from lack of sleep and the chapped lips from too much nibbling). But the other part? His essence? It was as if the Carter we knew and loved had transferred his shell to a completely different person.

Somehow, someway I had to reach him, to make him see that things would be alright. To that end, I flipped open the pizza box, shoveled a slice onto each of three plates, and then dealt them out like a deck of cards.

Carter took his and then tried to hand it back. "I'm not hungry, remember?"

"Humor me." I turned without accepting his plate, grabbed my glass of water, and pointed my grandfather and Carter toward the living room with my chin. "A two-person table with three people means we're eating in there tonight."

"If I'd known you had company, Sunshine, I would have—"

"You would have joined us just like you are now." I took the left side of the couch, Grandpa Stu took the armchair, and Carter hovered awkwardly between the two rooms. "Did you go to the theater today?"

Carter set his plate of pizza on the end table and stepped away from it as if it had teeth and growled. "I wish I hadn't."

"Why? Everyone still acting weird?"

Grandpa Stu stopped chewing long enough to wipe his face with his flannel shirt sleeve. "Who's everyone?"

"The people Carter works with at the theater. He's afraid it's because they think he killed Fiona."

"But he didn't," my grandfather countered.

Carter pressed his fist to his mouth and slowly lowered himself onto the opposite end of the couch. "You sound like you believe that, Stu."

"What? That you didn't kill her?" Grandpa Stu took another bite, moved his eyes to the beat of his chewing, and then swallowed. "Why wouldn't I believe that? Why wouldn't *anyone* with a working brain believe that?"

"Frank doesn't believe that!"

Grandpa looked a question at me.

"Frank Martindale—Fiona's uncle and Carter's boss." When I was sure my explanation had registered, I turned my attention to my friend. "That kind of grief has to make it hard to breathe, let alone think coherently. Give it time, Carter. He'll come around. He's worked with you long enough to know the thought of you killing Fiona is preposterous."

"You seem to have forgotten the wrath I unleashed on his precious niece just six days before she fell out of my chair. A wrath he would have fired me over if not for you giving her the Salonquility commercial."

My grandfather chased down his last bite of pizza with a gulp of water and then waved his glass at Carter. "It's like I told you on the phone that night, young man. Witnessing your tirade gave him an opportunity to unleash his own frustrations. You were simply in the right place at the wrong time. Or is it the wrong place at the right time?" He stopped, tapped his temple, and then brushed the air with his hand. "Eh, what difference does it make? Both work."

I glanced at Carter to see if he was as in the dark about what my grandfather was babbling about as I was, but his woebegone shrug told me otherwise. "Um, for the record"—I split my best stink eye between the pair—"I'm not sure I like you two having phone conversations without me. You only know each other because of *me*, which means *I'm* not the one who's supposed to be in the dark about things."

If I'd known it were possible for anything I said or did to make Carter look even more dejected than he already did, I'd have kept my juvenile bout of jealousy to myself. Since I didn't (and, therefore, hadn't), I evaluated my options and settled on a little good old-fashioned reassurance.

"There were four other people on the set that day, Carter. That means there are four suspects."

"Six, counting you and me," he whispered, just barely loud enough for me and Grandpa to hear.

I hiked my calf up onto the couch in front of me and spread my hands wide. "Well since *I* didn't do it, and *you* didn't do it, that leaves four. Rachel, Sara, Jeff, and Rocky."

"My money is on Rocky, with or without my granddaughter raining on my parade."

I met the question mark in Carter's eyes with a frustrated exhale deliberately aimed at the occupant of my armchair. "Grandpa, how many times do I have to tell you that just because Rocky sweats a lot doesn't mean he's a murderer."

"On its own, you're darned tootin'. But with what he said on the phone, I think it's a slam dunk."

"What did he say?" Carter asked.

I dropped my foot back to the ground and stood, my desire to clear Carter overshadowed only by my reluctance to get his hopes up before I had something concrete to take to the police. "Grandpa Stu heard Rocky telling someone on the phone that Fiona's death didn't make things better the way he'd hoped."

Grandpa Stu thumped his hand atop his knee. "Don't get much more incriminating than that, in my book."

"Sunshine? Is this . . . *true*? Am I off the hook?"

I both loved and loathed the hope I heard in Carter's voice, and hated the fact I had to be the one to temper it with caution. Squatting down next to his side of the couch, I pulled his hand off the throw pillow he was practically choking to death and held it tight.

"Would you have imagined Fiona's death causing this much upheaval in *your* life?" I asked.

"Not even close."

"And *you* didn't kill her. So we can't assume Rocky's feelings on the matter are any different." The sight of Carter practically folding in on himself in defeat tore at my heart. It was hard to see anyone sad, but Carter? No way. "If it helps, Sam and I have narrowed the window in which the hair color was compromised to that break you all took after the massage scene was filmed."

Carter unfurled his body enough to pin me with a wide-eyed stare. "How?"

"Wait!" I ricocheted upright once again. "I didn't show you yet, did I?"

"Show me? Show me what?"

I grabbed my backpack. "Sam and I went through the footage from the commercial, comparing what was filmed with the continuity shots taken just beforehand." I reached into the center compartment of my bag and pulled out the envelope containing Sam's pictures. "Sometime between the continuity and the start of the actual scene with you, the bowl of hair color was moved from one side of the tray to the other. Additionally, the brush went from *beside* the bowl to *in* the bowl, leading to my theory that the peanut oil was added to the bowl during that break. See?"

I handed the pictures to Carter as my grandfather moved in for a closer look. Together, they looked from one picture to the other and back again before Carter jumped off the couch so fast, he nearly knocked me over. "Then it couldn't have been me!"

My grandfather pried the pictures from Carter's hands and lowered them to his lap. "Did you think it was, son?"

"No. Of course not. But I wasn't there during the break! I was outside. With Jeff and Rocky."

I stepped into the kitchen long enough to secure a refill of pizza for my grandfather and me, and then returned to my original starting spot on the couch. "Jeff and Rocky were out there with you?"

"*They* were taking a smoke break. *I* was taking a Fiona break."

I laughed. "You hadn't worked with her yet."

"When it came to Fiona, you took your breaks when you could—before, during, after." Carter returned his focus to his own slice of pizza and, after a few seconds, grabbed the plate from the end table and took a small bite.

Progress . . .

"You sure Rocky was outside with you, young man?"

I swung my attention to my grandfather and the disappointment oozing out of his pores. "I'm pretty sure Carter would know."

"But was Rocky by Carter's side the whole time?" Grandpa Stu asked, mid-chew.

Carter shrugged. "Not the whole time, no."

My grandfather shook his pizza slice at me. "See?"

I rolled my eyes. "That doesn't mean Rocky killed Fiona. We still haven't accounted for Rachel and Sara yet."

"Or Jeff."

My grandfather and I turned, in unison, back to Carter. "You just said he was outside with you."

Carter gave me a half nod, half shrug and went back for a second, slightly bigger bite of pizza. "He was. For a little bit. But when I got waylaid, *he* hightailed it back inside."

"When was that, exactly?" I asked. "Meaning, how much break was left?"

"I don't know. Maybe three, four minutes?"

I met my grandfather's knowing eyes with a shrug of my own. "More than enough time to add a squirt of peanut oil, yes?"

"If we must assume Rocky didn't, then sure." My grandfather gnawed at his crust for a moment and then tossed the remaining bite or two back onto his plate. "But my money is on that one."

"If you end up being right, I'll buy you a-a..." I searched my memory bank for something that would please my grandfather and settled on one of two. "A ticket to a Cardinals game in the spring— complete with a stay here."

"Could we go to that dance place again?"

"Dance place?"

Carter grinned at the two of us over his now half-eaten slice. "He means The Car Crash in Westport. That place where we danced to 'YMCA' in the middle of the dance floor during his last visit."

I tried to wave away the memory but couldn't. It was, after all, seared into my brain. "Don't remind me. Please."

"Well, Sugar Lump? Can you add that into my prize package if I'm right?"

"Your *prize package*?"

Grandpa Stu polished off his water and set the empty glass next to his plate. "And one more thing. I'd like Martha to go with us to the game."

It was a good thing I wasn't still actively eating because if I were, I'd have choked. Carter, on the other hand, wasn't quite so lucky.

I scooted across the couch, motioned for Carter to lift his hands into the air, and began to smack him on the back the way my mother had always done to me when I ate a little too fast.

Carter coughed.

Carter sputtered.

And, eventually, he was able to eke out a "mercy" just loud enough for me to hear over the dull roar in my own ears.

It was one thing to have to deal with Ms. Rapple on the way up and down my front walkway. But to break bread (or, more likely, hot pretzels) with her at a ball game?

I looked at Carter, and he looked back at me, the terror I saw in his face surely a carbon copy of my own.

My grandfather clapped his hands. "Then it's settled. All we need now is the schedule for next year's ball games so I can pick the best one for us all to go to." He pointed at Carter. "You will join us, won't you?"

"He'd love to!" I met Carter's horrified gaze with a silent dare to disagree before turning back to my grandfather. "If you're right about Rocky, that is."

"Oh, I'm right. You mark my words." Grandpa Stu scooted forward on his chair, his smile a mile wide. "So what's next?"

I gathered up our empty plates and napkins while Carter collected the glasses. "For now? Bedtime. I'm exhausted."

There was no mistaking the way my grandfather's shoulders slumped in response or the guilt I felt in response to his response. But I needed to hold fast. Between work and Carter and Andy, I was running on empty.

Carter met me in the kitchen while my grandfather wandered over to the living room window to peek outside.

"If it ends up being Rocky, we're in trouble, Sunshine."

I set the glasses and plates into the sink to be washed at a later time and looked at Carter across my shoulder. "Tell me about it. Can you even *imagine* going to a ball game with her?"

"No. Just"—Carter sucked in a breath and released it in a disgusted huff—"*no.*"

As awful as the image was, there was some comfort in knowing I wasn't alone in my horror. Still, I needed to wipe the thought from my brain if I was to have any chance of sleeping.

"I'm glad you finally ate a little something." I raised up on tiptoes and kissed Carter on the cheek. "It won't do any of us any good if you don't take care of yourself."

"I know." He took my hands in his and squeezed. "So? What did it say?"

"What did what say?"

"The letter. From Andy."

"What letter?"

He released my hands and gestured toward my bedroom. "I saw it outside your door when I got home, and I was afraid Rapple would too. So I let myself in and stuck it on your pillow."

There was a letter from Andy.

On my pillow.

Suddenly I wasn't so sure I wanted to go to bed anymore.

Sure, I'd put on a good face the past few days, but it was just that—a face. Inside, it was taking everything I had not to fall apart. I cared about Andy. A lot.

"Go. Read it." Carter gently shoved me toward my room. "I'll stay here with Stu until you're ready to call it a night."

I took a few steps and then stopped, looking back at my friend as I did. "What happens if he's just confirming what I already know? That he really does want to be with Brenna?"

"Then he's a fool."

I felt the burn of waiting tears and did my best to blink them away. "I love you, Carter."

Chapter Twenty

I clicked my bedroom door closed and stared at the envelope propped against my pillow. Even if Carter hadn't told me it was from Andy, I'd have known the moment I saw it.

Even though we'd only been dating a short time, I'd memorized so many things about him already. Like the way he tilted his head when he smiled at me. The way he brushed his lips against my temple when we sat on the couch together. The way he always took the outside whenever we went for a walk together. And the way he underlined my name whenever he wrote it . . .

I stayed there, with my back to the door, eager yet scared to get any closer. More than anything, I wanted the contents of the envelope to be a love letter, yet I had the past week and a half to indicate otherwise.

Even before I walked in on my fiancé and the waitress he was cheating on me with, I'd never been a fan of surprises. I liked to be in the know all the time. As a toddler, I would often peek at the last page of whatever book was being read to me pages before we got there. As a preteen, I'd been known to snoop through my mother's closet in the weeks leading up to Christmas. As a high school student, I'd been famous for badgering my teachers for my grade on a test within minutes of turning it in. And as an adult, well, no one had ever succeeded in pulling off a surprise party for me, that's for sure.

Slowly, I parted company with the door and inched closer to my bed, my only two options at that particular moment front and center in my thoughts.

I could pick the letter up off my pillow and stuff it in a drawer . . .

Or I could read it.

Like a magnet to metal, I made my way over to the bed, my eyes glued to the envelope. When I was in line with my pillow, I lowered myself to the edge of the mattress, took a deep breath, and picked it up.

I ran my fingers across my name and imagined Andy writing it at his desk at Zander. Or maybe from atop his own bed with my picture next to him on his nightstand . . .

I discarded both images from my brain and turned the envelope over. Sliding my index finger along the edges of the flap, I opened it and pulled out the letter.

For a few seconds, I simply stared at the folded page, trying to imagine what he'd written. But when my curiosity won out over my imagination, I unfolded the paper and smoothed it out across my lap.

> Dear Tobi,
> I want to start this letter off by saying I miss you. A lot.
> You've become incredibly important to me these last few months, and not having you a part of each day, whether by phone or in person, is hard. That said, I heard the hurt in your voice the other night, and I realize I'm to blame for that.
> I can't really explain this thing with Brenna to you because I can't really explain it to myself, either.
> It wasn't all that long ago that I was in love with her. I truly thought she was the woman I was going to marry and spend my life with.
> When she ended it, I was pretty hurt. I doubted myself and my ability to know real love. I figured I'd concentrate on Zander and my friends and I'd be fine. If I dated, great. If not, that was okay too.
> And then I met you.
> When I'm with you, I'm happy.
> I smile more.
> I laugh more.
> And I'm content.
> All good things, I know.
> But then Brenna showed up at that restaurant last week, and I was thrown.
> And while I know you and I have been taking it slow and there haven't been any promises made, I don't know what's going on in my head right now. I'm trying to figure that out. I want to ask you to wait, to give me time to sort things out,

but I know that's not fair. That's why I'm going to have Gary handle things between Zander and you for now. It's not that I don't want to talk to you—because I do. It's that I'm not sure I can.

Please know you're in my thoughts all the time.

Please know these last few months have been special.

Fondly,

Andy

I tried to wipe away the tears before they made their way down my cheeks, but if the salty wetness I tasted on my upper lip was any indication, I'd failed. "I am such an idiot. Did I learn nothing from Nick?"

The words were barely out of my mouth before I was folding the letter and stuffing it back into the envelope. "Ugh! Ugh! Ugh!"

I pitched myself onto my back and stared up at the ceiling, the reality that was still clutched in my hand slowly eating away at my anger.

Andy wasn't Nick. He hadn't done anything wrong.

In fact, he'd done everything right by being honest and upfront. The fact that I didn't like what he had to say didn't negate that.

Did I hurt? Sure. So much so, it was actually hard to catch my breath. But I wanted honesty, and honesty he'd given me.

I let the tears flow for a while, and then, when I'd had enough, I made myself sit up, wipe my face, and set the envelope with Andy's letter in it into my nightstand drawer. Why I was keeping it, I wasn't sure, but I was.

I could examine the reason behind that decision later. When I was stronger.

A soft tapping at my door made me swipe at my face one more time before I left the bed completely.

"Tobi? You okay?"

I smiled in spite of the pain. I might be batting zero in the romance department, but when it came to friends like Carter, I was the home-run queen. And really, when push came to shove, wasn't that what really mattered?

Squaring my shoulders, I crossed to the door and opened it just enough to offer Carter as much of a reassuring smile as I could. "I'm okay. Or I will be . . . soon."

A cloud passed across his face. "So it's over?"

I tried to speak but couldn't. Instead, I nibbled in my lower lip and nodded.

"I repeat, he's a fool."

"I'd rather he be honest." And it was true. I did feel that way. Despite all the walls I'd put up in the wake of Nick's betrayal, I'd fallen for Andy. And I'd fallen for him because he was a decent guy. His letter was simply proof of that.

Carter reared back to protest, but I stopped it with a squeeze of his arm. "Really, Carter, I'll be okay. I think the best thing for me now would be a good night's sleep and to clear you of this whole Fiona thing."

"I hate this for you," he finally said.

"I know. But, really, I'll be okay. I have you and Grandpa Stu and Mary Fran and Sam. If you ask me, that makes me a pretty lucky girl." I stuck my head through the door and glanced into the living room. "Where's my grandfather?"

Carter closed his eyes.

"Carter?"

"He stepped outside."

"It's"—I glanced back at my bedside clock—"almost nine-thirty. The only person out at this time of night is . . ." I let the rest of that sentence go as the reason for my grandfather's nighttime stroll became crystal clear.

I groaned.

"It could be worse," Carter said.

"Oh?"

"He could marry her and she'd be your step-grandmother."

I gasped so loudly I swear it could be heard for miles. "Bite your tongue, Carter McDade!"

"If I thought it would help, I would. Trust me."

I grabbed hold of my bedroom door and used it to keep my balance. "We've got to do something to-to stop this."

Carter's gaze led mine toward my partially opened front door. There, just beyond the door, on the porch, were two people-sized shadows and one kick-me-dog-sized shadow. My stomach started to churn but stopped as the sound of laughter interrupted our collective and horrified silence.

It was my turn to squeeze my eyes closed and pray.

"Now don't get me wrong, Sunshine, I agree one hundred percent. I really do. But . . ."

When he didn't continue, I forced my lashes apart. "But what?"

"I think she makes him happy."

Our groans mingled and then drifted away, bathing us in a silence that went unchallenged by any laughter from the porch.

Curious, I glanced back toward the front door and the shadows just beyond. Two people-sized shadows melded into—

One?

I grabbed Carter's hand so tight he actually yelped. Though, in all fairness, the yelp might have preceded the squeeze. Either way, the shadows separated and blood returned to my head.

"Oh. My. God," I whisper-hissed. "Make. It. Stop."

The panic (read: desperation) in my voice was matched in Carter's. "But how?"

"We need to keep him busy."

"But how?" Carter repeated.

"We need to step up our investigation. It'll help you, and it'll keep him too occupied for-for"—I pointed toward the shadows—"*that*."

"Okay . . . okay." Carter pressed his left hand to his chest and waved his face with his right. "I'll take him with me tomorrow."

"What's tomorrow?"

"Fiona's funeral."

I took a moment to absorb that tidbit. I hadn't really known Fiona. I'd only given her the part in the Salonquility commercial as a favor to Carter. What I'd seen of her during the few hours I had spent with her hadn't been favorable.

Yet she'd died on the set of a commercial I'd set in motion. Surely that meant I too should pay my respects to the woman, didn't it?

"Do we have a time and place?"

"It's at St. Mary's at eleven o'clock."

"Eleven o'clock at St. Mary's." I took one last look at the shadows and mustered up every ounce of determination I could. "Grandpa Stu and I will be there."

Chapter Twenty-one

While I'd been blessed not to have to attend too many funerals in my life, there was one common denominator (besides the dead body) that always stood out to me while I waited for the processional to start.

No, it wasn't the tissues—although I saw plenty of those.

And no, it wasn't the sea of black clothing to my left and right.

It was the way the whole experience spoke to my senses. Sniffles echoed around me, dread sat in my mouth, incense tickled my nose, sadness lurked on every face around me, and every hand I shook was ice-cold.

"Well, well, well," Grandpa Stu groused just loud enough for me to hear. "So it's true what they say—the guilty party can't stay away."

I pulled my attention from the empty pews near the front to take in my grandfather. "What are you talking about?"

"He's here."

I took in the elderly couple on the opposite side of Carter, the family of four behind us, and the handful of single mourners who dotted the pew directly in front of ours. Not a single face I saw set off any bells of familiarity.

"He who?"

"The murderer."

I followed my grandfather's not-so-sly pointing finger to the other side of the church. And, sure enough, I spotted his number-one suspect sitting alongside the trio of people I had yet to discount. My shock at seeing them among Fiona's mourners lasted only as long as it took to step off my high horse.

Rachel, Sara, Jeff, and Rocky had known Fiona as long as I had.

Like me, they had played an active part in the last few hours of her life. Like me, they had been horrified at the sight of her lifeless body at their feet and the knowledge that she'd taken her last breath in their presence.

If I could sit there, awaiting her family-flanked casket, there wasn't any reason they couldn't as well. In fact, before Fiona had died, I'd come to enjoy the Starwood Studios team. They were funny, hard-working, and all-around nice people—the kind of people who would pay their respects to someone they'd worked with.

"Look at him," my grandfather said, jabbing me in the ribs with his elbow. "Do you see the way he keeps looking back over his shoulder? Like he's worried someone is going to figure it out?"

I held my response and did as I was asked. And, not surprisingly, Rocky did keep looking back. But so too did Jeff and Sara. I shifted my focus down the line of familiar faces until I reached Rachel. She was the only one who didn't look back. Instead, she looked forward, her profile visible yet difficult to read.

"Maybe, when this is over, we could stop at that fancy mall off that one exit that starts with a B. I need to find some new duds I can wear when we go to that club again. The store at home only seems to have things for old people."

I searched for a retort worthy of the moment but swallowed as the rest of his statement (and Carter's best uh-oh look from the other side of my grandfather) hit me like a poke to the eye. "You say that like going to the club is a surefire thing."

"The club *and* the ball game with Martha," he corrected.

A chill that had nothing to do with our surroundings and every-thing to do with the image now playing out in my head skittered up first my spine and then Carter's. "I wouldn't be so sure just yet, Grandpa."

"No?" Again he poked me in the ribs, and again I followed his gaze back to Rocky. "Lookee there, Sugar Lump. He hasn't stopped looking back since he sat down."

"Neither have Jeff and Sara. Or anyone else in this church except for maybe the three"—I stopped, leaned forward enough to see Carter, and then resituated my back against the pew—"I mean, *two* of us. And that's just because we're talking and you have me looking at Rocky instead of the vestibule."

The words were no sooner out of my mouth when everyone

around us stood, their gazes still fixed on the back of the church. Slipping my hand through my grandfather's arm, I helped him to his feet and directed his attention in the same direction as everyone else's.

The casket carrying Fiona's body was now in the back of the church with a half dozen pallbearers distributed evenly around its sides. Immediately behind it was a couple I guessed to be in their mid to late fifties, their pained faces leading me to believe we were looking at Fiona's parents. Behind them were three boys ranging from late teens to early twenties—Fiona's brothers, I surmised, although they didn't really resemble her in any way.

Around us, the first few notes of a familiar tune emanated from the organ pipes flanking the wall to my right. Some mourners reached for hymnals, while others dabbed at their eyes and kept their focus on the casket and the pallbearers walking alongside it.

I wanted to sing, I really did, but despite not really knowing Fiona, the lump rising up my throat made it next to impossible. The woman had been a shrew, there was no denying that. But shrew or not, she hadn't deserved to die the way she had. No one did.

Curious, I swung my attention back to the studio people. Rocky, Jeff, Sara, and Rachel were all watching the processional, their attention darting between the casket and the crying family following closely behind. I tried to see if my grandfather was right, if there was anything about Rocky that raised the hair on the back of my head, but there was nothing. He looked as uncomfortable at being there as the rest of them.

I let my attention linger on them for a few more notes of the hymn, taking care to really look at each player and consider what motive they might have had for killing Fiona.

Jeff looked every inch the perfectionist I knew him to be. His tie was centered, his shirt freshly pressed, and his jacket buttoned. He'd locked horns with Fiona a few times at the run-through, but he'd heard her out, accommodated her requests when they made sense, and held his ground when they didn't. She'd threatened his job briefly when he refused her demand for one particular angle, but he'd shut off the camera and kept it off until she backed down. He'd won that battle.

Rocky looked at the casket, closed his eyes, and appeared to be saying a prayer. It fit with my initial impression of the fortysomething Hispanic male, who was relatively new to his job as a key grip. Each encounter I'd had with the man to date had been pleasant, peppered with light conversation and a desire to learn from his colleagues. When he messed up—as he had with the wire and the nail polish bottles on the Salonquility set—he was hard on himself, taking the blame immediately and apologizing profusely as if he was worried about keeping his job. Had Fiona's reaction upset him? From what I'd been told on the set that day, yeah, but Fiona irritated everyone.

I made a mental note to see what I could learn about Rocky's personal life and immediately followed that up with a silent prayer for his innocence. I tried to tell myself the latter was because I found him endearing, but Carter and I both knew that wasn't true.

Shaking a ball cap–wearing Ms. Rapple from my mind's eye, I willed myself to move on to the young woman seated next to Rocky. Sara was doing exactly what Sara did—noting every detail, every nuance of the scene unfolding in front of them.

Standing there, watching her, I couldn't help but wonder if she ever relaxed, if she ever just shut down and let life's chips fall where they might. I wanted to think she could, yet I couldn't picture it. Sara was out for Sara. I'd seen that with my own two eyes on occasion. And if even half of the rumblings I'd heard around the studio were to be believed, she had no qualms about trying to make Rachel look incompetent at her job. The only thing I didn't know was whether she'd go so far as to murder someone to bring that fact home to studio executives . . .

I shifted my attention to Rachel, only to find her staring back at me with something that looked and felt a lot like controlled rage. Unsure of what to do or how to respond, I took the easy way out and looked back at the center aisle in time to see the casket go by and the grieving parents stop dead in their tracks at the end of our row, their collective gaze fixed on . . .

Me?

Before I could make sense of what was going on, the man reached into our row, grabbed Carter by his shirt collar, and ordered him to leave.

I'm not sure how long we sat in Carter's powder blue 1975 Ford Grenada before he finally spoke. Twenty minutes, maybe thirty. I tried to cheer him up. Grandpa Stu tried to cheer him up. Heck, I even found an old eighties station with some of his favorite tunes. But nothing seemed to reach him through his humiliation and his sadness.

Eventually, after I ran out of things to say, after Grandpa Stu's suggestion of a coffee shop went ignored, and after the first notes of Wham's "Wake Me Up Before You Go-Go" prompted me to give up on the notion of music as a distraction, we gave into the silence and retreated into our thoughts.

While I could only venture a guess as to what Carter and my grandfather were thinking, I was painfully aware of the one thing looping through my head.

Rachel hated me. Plain and simple.

And while I desperately wanted to throw up my hands and feign confusion, I knew why. I'd gotten her hopes up, only to rip them away just as quickly. If said hopes had been related to something unimportant, I could chalk her reaction up to petulance. But I knew what it meant to have a dream, and the Salonquility commercial would have been a chance for Rachel to live her dream of being an actress.

Had she called her mom and told her she was getting a commercial?

Had she touted the news on her Facebook page?

Had she taken herself out to dinner to celebrate?

I tried to tell myself no, to believe she hadn't uttered a word to anyone, but I knew the likelihood that was true was slim to none.

Yep, I'd not only broken Rachel's heart, I'd likely also humiliated her in front of her family and friends. Was it any wonder this woman hated me?

No.

Was there a chance that hatred had crossed the line into revenge? Maybe.

I stretched my right arm alongside the passenger window and released a long (read: dramatic) sigh. "I hate this. I hate that you're being blamed. I hate that Fiona is dead. I hate that I hurt Rachel. And I hate that Fiona's parents and siblings have to go through this kind of pain."

Carter pulled his chest off the steering wheel and gave me an odd look. "Fiona's parents and siblings?"

"The people who were behind the casket. The man who told you to leave . . ."

"That wasn't Fiona's parents, Sunshine. That was Frank—aka my boss, aka the Frankster—and Trina, his wife and Fiona's aunt. And those boys are Trina's sons and Fiona's cousins."

"Ahhh," Grandpa Stu said from the backseat. "The reaction makes even more sense now."

I held my grandfather off from any further commentary and took the conversation back to what Carter had said. "Then where were her parents? Shouldn't they have been the ones right behind the casket?"

"They were killed in a car accident when Fiona was eight, I think. That's when she went to live with Trina and her sons."

"Oh. Wow." I tried his words on for size and found that they only added to my depression. "So much tragedy in one family."

Carter nodded then let his head flop back against the headrest. "I know."

"That's why he acted out the way he did just now, son. Between the stress over the theater and the heartache over his niece, you're something concrete he can lash out at."

I looked from Carter to my grandfather and back again. "That makes sense, Carter."

"It does. Especially when you add in the fact that I'm the prime suspect at this point." Carter traced his finger around the steering wheel twice and then exhaled a burst of air. "If I were him and I was faced with the same stuff, I'd have probably thrown me out too."

"Knowing you the way I do, I'd doubt that, but you're different." I glanced at the church, and the hearse waiting out front to transport Fiona's body to its final resting place, before taking in Carter once again. "A *good* different, that is."

"We can do something for that man and his wife, you know."

Carter and I both turned to look at the bald man behind us and waited for him to continue. Grandpa Stu, of course, didn't disappoint.

"We can find the person who did this to their niece so justice can be served."

"That won't bring her back."

I reached across the vacant spot between us and closed my hand over the top of Carter's. "You're right, it won't. But at least then they can grieve Fiona without all the unanswered questions hanging over everything."

"You really think the peanut oil was added to the hair color during that break?" Carter asked.

"I do."

Carter bobbed his head slowly as if he was mulling my words. "And you weren't there during that?"

"No. First, I stopped in the restroom. Then I went in search of a snack but got sidetracked checking voice mail. I was at the vending machine when I heard you screaming."

Carter pulled his hand out from beneath mine and returned it to the steering wheel. "Sounds like it's time to pull up my big boy pants and do some more remembering, doesn't it?"

Chapter Twenty-two

I fingered my way through the stack of pink sticky notes on JoAnna's desk and was pleasantly surprised to see a message from the children's boutique I'd been courting for the past few weeks. I was also pleasantly surprised to read I had two hours before their requested callback window opened and I had to play professional business owner.

For now, though, I could move at my own pace. I could work if I wanted to, I could veg if I wanted to, or I could even eat my way through JoAnna's currently unguarded (thank you, dentist appointment) candy jar if I wanted to.

I helped myself to a butterscotch candy, a fun-sized Grand Bar, a bag of M&M's, and a Hershey's Hug, added them to my hand with the sticky notes, and made my way down the hallway toward my personal haven.

More often than not, when I covered the relatively short distance between point A and point B, my mind was somewhere else—on a pitch I was creating, on a client I was trying to woo, or on a call from Andy I was anticipating or even reliving in my thoughts. Today, though, I didn't have to hurry. I was between pitches, I had a two-hour break before my next woo, and, well, there would be no more calls from Andy for a while.

Determined not to spiral into glumness, I made myself stop at the shadow box Andy had given me when I created his company's winning slogan. I looked through the glass panel at the miniature closet system, the tiny skeleton hanging from a clothes bar, and my slogan engraved across a gold plate. It had been such a sweet and thoughtful gift from someone who knew how important my work was to me.

As I stood there, my thoughts flip-flopping between the shadow box itself and the man who'd given it to me, I realized one of the things I missed most about Andy. When you took away all the romantic stuff and the comfort that came with having someone think you're special, I'd treasured his friendship. He'd cared about who I was as a person. He'd gotten a kick out of the way I'd drift into Slogan Land (don't look it up, it's my own special happy place) in the middle of a date. And he'd been genuinely happy for me when I went on to land all of the clients I'd accumulated thus far, expressing his pleasure via chocolate, dinner out, and, most importantly, the best hugs ever.

I'd miss that. I really would. But I was in a better place now than I'd been when I met Andy. I was stronger, more centered, and generally okay. The walls I'd erected after Nick had come down because of Andy.

I stepped to my right and gazed at my New Town shadow box and stopped. I was proud of my work, proud of the slogans I'd created, but what I'd never realized until that moment was that each new slogan coincided with a change in me. My Zander Closet Company ad had marked a turning point in my life—both professionally and personally. Professionally, it had been the puff of air beneath my wings I'd needed as a brand-new business owner. Personally, it had helped me heal.

Landing New Town had been a coup. It verified that I had the talent and the right to go up against the big overpriced advertising firms. And it was a huge factor in why I was mere days away from adding car owner to my list of accomplishments.

I stepped to the right once again and smiled at the empty shadow box that would soon boast a scene commemorative of Pizza Adventure. As far as JoAnna knew, I was waiting to have it made until the restaurant opened its doors. But the main reason I was waiting was that I was having a hell of a time deciding how to illustrate the company. There were simply so many aspects I could pull out.

As for what the work on Dom and Gina's restaurant coincided with in my life, I'd have to say a new level of confidence in myself. When Nick betrayed me, I'd floundered, torn between wanting to scratch his eyes out and trying not to pick myself apart for deficiencies that might have caused him to cheat. Now, I knew I was okay. I was smart. I was creative. And I was quirky. I was okay with that. In fact, I liked it. The fact that it hadn't been enough to keep Andy from looking backward instead of forward had nothing to do with me.

I moved a step closer to my office and gazed at the empty box that would, hopefully, be filled with salon-related items soon. With Pizza Adventure and Salonquility happening at the same time, I'd have to give some thought to a second life-turning point . . .

I completed the remaining four or five strides to my office door and flipped on the overhead light. The winter sky outside my lone window hung heavy with the promise of snow, and for a moment, I wished I was at my apartment, snuggled under a blanket with a really good book in my hand. But as I looked toward my draft table and the slogans I'd been trying out in hopes the children's boutique would return my call, I knew I was someplace far better.

Sure, I loved to relax—who didn't? But I loved creating more. It gave me a purpose, a place to feel whole.

I was well aware of the smile spreading across my face, and let it be as I made my way over to my desk. Pulling back my chair, I sat down, dumped the notes and candies onto my desk calendar, and settled back for a little lunch (don't judge).

First, I ate the Grand Bar.

Thanks to its fun-size designation, I was done in two bites.

Next, I moved on to the bag of M&M's. Based on their size alone, I should have plowed through them with one, maybe two handfuls, but I'd been eating my M&M's by color since I was three, and now was no different. I poured some into my hand, arranged them in color groups against my palm, and then ate them one color at a time until I had one of each left. Then it was all about eating them in order of preference (yellow, my favorite, was always last).

Halfway through my second handful, I found myself wishing JoAnna's appointment was over just so I could strike up a conversation. Instead, I considered my various phone call options.

Carter was home, remembering.

Grandpa Stu was replacing burned-out lightbulbs for Ms. Rapple (*I know*, trust me).

And Andy was—

"Nope. Not gonna go there." I finished my M&M's, reached for my phone, and dialed the pet shop. I'd been so busy, I hadn't spoken to Mary Fran since Sunday.

She picked up on the second ring.

"To Know Them Is to Love Them; this is Mary Fran."

"*Mary Fran—Mary, Mary Fran!*"

I laughed at the sound of Rudder in the background and then grabbed the Hershey's Hug so it could stop taunting me. "Hey, Mary Fran. It's me—Tobi. Sounds like it won't be long before Rudder can start answering the phone, eh?"

"Ha! Might be a way to make him earn his kiwi." Mary Fran's voice was . . . *different*. But just as I was gearing up to ask if she was okay, she took control of the conversation. "Sam said Carter borrowed one of his ties early this morning. I'm not sure I've ever seen Carter wear a tie."

"We went to Fiona's funeral at St. Mary's."

"But I thought Carter was a suspect."

"He is. For those lacking a brain, of course."

"I'll try not to take offense."

"You were stressed and not thinking clearly. You get a pass."

"Thank you." A change in Mary Fran's volume indicated she'd wedged the phone between her ear and her chin and was moving about the shop, taking care of the animals. "So? How'd it go?"

"We got thrown out."

"Of a funeral?"

"Well, technically, *Carter* got thrown out, but Grandpa Stu and I left too. In a show of solidarity, you know?"

"Who threw him out? The cops?"

"No. Fiona's uncle."

"Oh. Wow. Okay. I guess that makes sense." I heard the refrigerator open and knew, based on the time on my desk clock, that Rudder and Baboo were about to get their afternoon snack. "I can't even imagine how out of my mind I'd be if something happened to Sam."

"I know. But Frank's anger is aimed at the wrong person." I pushed what was left of my Hershey's Hug into the left corner of my mouth and savored it until there was nothing left except the taste of residual chocolate on my tongue. "So . . . in other news . . . what's going on with you? Any new developments on Mr. Crankypants? Did you knock on his door again?"

"No. And no."

"Why?"

"I've been busy. I will be so glad when this reunion is finally behind me. I had no idea how much time it was going to take to make something like this come together."

"But it'll be worth it when you get to see Mr. Wonderful, yes?"

"When I'm awake and lucid, yes."

"Awake and lucid?"

"Not in danger of having a nightmare."

I laughed. "Uh-oh."

"Twice now, I've dreamt of him being bald, fat, and toothless."

"Oooh, yummy!"

"That's one word for it. But, really, I can't even think about that right now."

"Okay, so let's talk about something else. Has Rudder been behaving himself at night? At least enough to keep from racking up any more complaints against you and the store?"

"The second he starts getting rowdy, I give him the eye, and he stops."

I paused midway through my butterscotch unwrapping. "Wait. You mean you slept at the pet shop again last night?"

"I've slept at the pet shop every night since the complaint."

"But I thought it was just the one night—the night I was there."

"Nope."

I left the unwrapped candy on my desk and leaned back against my chair. Now the odd edge to her voice made sense. She was exhausted. "Mary Fran, you can't keep doing that. There's no way you're getting the sleep you need."

"I can't lose the shop, Tobi. It's my—"

"*Snort! Snort! S-nort!*"

Parting company with the back of the chair, I caught my head just before it actually made contact with the desk. "Tell me that little twerp didn't just snort when you said my name."

"He didn't snort."

"You're lying."

"Yes, yes, I am. But in my defense, you told me to."

There was no use in arguing. Not with her anyway. "When is he going to stop doing that every time he sees me or hears my name? And don't go off on the whole he likes repetitive sounds thing because I've made a conscious effort to cut down on my snorting, and you know that. Do I relapse once in a while? Sure. But I've gotten tons betters"

"Rudder is *smart*. You know that. He forgets nothing."

"He's lucky I'm not a violent person." I lowered my head all the way down to the desk and reveled in the feel of the cold surface against my skin. I stayed there for a few minutes, muttering some not so nice things about Rudder beneath my breath that obviously amused Mary Fran, if her laugh was an indication. "I'm serious."

"I know."

"I swear, if there's anything in this world capable of actually driving me to drink, it's that bird."

Mary Fran laughed again.

I sat up tall. "Why don't you let me take a turn sleeping at the store on Friday night? I mean, I don't have anything else to do, and you need your sleep."

"I don't think I'd sleep real well knowing you're alone with Rudder . . ."

"Oh, c'mon . . . What am I going to do? Deprive him of kiwi until he agrees to stop snorting every time he sees me?"

"Among other things, yeah." The sound of the kiwi knife smacking against the cutting board filled the temporary void left by Mary Fran's voice. When the smacking stopped, she turned her attention back to me. "That said, I sure wouldn't mind a do-over of our sleepover. One that doesn't include an unexpected visit from Carter and two uniformed cops watching my shop from a car parked across the street."

She had a point.

But still, if Mary Fran was there, I couldn't torture my feathered nemesis.

Decisions . . . decisions . . .

"Maybe we could have it on Saturday?" Mary Fran suggested. "When I'm back from my reunion? We could stay up all night talking about how it went and what everyone looks like now and . . . how it went with Evan."

How could I say no? Especially after the bazillion ways Mary Fran had helped me over the past few years with everything from a part-time job at the pet shop when I wasn't sure if I could keep paying my rent to loaning me her car whenever I needed wheels. And that wasn't even touching on the important things, like her friendship and her unwavering loyalty.

"Saturday night it is."

Mary Fran squealed so loudly, I actually had to pull the phone from my ear until she was done. When she was, I returned to hear, "Don't pack pajamas! I saw some in a catalog a while back, and I couldn't resist buying them. I was going to give them to you as one of your Christmas gifts come December, but this will be even more perfect!"

"Mary Fran," I protested. "You know you don't have to—"

"Silence! And I mean it, Tobi."

"*Snort! Snort! S-nort!*"

This time, I let my head hit the desk in controlled frustration, following it up with a groan.

Mary Fran giggled.

"Don't be surprised if, during our sleepover, I send you outside for something and then lock you out for . . . I don't know . . . maybe thirty minutes or so?" I made a mental note to Google fast torture techniques and then grabbed the butterscotch off my calendar and popped it into my mouth. "Don't worry, though. I'll let you back in when I'm done."

"Let's not and just pretend you did, shall we?" Mary Fran paused. "Sooo, switching topics, who are you bringing to the soft thingy?"

Jolted back into a reality that didn't include Rudder and a gallon of water, I sat up once again. "Soft thingy?"

"For that pizza place."

"You mean the soft launch? For Pizza Adventure?"

"Okay, sure."

"How did you—wait. Right. Sam. I wasn't thinking." I shifted so I was sitting sideways in my chair and then flung my legs over the armrest. "Wow. I'd forgotten about that. Do you want to go with me?"

"Sam is taking me."

"Oh." I worked the butterscotch around in my mouth and weighed my remaining options. "I think Carter would love it. But if my grandfather is still around, I probably should take him."

"What about Andy?"

I stopped sucking. "No."

"You're giving up too easily, Tobi. This Brenna shrew had her chance. She chose her career, remember?"

"First of all, to Andy, she's not a shrew. And, really, in this circumstance, his opinion is the only one that matters."

"But he's crazy about you. Anyone who's seen the way he looks at you knows that!"

I worked my candy over in my mouth a few more times and then finished it off with a few definitive crunches. "Apparently, his feelings for her are still very much alive and well."

"So you're just going to roll over?"

"I'm not rolling over, Mary Fran. He wrote me a letter. He told me he cares. But . . ." I sighed. "I need to respect his decision. I mean, isn't this what I wished Nick had done? That he'd had the guts to just tell me he didn't want to be engaged rather than humiliating me the way he did? Andy is doing that!"

"Oh, Tobi. I hate this for you. And for him."

I barely registered Rudder's trio of snorts in the background as I zoned in on Mary Fran's last few words. "You hate this for him? You mean *Andy*?"

"Of course I mean Andy."

"And you hate this for him because why?"

I heard the creak of Rudder's food door opening in the background and the answering squawks that always accompanied the up-close visual of his first kiwi. I wanted Mary Fran to answer me, but I also knew if she didn't concentrate, Rudder would find a way to shovel all of the kiwi into his cage, leaving the much sweeter Baboo kiwi-less.

So I waited until I heard Rudder's food door creak closed and Baboo's creak open. When Mary Fran was done cooing, I repeated my question in the event she'd forgotten. "*Ahem* . . . and you hate this for Andy because *why*?"

"Because he's making a life-altering mistake letting you go."

I laughed (and, yes, this time I snorted too). "Don't you think you might be overstating things just a little?"

"No, I don't. You two had the doe-eyed thing going on, sure. But he *listened* to your dreams. What guy does that? Certainly none *I've* ever met."

"Not true. There was Evan's brother—Drew."

Mary Fran's sad sigh lasted for all of about a second before she was off and running on my personal life again. "You and Andy also lifted each other up, you challenged each other to be better, and you supported each other in a way that very few people have in life with anyone, let alone a mate."

I was speechless, utterly speechless.

I mean, it wasn't that I hadn't thought those things inside my own heart, because I had. But I'd been known to misread things in the past. My complete shock at finding Nick with another woman had been proof enough of that.

And while I knew what I had with Andy had more layers, I still tended to err more toward caution when it came to listening to my heart. Yet, hearing that Mary Fran had picked up all the same things my heart believed to be true was wonderful, validating, and heartbreaking, all at the same time.

Resting my cheek against my chair, I squeezed my eyes closed against the tears I knew were coming. "I miss him, Mary Fran. I miss him a lot."

Chapter Twenty-three

As eager as I was to own a car, I made a mental pact with myself to walk to (and thus, from) work most days. It was good exercise, the smiles and waves I got along the way always put me in a good mood, and some of my best slogan ideas had come while walking the sidewalks of the Central West End.

But perhaps one of my favorite reasons not to give up walking entirely was the opportunity it afforded (in winter, of course) to throw back my head and catch a few snowflakes with my tongue. It always reminded me of growing up just outside of Kansas City. Grandpa Stu and I would look out the window behind my parents' couch and wait for the forecasted snow to start. And when the first few flakes began to fall, we'd race out the front door to see who could catch the first one.

When I was really little, I always won. At the time, I actually believed I was faster. But as I got older, and I took stock of how many times my grandfather would "bump into something" on the way, I realized I was being humored. Once I called him on it, though, things changed. Catching that first flake still entailed giggles and triumph, but it also included elbows, tickles, and out-and-out trickery, and I loved every minute of it.

Granted, if I already had my car, I could be home, racing my grandfather out the door and down the porch steps right now, but at that moment, I needed a little time to detox even more. I'd gotten a lot of stuff done after my call with Mary Fran, but even so, I'd also done my fair share of revisiting all the things she'd said about my relationship with Andy. It didn't help matters, of course, when JoAnna finally returned from her appointment and essentially said all the same things.

Yes, I knew Andy and I had had something special, something

pinch-worthy. But dwelling on what wasn't to be in the end really didn't do me any good. Instead, I wanted to use that experience to remember that not all men were like Nick, and if I could find one Andy, I could find another.

At least I hoped I could.

When the time was right.

I lowered my chin to keep from running into anything, walked the remaining block to the bakery, and looked in at all the chocolate goodies inside. I waved back at the cashier, who was poised and ready to take my money, but felt no pull to actually go inside.

Hmmm . . .

I counted to ten to see if the historic event would hold and, surprise-surprise, it did.

Double hmmm . . .

Guilt, rather than desperation, pulled me inside, and I ordered up two chocolate-chip cookies—one for my grandfather and one for . . . well, in case I came to my senses after the bakery was closed and locked for the night.

Once they were bagged and in my hand, I headed back outside. The flurries had picked up a little, but they seemed more interested in floating around rather than actually sticking to anything. I took that as a sign to pick up my pace before they changed their mind and made the concrete sidewalks treacherous for those wearing heeled boots (read: me).

Still, as I moved between streets and around corners, I made time to breathe, to rid myself of a malaise I didn't want to feel anymore. Yes, I hated that Andy and I were done. But I had so many things to be grateful for, starting with my posse of supporters—two of whom I was determined to feed with a meal that didn't include cheese or Cocoa Puffs. What that meal was going to be, I wasn't sure, but I'd figure something out.

I turned onto McPherson and instantly felt my spirits soar. In just the two short years I'd been living there, I'd come to embrace this street as home. I loved its sounds—the occasional bark of a dog (as long as it wasn't Ms. Rapple's), the chatter of neighbors out on the lawns, and the laughter of children on their front stoops. I loved its smells—lilacs in the late spring, barbecues in the summer, apple pies baking in the fall, and wood-burning stoves in the winter. And I loved its quaint, close-knit aura—soup that would show up on the doorstep of the sick, animals that would be looked after during vacations, and eyes that were always on alert for—

I stopped in line with Mary Fran and Ms. Rapple's place and noted the navy blue car parked across the street from the two-family house I shared with Carter. Despite the flurries and the cold temperatures, the driver's-side window was open. As I drew closer, I realized the car's lone occupant was sitting behind the steering wheel looking up at my house, with a mixture of intrigue and apprehension.

I paused for a second to take in the man's overall appearance—an inspection that wasn't as painful as one might think. His hair was dark and full, like a Greek god's. And while I know it sounds very romance novel-y, his cheekbones were, in fact, chiseled.

Focus . . .

Squaring my shoulders, I walked right up to the car, and despite the momentary loss of breath (mine) at the bluest eyes I'd ever seen (his), I put on my best tough-girl face.

"I know why you're here, you know." I shook my bag of cookies at him and—wham!—my need for sugar returned.

Damn.

Focus . . .

I brought my gloved hand (and thus the cookie bag) down to my hip and made myself breathe. "And I just want you to know that you and the rest of your little cohorts are wrong—completely, utterly, absolutely, *undeniably* wrong."

He blinked once, twice, and then, just as he was opening his mouth to respond, my phone vibrated inside my coat pocket.

"Oh. Sorry. I'm getting a call." I handed him the bag to hold, pulled off my glove, and retrieved my phone.

"Hey, Carter, what's up?"

"I remembered something!"

Aware of the man sitting in front of me, I tried to hide my confusion. "Um . . . okay . . ."

"In other words, stop flirting with the man in the car and get in here so we can put this Fiona thing to rest once and for all."

"Seriously?"

"I said it, didn't I, Sunshine?"

"I'm on my way." I reached through the open car window, took back the cookie bag, and backed away from the car while simultaneously soaking up the attractiveness of the man now staring at me like

I was completely nuts. "See? There you go. It's official. He remembered something. So you're free to go."

I tried to focus on Carter, I really did. But walking into my living room to find Ms. Rapple sitting on my couch with my grandfather was rather disconcerting, to say the least.

What was even more disturbing than her presence, though, was the fact that my grandfather's arm was draped across the back of the couch right behind Ms. Rapple's shoulders.

And if that wasn't vomit-inducing enough, my grandfather sported an eggplant-colored, hand-knit sweater identical to the one Ms. Rapple and her kick-me dog, Gertrude, were wearing. It was my worst nightmare come to life . . .

I closed my eyes, counted to ten in my head, and then opened them.

Ms. Rapple was still there.

Gertrude was still there.

And Grandpa Stu was still wearing eggplant . . .

"Oh. My. God."

"I know," Carter gushed from his spot on the edge of my coffee table. "I was having such trouble remembering that break—like I'd blocked it out or something. So I decided to scrub my bathroom from top to bottom, and as I was polishing the mirror, it came to me."

It took me a minute to realize Carter and I weren't on the same train. Once I did, though, I spared my eyes the spectacle playing out on my couch and hopped across the tracks onto his car. "I'm sorry, I need you to tell me again. Slower this time."

Carter stopped flapping his hands and took a long, audible breath. "Okay. Sorry. Anyway, as I told you before, the second we were given the green light for a break, I went outside. With Rocky and Jeff."

My grandfather pointed (with the finger of the hand that wasn't attached to the arm around Ms. Rapple's shoulders) at me. "Eh? See? He said Rocky."

"Rocky *and* Jeff," I corrected. "And, in case you missed it, they were outside . . . *with Carter*."

Carter flapped again just enough to reclaim our attention and then continued. "I have no idea where Rachel and Sara went."

"I told you this already, remember? Rachel went to her office to make a call. I even followed her as far as the bathroom."

Carter paused, considered my words, and then moved on, his face set in determined lines. "That still leaves Sara. And according to what Sam told me, you're not really sure what Sara was doing when she wasn't telling the Frankster where he could find and threaten me."

I pulled my imagination back long enough to offer the same answer I'd given Sam on the subject. "She was looking at Rachel's clipboard when Rachel and I headed down the hall. I saw her again in the hall a little later, when I was searching for coins at the bottom of my purse, but you're right, I can't say for sure where she was in between those two—"

I stopped as Carter's words registered. "Wait. Your boss threatened you? When? Where? How? And, more importantly, why didn't you tell me?"

"Probably because the next time I saw you, Fiona was lying on the floor—dead."

"Good point." Still, I hated being left out of the loop. Especially when my grandfather chimed in that *he* had known. "But seriously, what happened?"

"He wanted to make sure I was well aware of the fact that my job at the theater—as long as there *was* a theater, anyway—was riding on Fiona's experience on set with me." Carter hiked his left ankle across his right knee and made a face. "Of course, I was already well aware of that fact, thanks to the bajillion times Fiona mentioned it in passing that day."

"Tell her what Rocky did," Grandpa Stu said.

I looked back at Carter and waited.

"Rocky got a little nervous and took his cigarette around the side of the building."

"Eh?" My grandfather elbowed the invisible person on his non Ms. Rapple side. "See?"

"There are no doors to the set on the side of the building," I said. "And if he'd come around to the front, I was eyeballing the vending machine by that point, and I would have seen him go by."

"He didn't. He came back around the corner to finish the last puff or two of his cigarette once he was sure Frank was long gone."

Hallelujah, no ball game with Ms. Rapple...

I tried to catch Carter's eye so we could share the celebration but stopped when I noticed my grandfather's shoulder droop.

"So Rocky is out?" Grandpa Stu murmured.

For some strange reason I'd need to examine at a later time, I felt bad having to nod. "Yes."

Then, switching my focus back to Carter, I got back to the business at hand. "And what about Jeff? You said the other day that he went inside after a while. Was that before or after Frank showed up?"

"Within a few seconds. I think he wanted to stay and help me out, but he got a call from his wife, and he went back inside." Carter bobbed his foot a few times and then dropped it back down to the ground. "He was wrapping up his call with her when he stuck his head outside to tell us break was wrapping up. And I could be wrong, but I think if you were setting the stage to kill someone, you probably wouldn't be talking to your wife while you did it."

He had a point.

Still, it wouldn't hurt to stop at the studio and check in with Jeff . . .

"So if Rachel was in her office, Rocky was outside, and Jeff was either outside or on the phone the whole time, that just leaves Sara, doesn't it?"

I let my grandfather's summation and Carter's answering flurry of preening marinate in my thoughts for a few minutes before sputtering out a fact I'd missed until that moment. "Wait. I realize filming had already started when I heard you screaming, but I was at the vending machine for a while, and I only saw Sara that one time. Wouldn't I have seen Rachel again if she'd really been in the office the whole time?"

Silence filled the living room as they tried on my words. Eventually, Carter shrugged, the enthusiasm that had been so prevalent in his phone call muted. "So it might not be Sara?"

"Exactly."

Carter flapped his hands again, only this time it was clearly out of frustration rather than excitement. "I thought I had it!"

"Hey, two is still better than four, right?"

Chapter Twenty-four

I called JoAnna to let her know I'd be a little late, though when she asked for a reason, I wasn't able to provide one. I just knew I needed to start my final workday of a hellish week at the pet shop.

If this had been four months ago, it would have made sense. Sadie, the shop's resident calico cat, had been my very favorite animal in the whole store. No matter how busy any given day may have been, I always found time to stop by for a little cuddle time whether I was moonlighting at the shop or not. In fact, I loved her so much, I'd have brought her home myself if it weren't for my landlord's explicit rule against pets.

But it wasn't four months ago, it was now—a now that had Sadie living in a real home with blankets, a window hammock, no squawking bird in the background, and . . . *Brenna*.

Feeling my mood begin to plummet, I turned up the pathway for To Know Them Is to Love Them and took a long, slow breath. What I really needed at that moment was a little familiarity and a reason to laugh. Mary Fran and her shop's menagerie of animals was the closest thing I could think of that fit the bill.

I cupped my hand over my eyes and peeked around the CLOSED sign that would remain in place for roughly another thirty minutes. A few lights were on near the back of the main room but not enough to give passersby the false impression the shop was open for business. I scanned the area behind the register, and when I didn't spot Mary Fran, I looked to the birdcages on the left, ducking as Rudder turned his little bird beak in my direction.

Any question as to whether I'd moved fast enough was erased from my thoughts when I heard his faint little bird voice through the closed door.

"*Snort! Snort! S-nort!*"

I did my best to control my retort lest someone I knew happened to stroll by, but as I straightened up I came face-to-face with Mary Fran through the front door's glass pane.

She unlocked the door, looked past me to the walkway, and then pulled me inside. "I figured you were out there."

I started to ask how until Rudder provided the answer. "*Snort! Snort! S-nort!*"

My hands clenched reflexively at my sides. "You know, I've been thinking . . . Rather than meet you at my place after the reunion on Saturday night, how about I just meet you here? I could come a little early and make sure everything is okay."

Mary Fran's tired eyes lit up with her laugh. "Uhhhh, no. I want to enjoy my reunion, not spend it worrying about Rudder's safety."

"Oh, c'mon. Do you really think I'd hurt him?"

"I think I'll leave that one alone." Mary Fran hooked her thumb in the direction of the back hallway. "I know coffee isn't your thing, but would you like a Danish?"

My ears perked. "What kind of Danish?"

"Cinnamon."

"Sure. Sounds good."

I followed her into the office that was currently doubling as her bedroom and shook my head at the sight of the sleeping bag stretched across the floor behind her chair. "I still can't believe you're sleeping here. Oh, and by the way, has Sam been sleeping here, too?"

"No. He needs his rest for school."

"And *you* need your rest for *work*."

Mary Fran liberated a cinnamon Danish from a box, set it on a napkin, and handed it to me. "I'm fine. Really. Besides, I've been so busy with last-minute reunion stuff, I haven't been sleeping much, anyway."

"Still."

"I'm fine, Mom."

I made a face and then followed her back into the pet shop. "Maybe Mr. Crankypants feels bad about filing that complaint and that's why you haven't seen him."

"I wish. But George Potter, the tenant who lives above the deli next door, says he thinks the guy was getting back from some sort of work trip last night."

"So maybe he really *wasn't* there when you knocked that one time."

"Perhaps." Mary Fran stopped beside the fish tank, shook some food in, and moved on to the bunny pen. "Needless to say, after hearing that from George, every time Rudder moved so much as a feather during the night, I was in here, reminding him to use his inside voice."

I stopped chewing and stuck my tongue out at the subject in question. "You say that like he has one."

"Snort! Snort! S-nort!"

"Saturday night, pal. Saturday night." I took another bite of my Danish and looked around, my gaze coming to rest on an open book atop the counter. Even from a few feet away, I could tell it was a school yearbook. "Hey, is that one of Sam's yearbooks?"

"No. It's mine."

"Ooooh, fun!" I made a beeline for the book, pointing at it as I did. "May I?"

"Would you listen if I said no?"

"Probably not." I scanned the open page and its potpourri of casual pictures, and instantly found Mary Fran. She was leaning against a series of lockers, laughing with about a half dozen other cheerleaders. "Wow. You really haven't aged at all."

Mary Fran laughed. "You lie, but I love you for it."

"No, I don't. I'm serious." I turned through the next half dozen or so pages devoted to clubs and activities, but other than the official team photo with the girls and their pompoms, I didn't see any more shots of Mary Fran.

I could feel her watching me from time to time as she straightened product shelves and moved around the shop communicating with the various animals. When I got to the pages devoted to her senior class, she gave up and came to stand beside me at the counter.

Page by page, I worked my way through portraits of teenagers on the cusp of becoming adults. There were the jocks, the geeks, and the in-betweens, just like at any school in any state. On occasion, if I wasn't sure which category the student filled, the quote underneath the photo made it clear. The jocks tended to pick quotes related to freedom or partying. The geeks tended to pick the kind of quotes a person had to read twice to understand. And the in-betweens, well, they ran the gamut from lighthearted to poignant.

"That's him. Third one down on the left."

I looked up at my friend and then back down at the book, my eyes seeking and finding Mary Fran's quarterback. I took in his blond hair, his blue eyes, his tanned skin, and his mischievous smile. His quote—"Rock on"—was short and sweet, yet told me little. I took a moment to read the paragraph below—the friend-centered memories, the inside jokes I didn't understand, and the innuendos that had surely shocked his mother when she saw his yearbook for the first time. Near the bottom I saw a nod to Mary Fran and the backseat of a 1968 Mustang I chose to leave alone.

"He's . . . cute." I tried to infuse sincerity into my voice, I really did, but it was hard when Evan Murran was exactly the kind of guy I'd avoided like the plague in high school and in life (with the lone exception of Nick, of course). "And you've had no contact with him at all?"

"Only via the registration letter and check I picked up at the class PO box a few months ago. He attached a note that said he was traveling and in the process of moving back to the area, but that he'd be there."

"He hasn't looked you up personally?"

"Different last name now, remember?"

Ahhhh. Yes. Mary Fran was a Wazoli now, thanks to Sam (or, rather, Sam's father—aka the first of her three husbands).

"Besides, there's something exciting about seeing him for the first time in twenty-five years in the same place where we first met."

I followed Mary Fran's gaze back to Evan's photo and the rest of the pictures on the page. "What was your maiden name again?"

"Tucker. I'm on the next page."

I flipped the page and found her immediately. "Ah, here we go . . ."

Just as I'd already noted in the two pictures I'd seen, Mary Fran hadn't changed much. Her hair was shorter now, and there were some lines around her eyes that hadn't been there when she was eighteen, but the smile and the aura were still the same. If I was seeing her picture with no heads-up, I probably would have known she was one of the "it" kids, yet still there was a depth behind her eyes and her smile that hinted at something more.

I took a moment to process the younger version of my friend and then moved on to her quote. "Love is a four-legged word," I read aloud. "Okay, that's adorable and so very perfect for who you are."

Mary Fran shrugged. "I always thought so. Though Evan thought it was weird."

"Why?"

"He thought I should've picked something . . . I don't know—"

"More lame like his?" The second I uttered the words aloud, I felt ashamed. Mary Fran had liked this guy. A lot. "Actually, that was out of line. I'm sorry."

She waved it off like it didn't matter, but I still felt bad and quickly turned the page. I perused the rest of her classmates before moving on to yet another section devoted to the seniors.

Here, each member of the graduating class was depicted in a trio of photographs through the years. "Oh, this is fun."

"I picked out my own, but some of my classmates let their parents do it. A few who did regretted it, while others loved it."

Sure enough, some students had adorable baby photos, first day of school shots, and one with their friends. Others had silly baby photos, awkward middle-school pictures, and family ones too. Page by page, I thumbed through them, laughing out loud at a few.

I turned to Evan's page and smiled at the image of the chubby, bald baby he'd once been.

"His mom picked out that middle-school picture, and he hated it." Mary Fran reached around me to tap the middle photograph—one with the future high school quarterback fast asleep on a couch with his mouth open and a droplet of drool making its way out of his mouth. "Everyone else thought it was funny, which infuriated him even more."

"I can imagine. Wow." I was just sliding my eyes one more picture to the right when Rudder let out a squawk so loud we both turned. "Geez. What was that?"

"Geez! Geez! Snort! Snort! S-nort!"

Mary Fran glanced down at her watch and immediately abandoned the yearbook in favor of the refrigerator. "Rudder is right; it's time for his morning kiwi."

"For which Rudder"—I glared at the bird—"can wait five minutes."

"It's okay. I've looked through that book close to a million times these past few months. Now I just want to see everyone as they are today." Mary Fran removed the Tupperware of kiwi from the refrigerator behind the counter and popped open the lid. "Besides, it's coming up on time to open, so I really should cross him off my to-do list."

I met Rudder's challenging (no, seriously) glare with one I hoped was equally challenging and held it while his kiwi was cut into little bird-sized pieces. When it became clear he had no intention of backing down, I pointed at him across the shop. "Just you wait until Saturday, pal. Just. You. Wait."

"*Snort! Snort! S-nort!*"

Half laughing, half seething, I turned back to the yearbook as Mary Fran delivered Rudder's kiwi. My gaze immediately returned to Evan Murran's baby picture . . . his napping photo . . . and what was obviously a family photograph.

I studied the faces of his parents, noting the hairline he shared with his dad and the smile he shared with his mom. Over his right shoulder, just behind his mom, was a younger sister. Over his left shoulder, and behind his dad, was the older brother who had—

I heard my answering gasp a split second before the plate Mary Fran was holding hit the ground and scattered Rudder's kiwi across the floor.

Chapter Twenty-five

I was still patting myself on the back for the cockamamie reason I'd given Mary Fran for my kiwi-spilling gasp when I pulled open the door to my agency and came face-to-face with Rachel Clark.

Quickly, I made a mental note of the Tobi Tobias Advertising Agency notepads stacked on a small table in the waiting area of JoAnna's office and tried not to imagine the fate that had likely befallen them while I was making false spider reports to Mary Fran and offering halfhearted apologies to a pissed-off bird.

"Oh. Hey. I-I'm glad I caught you." Rachel turned her back parallel to the hallway wall and waited for me to step all the way inside. "I was just talking to your secretary, trying to get a handle on when you might be in."

"Sorry. I had to make a stop this morning."

Granted, *had to* was a bit of a stretch, but to correct her would be silly. Besides, based on Rachel's anger issues, I really should concern myself with more important things, like JoAnna's whereabouts and—

I cocked my ear toward the end of the hallway and sagged with relief at the tap-tap of my secretary's keyboard.

Phew . . .

"Tobi? Are you okay? You look a little funny."

"No, no, I'm fine." I inhaled myself up to my full height and threw my shoulders back a smidge to assist in the strong and capable aura I felt a sudden need to exude. "So what brings you by?"

I hoped I sounded a bit more natural than I felt, but in the event I didn't, I opted to disguise it with a halfhearted wave toward the reception area.

Rachel, unfortunately, followed. "I was hoping maybe we could talk for a second? In private?"

192 • *Laura Bradford*

"Uh, sure. We can do that."

When I stepped into sight of JoAnna's desk, I made sure she saw me and then continued down the next hallway and into my office. With any luck, JoAnna had seen me wiggle my eyebrows as we passed and was subsequently poised and ready to call 9-1-1 if necessary. If she hadn't noticed, I always had a few sharpened draft pencils I could use . . .

I motioned my unexpected guest toward the chair across the desk from mine and then closed the door enough to afford Rachel the privacy she requested while still making my shouts for help audible to JoAnna.

With heavy feet, I made my way around the desk to my chair and slowly lowered myself onto its front edge. "So what can I do for you?"

"You can accept my apology."

I'm not sure what I was expecting her to say in response, but that definitely wasn't it. So after I composed myself (aka gained control of my gaped mouth), I stepped back into the conversation. "Your apology? For what?"

"For being a little rude the other day when you stopped by with those treats from the bakery." Although her hands were out of view on her lap, I could tell she was fidgety. "I mean, it was really a very nice thing to do, and you were right, I was a little wigged out by everything that happened last Friday. Still am, in a lot of ways."

"That's understandable."

"I mean, did you see how sad that woman—her aunt, I believe— was when they were walking behind Fiona's casket?"

I cast about for the smartest answer I could give, but opted for the one that found its way out of my mouth. "I did, but honestly, the last thing I remember before Carter got thrown out was seeing the way you were looking at me. You . . . you looked angry."

Rachel shifted awkwardly in her chair, her cheeks growing crimson. "I know. And I'm sorry for that too. I guess I was just afraid that you'd heard and that you would say something to my boss."

Once again I was caught off guard. And, once again, I found myself having to force my jaw back into a more normal position. "I'm sorry, I'm not sure I'm following. What would I tell your boss?"

"That I was interviewing for another job."

This time when my jaw went slack, I just let it go. If nothing else, it gave me time to think.

"They called about the second interview when you came to my office with the brownies and stuff. The first call—the one you walked in on—was the man who'd interviewed me, calling to tell me he wanted a second one. The second call—the one I took while I was locking the back door—was from his secretary with a time and date for that interview."

"Why would I tell your boss that?" I managed to ask over the odd roar in my head. "What you do is your business, not mine."

Her hands stopped fidgeting just long enough for her to shrug. "I just know that you've established a relationship with the studio these past few months and . . . I don't know . . . I was just concerned."

I'm not sure why, exactly, but at that precise moment it finally dawned on me I'd never finished the cinnamon Danish Mary Fran had given me and I was still hungry. So I popped open the bottom left drawer of my desk, pulled out a bag of pretzels and a handful of napkins, and offered some to Rachel. When she nodded, I poured some onto a napkin and pushed it in her direction. "So? Did you get the job?"

"I did. I start on Monday."

I looked at her across the pretzel I was dying to eat. "Monday? Wow. That's really fast."

"I have to get away from Sara. She's driving me insane." Rachel broke her pretzel in half and nibbled on one of the pieces. "I kept thinking she'd go away, but she didn't. And then when it became apparent she was more than willing to cast a shadow on Jeff and Rocky's work in order to get my job, I knew I couldn't stay. Those guys need their jobs even more than I do, and they're good at what they do."

"That was in doubt?"

"She was picking apart the work they were doing so she could make me look bad. And while the making me look bad was infuriating all on its own, there was occasionally some merit to it. But not those two. Not ever."

I swallowed my second pretzel and pointed my third at her. "*You* are top-notch to work with. Always. Don't you dare sell yourself short. You were a professional from start to finish every time we worked together."

Her face flamed red again at the praise. "Thanks."

"So what kind of job did you get?"

"Same work. Just at a studio on the other side of town."

"Lockman Studio?"

Rachel nodded.

"Congratulations—really. But . . ." I stopped, ate another pretzel, and then continued. "I thought your ultimate goal was to act."

"It is—I mean, was. But it's not meant to be. And that's okay."

I heard the words.

I saw the forced smile.

But I wasn't buying it. "You have to know I'm so sorry about taking the Salonquility commercial from you the way that I did. But I truly did plan on giving you the next suitable commercial gig I got."

"It's okay, Tobi. Really. I'm over it. I think part of my initial anger at what you did stemmed from my desperation to get away from Sara." Rachel nibbled back her second pretzel half and then smiled. "Now, thanks to the job at Lockman, I get to do that."

"Okay, but if a commercial comes up in the future that I think is right for you, can I still call you?"

"Sure, I'd be honored." Rachel helped herself to another pretzel and then stood. "And if I manage to entice Jeff and Rocky over to Lockman, maybe your agency will come, too?"

"I'd certainly give it some serious consideration." I started to stand but stopped as my gaze fell on the notepad to the left of my desk phone—a Tobi Tobias Advertising Agency note pad. Swallowing, I looked up at Rachel. "I'm sorry I made you so angry."

Rachel waved her hands back and forth. "I'd say I was more hurt than I was angry. But I get it. I really do. You were looking out for a friend. How can I fault you for that?"

For a brief moment, I considered letting her version of reality go. After all, she seemed more at peace now, and that's really all that mattered. Then again, no matter how much she tried to dress it up now, Rachel had been bothered by my decision to use Fiona. And, lest I forgot, Fiona was still dead . . .

Before I could change my mind, I pulled open my top desk drawer, grabbed the mutilated notepad from its depths, and held it out for Rachel to see.

I watched her blink.

I watched her step toward the desk.

And I watched her take a closer look as I relinquished the pad to her outstretched hand.

"What is this?" she asked.

I studied every nuance of her face as she continued to look at the pad of paper, her confusion evident in her eyes and her posture. The only question was whether her reaction was real or an indication of just how good an actor she could be.

"One of the notepads I gave you when I inked Starwood for the Salonquility spot."

Her eyes dropped from mine to the pad. "Really?"

"My name used to be where that hole is now."

Rachel pulled the pad closer to her face. "Wait. It says *hate* above the hole . . ."

"It sure does."

"Who did this?" Rachel asked, meeting my gaze once again.

"You, I thought."

Rachel's hand dropped to her side. "Me?"

"It was in your desk drawer."

"I"—she shifted from foot to foot—"I don't know what to say beyond I didn't do this."

"Then how did it end up in your desk?"

Rachel looked back down at the pad before tossing it on to my desk. "I don't know. Maybe Sara does."

"Sara?" I echoed.

"She likes to sit at my desk every bit as much as she likes trying to do my job."

"But why would Sara do that to my name?"

Rachel stared at me so long I actually reached up and felt around for the second head I must have grown.

Fortunately, there wasn't one.

"Because if I'd been in the commercial, she would have stepped into my job—for real, not just in her head—for that shoot. And as excited as I was to be in a commercial, I'd have to say Sara was ten times more so to be in charge."

Suddenly it all made sense.

Sara had been pissed off . . .

Sara had been on the set alone when that final break first started . . .

Sara was the one I needed to talk to . . .

In lieu of the dance I wanted to do, I crumpled up my empty napkin and tossed it into the wastebasket underneath my desk. I had one more thing I wanted to know, so I went for broke. "One more question. The day Fiona died . . . you went to your office to make a call during that last break, and I went into the bathroom. When I came out, you weren't in the office any longer, and I'm not too sure where Sara was, either. Do you remember?"

"I do. Sara came into the office a few minutes after I did, and I was pretty fed up. But just as I was revving up to let her have it, Fiona's uncle came in and wanted to know how he could find Carter. Sara pointed the way." Rachel's focus drifted to my window. "By then, I knew you had to be finishing up, so I decided to have a little powwow with Sara in one of the sound rooms. And boy, did it feel good to call her on her crap."

"So she was with you right up until it was time to start filming?"

"Yes."

And just like that, yet another (and, quite frankly, my last) suspect disappeared—*poof!*

Chapter Twenty-six

If the way I muddled through the rest of the day was any indication, I think I qualified as depressed.

I tried to hide it from JoAnna by making sure I was hunched over my draft table every time she came into my office.

I tried to hide it from my voice when Gina Paletti called to remind me of Pizza Adventure's soft launch and to see who I was bringing.

And I tried to hide it from Sam when he stopped by the office on his way home from school to see how his pictures looked on my mock-up of the restaurant's ad.

But now that it was just me and I was poised to unlock my front door, I stopped trying. We were back to square one where Fiona's death was concerned, and it was, well, *depressing*.

I slid my key into the keyhole and realized—as the door refused to open—that it had already been unlocked.

Grandpa Stu . . .

I turned the key until the lock disengaged again and then pushed open the door. Like Pavlov's dogs with the bell, I felt my tongue leave my mouth at the first inhale of my grandfather's one true cooking success—his famous chicken noodle soup.

My stomach gurgled.

"Sugar Lump, is that you?"

I dropped my keys onto the table and my backpack onto the floor and followed my stomach into the kitchen. "How did you know I needed your chicken noodle soup today?"

His gaze dove down to the floor before returning (rather sheepishly, I might add) to the soup he'd been in the process of covering when I walked in. "Lucky guess?" he muttered.

I stared at him for a minute, maybe two, and then slowly made my way over to the wall and the support I needed. "You aren't making it for me, are you?"

He busied himself with the pot lid again—removing, replacing, removing, replacing. Eventually, he stopped and pointed me over to the kitchen table. "Why don't you sit for a spell. You look mighty worn out."

"Long day."

"Anything you'd like to talk about?"

I wanted to say yes. I needed to say yes. But at that moment, all I could think about was the soup simmering on my stove that hadn't been made for me.

"Who is the soup for?" I asked outright.

Grandpa Stu cleared his throat. "Martha. She's coming down with a cold."

I didn't want it to bother me, but it did. "Oh."

"She's a good woman, Sugar Lump."

"A good woman?" I heard the shrillness in my answer and regretted it the second I saw my grandfather's smile falter. "I'm sorry, Grandpa. I just had a lousy day, and I'm on edge, that's all."

I stood. "I think I'm just going to go into my room and be by myself for a while so that I can refrain from biting your head off during dinner."

"You know I'm always willing to listen."

"I do. And I love that about you." I met him in the center of the kitchen and kissed his cheek. "But right now I want to be alone."

It was nearly seven-thirty when I finally emerged from my self-inflicted time-out. I was still down in the dumps, but my stomach had reached a point where I could no longer ignore its hunger pangs.

I peeked around my partially opened bedroom door and scanned what I could see of my living room. When I saw no sign of my grandfather, I turned my head to my right and looked toward the kitchen.

Grandpa Stu waved at me over the top of his newspaper.

"Feel better?" he asked.

I abandoned the safety of my bedroom, shuffled into the kitchen, and dropped onto the empty chair. "Not really. But other than half a Danish at the pet shop this morning and about a dozen pretzels at my desk an hour or so later, I've had nothing to eat all day."

He snapped closed the paper, folded it in half, and laid it on the table while he stood. "Chicken soup coming right up, Sugar Lump."

"Nah, that's for Rap—I mean, Ms. Rapple."

"I took a bowl over to her about twenty minutes ago."

"You didn't stay?"

"Nope. I wanted to be here in case you needed me." He crossed to the cabinet, extracted a bowl from the first shelf, and carried it over to the stove.

I propped my right elbow atop the table and rested my cheek in my hand. As a little girl, I'd always loved watching my grandfather. It didn't matter if he was swinging a hammer, whittling a stick, or ladling soup, watching him concentrate had always been a comfort.

"We're back to square one, Grandpa," I said as he set the bowl and a spoon at my spot. "We're no closer to figuring out who killed Fiona than we were on Friday."

He stood guard while I tasted the first spoonful and then returned to his chair and his paper. "We've got the two girls, remember?"

"I don't think they did it."

His eyebrow lifted. "Oh?"

Slowly, I made my way through the soup, its welcome familiarity making it easier to talk. And talk I did. When I was finished taking him through my visit with Rachel and everything I'd learned, he leaned against the back of his chair and bobbed his head just enough to let me know he'd heard every word I'd said and was now digesting it. The part of me that had been carrying this burden all afternoon wanted him to say something—to share a thought or draft a plan that would make it all work out. But the rest of me knew it was best to give him time. Still, I couldn't help but share the part weighing most heavily on my heart. "I hate this for Carter. I really do. I mean, first he was worried about the theater as a whole, then he was worried about his job after the run-in with Fiona, and now he's worried about being charged with Fiona's murder."

"Remember what I always used to tell you when you were feeling overwhelmed?"

I looked at him over my soup spoon. "You told me to take it one step at a time. That, step by step, I'd get where I wanted to go."

"Well, the same holds true for Carter." He spun the paper around so the headlines and articles were right side up for me, but upside down for him. "He doesn't have to worry about the theater anymore, and you smoothed things over for him with Fiona by offering her the commercial."

"A commercial she was shooting when she was murdered," I interjected.

He brushed my words from the air. "All that's left for Carter to worry about is finding out what really happened on that set. And he's not alone in that. He has you and me helping him."

"I don't feel like I'm helping. I'm certainly not getting us anywhere." I helped myself to another spoonful of soup and then pointed my empty spoon at my grandfather. "Wait. Why did you say he doesn't have to worry about the theater anymore?"

"Because of this."

I followed my grandfather's index finger down to a news article on page three. "Okay . . . what about it?"

"Carter's boss will be paying off the debt on the theater."

"Really?" I set my spoon in my bowl and then leaned over both so I could get a closer look at the latest story about Fiona's death. Two paragraphs in, I felt the blood leave my face.

> "Theater was my niece's passion, her purpose," Martindale said. "And while nothing can bring her back, my wife and I take comfort in knowing that the lives of so many people in and around the metropolitan St. Louis area will continue to be enriched because of our beautiful Fiona."

The article went on to explain that Trina Renoir-Martindale, with the help and guidance of her husband, had decided to donate the trust left to her in the wake of Fiona's death to the theater.

> "It's what Fiona would have wanted," Renoir-Martindale said.

My head reeling, I continued to read, doubling back on occasion when I wasn't sure I'd truly absorbed something.

Soon enough, I reached the final paragraph. There, I learned that the couple's initial inclination to rename the theater after their niece had been discarded. Instead, in a nod to tradition, it would remain the Central West End Theater.

"Oh my God."

"Is something wrong with the soup, Sugar Lump?"

I wanted to answer, to assure him his chicken noodle soup was as good as I remembered growing up, but at that moment I could really only focus on one thing...

I knew who killed Fiona.

Chapter Twenty-seven

I hit the horn a third time, earning myself a raised fist from Ms. Rapple that magically morphed into a friendly wave as my grandfather finally emerged from my front door with Carter in tow. I knew I needed to find a way to come to terms with the fact my grandfather had real feelings for my perpetual thorn, but now was not the time.

Carter pulled the flaps of his Gomer Pyle–style hat closer to his ears and trotted over to the car, opening the door for my grandfather before he, himself, slid into the back. "So where's the fire, Sunshine?"

"No fire."

"Can I state, for the record, that I'm not really in the mood for a chocolate run?"

I watched as my grandfather fiddled with Carter's defroster, my thoughts ping-ponging between his need to be in control at all times and Carter's need to be in the know. "We're not going on a chocolate run."

"I'm pretty sure I'm not allowed to leave town at the moment, for obvious reasons, although I am impressed that you managed to find the spare set of keys for my car in that bottomless pit you call your backpack."

"Buckle up." When I heard the answering click of first my grandfather's and then Carter's seat belt, I shifted the Grenada into drive and pulled onto the active roadway, looking at the occupant of the backseat in the rearview mirror. "Do you know where Frank lives?"

Carter's eyebrows furrowed. "Frank as in my boss Frank?"

"Yes."

"On Summerton. Off Euclid."

"Summerton, off Euclid. Got it." I turned left at the stop sign and accelerated, sweeping a glance toward my passenger seat as I did. "You have your phone, yes?"

Grandpa Stu patted the front pocket of his flannel shirt. "I sure do."

"Where are we headed?" Carter asked.

"Summerton. Off Euclid."

"Why?"

"Because you just said that's where Frank lives." I stopped at the next four-way stop and readied my turn signal.

"He does, but if you want to see him, he's at the theater right now."

I took in the dashboard clock and noted the time: 8:25. "Now?" I asked, looking back at Carter.

"It's where he can talk to his bookie without Trina overhearing."

"His *bookie*?"

"Why do you think the theater started hemorrhaging money the way it did shortly after Frank and Trina got married?" Carter reached across the front seat, lowered the heat setting, and peeled off his hat. "According to Mimi, who overheard a conversation he had a few weeks ago, the theater wasn't the only thing he was in danger of losing."

I was mulling this latest revelation when Carter unknowingly dropped the final nail in Frank Martindale's coffin. "But Frank covered the problems by pointing to poor ticket sales and a lack of advertising dollars as the reason—though not even his beloved niece Fiona bought that."

It was all falling into place—means, motive . . .

"What's going on, Sugar Lump?"

I changed my turn signal to go right and made myself take a deep breath. After all, hyperventilating while taking down a murderer would probably be considered bad form.

"I know who killed Fiona."

Carter's gasp from the backseat was followed by a rapid hand-clapping (his), a squeal (also his), and a noticeable sigh (Grandpa Stu's). "Who?"

"Frank."

All hand-clapping and squealing stopped. "But he's Fiona's uncle!"

"Her stepuncle," I corrected. "Whose wife is the beneficiary of Fiona's trust."

I understood the silence from the backseat in the wake of my words, but to hear it matched by my grandfather gave me pause. "Grandpa? Is there something wrong?"

He waved off my question and, instead, directed my attention to the theater, which was now less than a football field away. "When should I call the police?"

I pulled to a stop in front of the theater and pointed toward the one lone car in the side parking lot. "Is that Frank's car?"

Carter nodded.

I cut the engine and tossed my grandfather the keys as I reached for the door handle. "Call them now."

By the time I was out from behind the wheel and standing on the sidewalk, Carter was next to me, his hat back in place and a determination on his face I'd not seen outside a debate on the merits of green leafy vegetables. "Back me up, okay, Sunshine?"

"You want *me* to back *you* up?" I asked.

"I'm the one he tried to frame for her murder."

He had a point . . .

I trailed him into the building and down a hallway, a lit office on the left-hand side our obvious destination. I tried to catch up with Carter before he made our appearance known, but he was a man on a mission.

When he reached Frank's office, he stopped and cleared his throat until the object of his mission looked up and saw us.

"How dare you show your face here!" Frank bellowed.

"It's a shame you didn't audition for the role of Scar when we did *The Lion King* last spring, Frank. You'd have been fantastic in the part."

Clearly caught off guard, Frank drew back. "What are you talking about?"

"You know Scar, yes? Mufasa's brother? The one who killed him and tried to make it look like Simba did it?" The telltale sound of a police siren, followed by a screech of tires, propelled Carter forward while I remained where I was, wishing for some popcorn and a box of Milk Duds for the final scene. "You see, drawing on one's real-life experience always makes a performance so much better, don't you think?"

Frank swallowed and looked at me. I waved my hands back and

forth in the universal *don't look at me* motion. The sound of running footsteps, drawing closer and closer, brought his attention back to Carter. "What the hell is going on?"

"You, my non-friend, are about to be arrested," Carter said, folding his arms across his chest. "For murder. *Fiona's* murder."

Chapter Twenty-eight

I sat on the counter, arms crossed, and waited for him to break. On some level, I knew what I was doing was a wee bit over the top, but I'd been raised on the whole consequences-for-your-actions thing, and it certainly had its merits.

Besides, it wasn't like I was going to actually let him starve to death. I just wanted him to *think* I was, that's all.

"I take it your Internet search on the effectiveness of waterboarding an African grey parrot turned up nothing?"

Keeping my eyes locked with Rudder's, I threw a "nah" at Sam. "However, if he doesn't promise to stop snorting every time he sees me or hears my name, I might be willing to post the first report."

"You realize Rudder knows you're all talk, right?"

I spun my head around to face Sam. "He does not—"

"*Snort! Snort! S-nort!*"

Sam's laugh echoed around the shop before being mimicked by Rudder himself. "See? You're not the only one he imitates, Tobes."

"I'm the only one he snorts at."

Sam opened his mouth, closed it, and then held back his grin with his top teeth.

"What?" I asked.

"Nope. Too easy."

I propped my hands atop my hips and gave him the same glare I'd been giving Rudder. "Say it."

"You're the only one who snorts."

Touché.

Releasing the groan I'd been holding back for close to an hour now, I turned my attention to the ceiling directly above my head. "I was so close to getting him to stop."

"No you weren't."

"Yes I was."

"No you weren't."

I knew we could go on that way for hours, but in the interest of my last shred of sanity, I gave in first. "I just want him to stop."

"Maybe you need to start looking at his response in a different way." Sam pulled one of two stools out from behind the counter and set it halfway between the counter where I was sitting and the cage where Rudder was starting to get antsy over the kiwi I'd purposely set on the counter next to me.

"Meaning?"

"He knows you—he knows you by sight and by name. If you ask me, that's pretty darn cool."

I sneaked a peek at Rudder.

"And he gets excited at both. Again, pretty darn cool."

I swallowed.

"The alternative is that he could see you as nothing special. Like just any old person who comes into the store in the course of a day." Sam spread his hands wide. "But he doesn't. In fact, you're special enough that he has a sound just for you."

I tried not to pout my lip, but I'm pretty sure I did anyway. "Maybe he could find a different sound?"

Sam looked at Rudder and then back at me. "Yeah, I'm thinking that's not gonna happen. This is Rudder Malone we're talking about. Stubborn is his middle name."

I considered sharing the middle name I'd invented for my beaked enemy, but in the interest of Sam's age and my refusal to curse around him, I opted to keep it to myself.

"Fine." I slid off the counter, grabbed the plate of kiwi, and carried it over to Rudder's cage. "Fine!"

When my feathered nemesis was happily occupied, I turned to Baboo and rewarded the quieter, sweeter bird with his favorite kissing sound—a sound he mimicked back. "Thank you, Baboo. There's hope for your kind yet."

Sam returned to the counter, retrieved the second stool, and set it on the ground next to his. "Come. Sit. Tell me what happened with the cops."

"It was in the paper and all across the news yesterday." I set Rudder's plate down and joined Sam as per his request.

"I know. But I want to hear it from you."

"Fiona's uncle was in debt up to his eyeballs—gambling debt, as it turns out. The bank sent its final warning letter, letting him know he had thirty days to pay up or they'd have to foreclose on the theater. Sadly, as is the case with the more serious gamblers, the bank was only one of a handful of folks Frank owed money to. He was afraid if he didn't make things right with those people, they'd come after him. Physically. He knew about the policy left by Fiona's parents to Fiona, but he'd only recently learned that it would go to Trina in the event of Fiona's death. He was already giving some thought to killing her when Carter exploded on her two weeks ago."

"And suddenly he had someone to pin it on?"

I repositioned myself on the stool so as to alleviate the stiffness I felt building in my back. "Yep. And he used said explosion as a reason to show up at the studio that day. Apparently, he'd been hanging around in front of the studio pretty much the whole day, and when Fiona texted that they were getting ready to shoot the scene with her and Carter after a fifteen-minute break, he made his move.

"Fortunately for him, Sara pointed the way to the back door, and he had just enough time alone on the set to add peanut oil to the bowl of hair color. Since he'd been there when the cat scratched Fiona's ear the day before, he knew it would get into her system faster, and he was right."

"Wow," Sam said. "That's sick."

"Yes, yes it is."

Sam played with his hands for a minute before engaging me in eye contact once again. "Was her aunt in on it?"

"No. Thank God. She simply believed Frank when he blamed the theater's money troubles on poor ticket sales, lack of advertising, and a host of other things that really weren't true."

When he didn't respond, I stepped down off the stool and wandered back over to the counter. "Your mom looked beautiful tonight. I really hope this reunion is everything she wants it to—"

A knock at the front door caught us both by surprise, but before I could get a clear enough view of the front stoop, Sam was on his feet and looking at me with an odd expression. "Do you want me to let him in, Tobes?"

I heard Sam, even registered the name he said when I questioned him, but for whatever reason, I needed my own confirmation. Stepping out from behind the counter, I walked toward the door, where Andy's blue eyes were staring back at me from atop the closed sign.

I wish I could explain what I felt at that moment, but I couldn't. Not to me, not to Sam, not to Rudder. Instead, I disengaged the lock and opened the door.

"Is Sadie okay?"

He started to draw back but stopped. "Sadie's fine. But I'm not here for her. I'm here for you."

"Me?"

"I stopped by your place. Your grandfather told me you were here." Andy stopped, peeked around me to wave at Sam, and then gave me his complete attention once again. "He was there . . . with Ms. Rapple."

"I know."

He looked like he wanted to balk, but he didn't, and I was glad. At that moment, all I could really process was his proximity to me and the fact that I wanted so badly for him to pull me in for a hug.

"Tobi, I'm sorry. I'm sorry for backing off like I did. But as I said in my letter—you did get that, right?"

I nodded.

A flicker of relief passed across his face, and he reached for my hand. "I needed to be sure I was done with Brenna. So if you asked, I could answer completely and truthfully."

Be sure I was done?

"I was caught off guard when she showed up at the restaurant that night, and I knew I didn't like it. But I wasn't sure if I didn't like it because she showed up when I was with you, or because she showed up at all. I wanted to figure that out. I tried not to give it too much thought when I was in L.A. for the convention, but I also knew you'd want to talk about it if you and I spoke, so I didn't call. I know that was probably stupid, but I didn't want to risk saying something that would mess us up. And then, when I got home, she was at my doorstep, wanting to catch up. So we caught up. She told me about her job and her successes, and I told her about mine. She suggested we try again, and all I could think about was you. But Brenna was a part of my life for a long time. I'd wanted to marry her. And I'd been crushed when she said no. I needed to know, beyond a shadow of a doubt, that I was over her, but I didn't think it was fair to make you—"

I pressed my index finger to the front of his lips and held it there until he stopped. When he did, I asked the only question that mattered.

"And? Are you?"

"Am I what?"

"Over her?" I asked.

"Yes."

I felt my breath hitch but willed myself to remain calm. "Are you sure?"

"I've done a lot of thinking over the past week or so, and I'm pretty sure I was over her the minute I laid eyes on you." He recaptured my hand and held it tight. "As for how I can say that—it comes down to this. I've been the happiest I've ever been since you've been in my life. Period."

I'm not sure who stepped forward first—me or Andy. All I know is that his arms opened wide, and I flew into them.

"*Snort! Snort! S-nort!*"

By the time Mary Fran returned from her reunion, our girls-only slumber party was ready to go.

The Dating Game was waiting on the counter . . .

I'd set out chips and pretzels . . .

I was wearing the striped pajamas she'd given me when I'd helped her with her hair earlier in the day . . .

Rudder was wearing his matching nightcap (applied with a little kiwi-bribery, thankyouverymuch) . . .

And I'd managed to make enough room in her office so that our sleeping bags could fit side by side.

But all of that went right out the door the second I saw her face. Mary Fran was pissed. Beet-red pissed.

"Mary Fran?" I stepped over the Twister board I'd set up in the middle of the floor and met her before she was even three feet into the shop. "What on earth happened? Are you okay?"

"It's him!"

"Excuse me?"

I followed the path forged by her finger, and when I saw nothing anger-worthy on the ceiling, I looked back at her and waited.

"Mr. Crankypants."

"You saw him?"

"He was at my reunion!"

My confusion must have seeped out of my pores or something, because she raked her hands through the curls I'd painstakingly placed all around her head and unleashed a blood-curdling scream that was really quite impressive.

"Talk to me, Mary Fran."

"Remember how I told you Evan was supposedly moving back to town?"

"Yeah . . ."

"Well, he did."

"He's married, isn't he?" I said between swallows.

"Nope."

"Okay, then what's the . . ."

Again, she pointed at the ceiling, only this time I kept my gaze squarely on her face. "He lives upstairs. Above the store."

"But that's where Mr. Crankypants . . ." I stopped, replayed everything she'd said so far, and blurted out my best interpretation. "Wait. Are you saying Mr. Crankypants is your quarterback?"

"That's exactly what I'm saying."

Uh-oh.

Mary Fran kicked off her sparkly high heels, stomped across the shop, and then, just before she reached the hallway, spun around, hands on hips. "This is why I've sworn off men. Because they're all jerks. Every. Last. One. Of. Them."

"Andy isn't."

Her hands slipped off her hips. "Andy?"

I nodded. "We're okay."

"For real?"

At my nod, she ran back, gave me a little spin, and then stepped back for one of her fast claps. "I knew it! I knew it! I knew you found a good one."

"And you can too."

"Nope. I'm letting that ship go. I have Sam. He's more than enough."

I snuck a look at the clock and then back over my shoulder at the road. Sure enough, the headlights I'd hoped to see (thanks to my superior sleuthing, Sam's ability to track down the correct Kelly Flannigan, and Andy's familiarity with the neighborhood in which the

Murran boys grew up) were just going dark in front of the shop. "I agree Sam is pretty special. I really do. But I don't believe he's the only one."

Mary Fran tapped me on the nose. "You really oughta think about cutting down on those Cocoa Puffs. The sugar is going to your head."

"Remember all those things you said about Andy and me? How he listens to my dreams and encourages me to pursue them?"

"Of course."

"You had someone like that once."

Mary Fran laughed. "In my dreams, sure. In reality, not so much."

I heard them outside the door but kept my focus squarely on my friend. "He was the first person you ever told about wanting this shop. And just as you never forgot that, he's never forgotten you." I peeked past her and instantly recognized the same attractive man I now knew had been staring up at my house by mistake three days earlier—a man I'd been convinced was yet another cop tasked with keeping tabs on Carter.

"What are you talking about, Tobi?"

"I'm talking about that—I mean, *him*." Grabbing hold of her shoulders, I turned her around to face the door and the man now standing just inside the pet shop, his gorgeous blue eyes trained on no one but Mary Fran.

"Drew?" she whispered.

"Hello, Mary Fran."

Before she could move, before she could utter another word, I brought my lips to her ear for one last piece of advice. "You know what they say. If you kiss enough frogs, you'll eventually find your prince."

DEATH IN ADVERTISING

When Tobi Tobias decided to open her own ad agency, having to moonlight in a pet shop wasn't part of her vision . . . of course, neither was murder.

Sometimes when opportunity knocks, the door you open leads to a closet. That's certainly the case for Tobi, whose weekends spent cleaning cages in her best friend's pet shop may soon be over. She's just landed her first big break—Zander Closet Company needs a catchy campaign slogan ASAP, and Tobi thinks she's got the right hook to knock 'em dead: "When we're done, even your skeletons will have a place."

But when a real dead body topples out of a showcase closet, she's about to discover there *is* such a thing as bad publicity. To save her fledgling business and not get killed by the competition, Tobi takes on a new pet project: solving the murder. But with a stressed-out parrot as the only witness to the crime, Tobi will really have to wing it to put the cagey killer behind bars

DEATH in ADVERTISING

First in a New Series!

A TOBI TOBIAS MYSTERY

LAURA BRADFORD

As a child, Laura Bradford fell in love with writing over a stack of blank paper, a box of crayons, and a freshly sharpened #2 pencil. From that moment forward, she never wanted to do or be anything else. Today, Laura is the national bestselling author of several mystery series, including the Tobi Tobias Mystery Series, the Emergency Dessert Squad Mysteries, and the Amish Mysteries. She is a former Agatha Award nominee, and the recipient of an RT Reviewer's Choice Award in romance. A graduate of Xavier University in Cincinnati, Ohio, Laura enjoys making memories with her family, baking, and being an advocate for those living with Multiple Sclerosis.

Visit her at www.laurabradford.com or on Facebook.

CPSIA information can be obtained
at www.ICGtesting.com
Printed in the USA
BVOW09s1838070817
491374BV00001B/3/P

9 781516 102099